The bronze giant, who with his five aides became world famous, whose name was as well known in the far regions of China and the jungles of Africa as in the skyscrapers of New York.

There were stories of Doc Savage's almost incredible strength; of his amazing scientific discoveries of strange weapons and dangerous exploits.

Doc dedicated his life to aiding those faced by dangers with which they could not cope.

His name brought fear to those who sought to prey upon the unsuspecting. His name was praised by thousands he had saved.

DOC SAVAGE'S AMAZING CREW

"Ham," **Brigadier General Theodore Marley Brooks,** was never without his ominous, black sword cane.

"Monk," **Lieutenant Colonel Andrew Blodgett Mayfair,** just over five feet tall, yet over 260 pounds. His brutish exterior concealed the mind of a great scientist.

"Renny," **Colonel John Renwick,** his favorite sport was pounding his massive fists through heavy, paneled doors.

"Long Tom," **Major Thomas J. Roberts,** was the physical weakling of the crowd, but a genius at electricity.

"Johnny," **William Harper Littlejohn,** the scientist and greatest living expert on geology and archaeology.

**WITH THEIR LEADER, THEY WOULD
GO ANYWHERE, FIGHT ANYONE,
DARE EVERYTHING—SEEKING
EXCITEMENT AND PERILOUS
ADVENTURE!**

Bantam Books by Kenneth Robeson
Ask your bookseller for the books you have missed

DOC SAVAGE®

Two Complete Adventures in One Volume

HELL BELOW

and

THE LOST GIANT

Kenneth Robeson

HELL BELOW / THE LOST GIANT
*A Bantam Book / published by arrangement with
The Condé Nast Publications, Inc.*

PRINTING HISTORY

*Hell Below was originally published in Doc Savage Magazine,
September 1943. Copyright 1943 by Street & Smith Publications, Inc. Copyright © renewed 1971 by The Condé Nast Publications, Inc.*

*The Lost Giant was originally published in Doc Savage Maga-
zine, December 1944. Copyright 1944 by Street & Smith Publications, Inc. Copyright © renewed 1972 by The Condé Nast
Publications, Inc.*

Bantam edition / October 1980

*Bantam Books are published by Bantam Books, Inc. Its trade-
mark, consisting of the words "Bantam Books" and the por-
trayal of a bantam, is Registered in U.S. Patent and Trademark
Office and in other countries. Marca Registrada. Bantam
Books, Inc., 666 Fifth Avenue, New York, New York 10103.*

PRINTED IN THE UNITED STATES OF AMERICA

0 9 8 7 6 5 4 3 2 1

Contents

HELL BELOW

CHAPTER I
The Old Thief

"I used to fight Indians," the old gentleman said. "I used to eat their ears. I would stew their ears, then eat them with salt."

He stopped and looked at the man across the desk while he tried to think of something that would express his feelings.

"But I wouldn't feed your ears to my dog!" he finished.

The young man said, "Hah, hah!" Then he waved at a chair. "Go sit down, pop. Go sit over there and have a good cuss."

"I wasn't trying to amuse you," said the old gentleman.

"I wasn't amused," said the young man. "You can rest assured of that."

The old gentleman spat. You could tell from the look of him that he had come from a hard, bleak desert country, and he spat the way he would spit to kill a bug on the sun-baked earth.

"I'm old Too-Too Thomas," he said. "And to think I would sink to taking sass off a clerk in a Washington bureau."

"I'm not sassing you, old-timer," said the young man back of the desk. "I'm just asking you kindly, please go over there and sit down. Cuss, chew tobacco, spit on the floor, but just leave me alone."

"I want to see the main guy."

"No."

"Listen, pup, I tell you—"

"Sit down. The head guy can't see you. He's got troubles of his own right now."

Old Too-Too Thomas gave his tooled leather belt a hitch, the belt that had an enormous silver and gold buckle set with diamonds of respectable size. He crossed the room

3

and took a chair, stretched his feet out in front of him and scowled at the toes of his embroidered cowboy boots.

Then he frowned at the door of the inner office. There were voices behind the door, and he had noticed that they were getting a little louder.

"I been in Washington seven hours," he said. "And as near as I am to that door is as close as I've got to anybody who amounts to anything."

"Believe me, pardner," said the young man, "some fellows are in Washington seven months and don't get that close."

"Mule feathers!" said Too-Too Thomas.

Suddenly there was no question about the voices getting louder in the inner office. They were very loud. They were angry.

One voice said: "You're not going to get in the shooting end of the war. That's the decision. You keep right on with what you are doing."

"Who's that?" asked Too-Too Thomas.

"The head guy," said the clerk.

A second voice said: "That is the same song and dance you've been giving us since the war started. My five aides are tired of it. I'm tired of it. We want action!"

"Who's that?" asked Too-Too Thomas.

"A man who wants to fight," said the clerk.

"That makes two of us," said Too-Too Thomas. "Who is he, besides a voice that's shaking the building?"

"His name," said the clerk, "is Doc Savage."

"Doc Savage, eh?"

"Ever hear of him?"

"No."

"Bless us!" the clerk said. "Where did you say you came from, the planet of Mars?"

"I came from the Dirty Man Rancho in the foothills of the Sierra Santa Clara in Lower California, where the pigs chase mountain lions," Too-Too Thomas said. "A man's country."

"Oh!"

"Is this Doc Savage going to get to fight?"

"Not," said the clerk, "if we can help it."

Too-Too Thomas listened to the voice of Doc Savage which was causing the door to bend on its hinges. He chuckled and said, "I'll bet you he does. I'll just bet you."

Then he leaned back to listen.

The head man was speaking, trying to soothe Doc Savage.

He was saying, "You're doing the work we want you to do. It's the work for which you were fitted when you were placed in the hands of scientists, as a child, and given the remarkable training which lasted until early manhood. You were given that specific training to fit you for the job of righting wrongs and punishing evildoers who are outside the law, and to do the job in the far corners of the earth if necessary. We want you to go right ahead."

Doc Savage said loudly, "There's a war going on!"

"Yes, a modern war," the other said. "A war being fought on the home front just as much as in the foxholes and behind bombsights."

"The home front," Doc Savage shouted, "is getting along extraordinarily well! Capital and labor and other special interests now and then try to push across one of their pet greedy ideas under cover of the war excitement, but the newspaper publicity and the people are taking care of that very nicely. The war is where the shooting is. We want to be in it."

Doc Savage had a remarkable voice, a voice that was full of controlled power, deep and modulated, giving the impression of vast strength and ability.

"You are not feeling very reasonable, are you?" the head man asked.

"Not particularly," Doc said. "Not to the brand of reasoning you are offering."

Now the other became indignant.

He shouted: "There is more to this war than just shooting Japanese or Germans. They can sink a battleship and we can build another one. But if they kill you, where would we get another man with your inventive skill and your thinking equipment? Where would we get a man with your almost fantastic ability to ferret out the most remarkable plots and intricate schemes?"

"You won't," asked Doc, "assign us to active service?"

"I will not."

Another voice, a small, squeaky one that the owner should have outgrown about the age of twelve, burst into the discussion. "What about me?" it demanded angrily.

Old Too-Too Thomas glanced at the clerk and asked, "Who's that one?"

"They call him Monk Mayfair," the clerk said. "But he is Lieutenant Colonel Andrew Blodgett Mayfair, one of the world's most able chemists."

Inside, the voice of Monk repeated, "What about me?"

"No."

"Why not?"

"Let a chemist of your ability waste your time packing a rifle? Anyway, you're a Doc Savage aide."

A fourth voice, a cultured Harvard voice, said, "I take it you are going to include me in this ridiculous refusal?"

"We are and we have!"

Outside, old Too-Too Thomas looked questioningly at the clerk.

"That one," said the clerk, "is Brigadier General Theodore Marley Ham Brooks, a lawyer."

Inside the office, Doc Savage said loudly, "This quarrel over whether we see action has been going on since the war began."

"That's right," said the head man.

"And the answer is still no?"

"It's still no."

"We're disgusted."

"If it's action you want," the head man said, "you get plenty of it the way things are."

Monk Mayfair said, "That's no argument—"

"How many times," demanded the other, "were you shot at in the past six months?"

"Not over a dozen times," Monk said. "What has that—"

"More than half the soldiers in the army never hear an enemy gun explode!" yelled the head man.

Doc Savage, in a quieter voice, said, "Come on, fellows. We're wasting breath."

They walked out of the inner office and old Too-Too Thomas stared at them in astonishment. He was impressed.

"They look even more capable than they talked," he said.

"They are," the clerk said.

"I got me an idea," said Too-Too Thomas.

Doc Savage, Monk Mayfair and Ham Brooks were walking angrily down the impressive hallway when Too-Too Thomas overtook them.

"My craw," said Too-Too Thomas, "is stuck plumb full of red tape."

Monk Mayfair examined the leathery old Westerner. Monk was a short man who gave the startling impression at times of being as wide as he was high. He had a large crop of rusty hair, a big grin, and affected the manners of a circus clown.

"Tsk, tsk," Monk said, shaking his head. "Poor fellow. But I guess it happens often."

Too-Too Thomas scowled. "You think I'm crazy, pardner?"

"Yes, and you have my sympathy," Monk said. "I'll bet you're not the first one got twittery trying to get something done."

"If you wasn't so homely," Too-Too said, "I would pop you right in the eye."

"You're offended?"

"Yeah, mad as a hornet. I ain't no crazier'n most."

"We're perfect strangers," said Monk. "You walk up and start talking about your craw. What do you expect us to think?"

"Don't care what you think," said Too-Too Thomas. "You fellers want action?"

"Action?"

"Heard you talkin' to that guy back there." Too-Too eyed them speculatively. "Right likely lookin' fellers, you-all. Figure you've sort of been up against a thing or two in your time."

Monk grinned. "Old-timer, I'll bet you've eaten a few tacks yourself. What's on your mind?"

"Craw's full of red tape, like I said. Got a job that has to be done, and there ain't time to fool around no more about doing it. Need help."

"What kind of help?"

Too-Too Thomas winked. "Kind you can give me, I expect." He gestured. "C'mon. Let's get outa this wickiup so we can talk."

They walked through numerous corridors and showed their passes to watchmen, took an elevator down, ran the gantlet of more watchmen, then finally stood on the street.

"Now, old-timer," Monk said. "What's this bur you've got under your saddle."

Too-Too Thomas eyed them intently.

"Know anything about submarines?" he asked.

Monk said, "Sure. Why?"

"Fine," said Too-Too Thomas. "Now the first thing we do is steal a navy airplane with some bombs on it and a can of quick-drying paint."

Doc Savage was a man with more qualities than a remarkable voice. He was a giant of a man who was so symmetrically proportioned that his actual size was not evident until one stood close to him; then it became startling. When he moved, the play of sinews in his neck and wrists indicated strength that was equally startling. His skin was a deep bronze color, his hair was straight and slightly darker, and his eyes were like pools of flake gold always stirred by tiny winds.

Until now he had, as was his habit, remained silent and expressionless. But the old Westerner's calm mention of stealing a navy plane was unusual enough to bring a startled expression to his face, and cause him to speak.

"Steal a navy plane?" he said.

"That's the only chance we got to make it in time."

"Stealing a navy plane is something they shoot you for," Doc reminded.

Too-Too Thomas shrugged, not impressed. "Done things I could've been shot for before."

A small park, pleasant in the sunlight, was across the street. Indicating the park, Doc said, "We had better go over there and sit down while you explain this."

They crossed the street, dodging traffic, which was thick. There were benches along the sidewalk, one of which they selected.

Too-Too Thomas took a deep breath.

"Lives," he said, "have a relative value, I've noticed. In wartime, they somehow ain't as important. But these are important to me. They're my friends, the ones that'll die right away. The other ones, the ones who'll die later, ain't people I know, probably, but they'll be nice folks."

Doc Savage said patiently, "The best way to tell a story is the way you read a book. Begin at the beginning and don't leave anything out."

"I do it a little different," said Too-Too Thomas. "You savvy what I'm telling you? I got to save some lives.

They'll die right away, tonight probably, if I ain't fast enough on my feet. Later on, more will die."

"Where?"

"I'll take you to the place."

"Where is it?"

Too-Too Thomas looked at Doc Savage steadily. "Don't push me."

"Are you," Doc asked, "going to tell us the whole story?"

"Not now, I ain't."

"Why not now?"

The leathery old man thought about the question for a few moments, then shook his head.

"There's somebody I don't want to involve until I'm danged sure," he said. "That's why. I just ain't going off half cocked, that's all."

"Do you," Doc asked, "expect us to steal a navy plane and a can of paint on the basis of no more than you're telling us?"

Too-Too Thomas got to his feet.

"You could buy the paint, not steal it," he said. He shook his head slowly. "Reckon it was a kind of a locoed idea I had. I was feeling kind of desperate or I wouldn't have tried it. Feel like the time the Yaquis chased me into the ocean and I couldn't swim a lick."

He eyed them and shook his head some more.

"You're right likely lookin' gents, too," he said. "Well, so long. I would tell you not to take any wooden nickels, only I can see you wouldn't. So long."

He walked off and left them.

Doc Savage, as soon as Too-Too Thomas was out of earshot, said quickly, "Monk, follow him. He is going north. Ham will go west, in case he turns in that direction. I will go east."

"I didn't think the old fellow was kidding, either," Monk said, and got to his feet.

Monk was rather proud of the job he did shadowing Too-Too Thomas. He ambled casually across the sidewalk as if he was going back to the building they had just left. In the street, he got into a taxicab. He felt sure he had disappeared in the street, as far as Too-Too Thomas was concerned, as if by magic.

Following Too-Too Thomas wasn't too tough, although the leathery-looking old gent behaved in a way that showed he was afraid he was being trailed. He walked fast, took a cab, and the cab went in and out of streets.

Doc Savage and Ham Brooks did not appear, for the simple reason that they'd had no chance to catch sight of Too-Too Thomas.

Washington is a city of contrasts, where a remarkably shabby street often adjoins a fine one. Too-Too Thomas picked one of the most ragtag thoroughfares to leave the cab.

He walked to a narrow alley and entered, striding along rapidly as if he knew where he was going.

Before Monk entered the alley, he cautiously used the shiny inside of the lid of his large silver watch as a mirror, and examined the alley periscope fashion. He saw no sign of his quarry.

However, Monk found after he had walked about twenty feet into the alley that he had walked against a gun. The gun was an impressive weapon of the type called a hogleg by cowboys. Too-Too Thomas, who held it, had stepped from a niche that Monk hadn't noticed.

"If this gun was to go boom-boom," said Too-Too Thomas, "it would blow you right out of this alley."

Monk didn't doubt it. As a matter of fact, Monk was wearing a bulletproof vest, but thinking about the kick that old gun would give his middle made him turn green.

"Figured one of you gents would trail me," said Too-Too Thomas. "Trapped you neat, didn't I?"

"What do you want with me?" Monk asked.

"Why, you're gonna run that submarine for me," Too-Too Thomas told him.

CHAPTER II
The Scared Men

Monk was not concerned so much about the submarine as he was about what might come out of the pistol. "You know about them things?" he asked uneasily. "They make a loud noise and a piece of lead flies out."

Old Too-Too Thomas chuckled. He was quite calm, a man who had walked in the path of danger before. He was somewhat proud of himself, too.

"Before you start something," he said, "just tell me where to send the body."

They walked to the other end of the alley. Just before they reached the street, Too-Too Thomas stowed his enormous piece of hardware inside his coat.

"We're going to take a ride in a taxicab," he said. "Behave yourself. If you don't, I give a sort of twitch, and the bullets fly around."

"A model boy," Monk assured him, "is what they always call me."

They found a taxicab, although it was a job. Cabs were not plentiful in Washington, and the drivers had more business than they could take care of.

Monk was familiar with the address which Too-Too Thomas gave the cab driver. It was a military air field.

The cab got moving, and Monk said, "Since we're partners, you might tell me what we're undertaking."

"Shucks, I don't see what makes you think we're partners," old Too-Too Thomas said. "We're man and lackey, that's what we are. You're the lackey."

"We going to steal a plane?"

"Sure."

They did not steal a plane immediately, though. They did not steal one from the military field at all. They got out and dismissed the cab and Too-Too Thomas looked the flying field over.

11

The man was evidently an old campaigner, because he correctly surmised that there were too many sentries and armed men around the place.

"Even if the guards were that many Yaqui Indians, the chances would be too long," he said. "And these soldiers may be tougher than Yaquis."

"So now I can go home?" Monk asked hopefully.

"No, no," said Too-Too Thomas. "I'll work the pump on my resources some more."

They went back to the city of Washington. This proved to be tiring, because they could not find a taxicab until they had walked through the heat and the dust for about a mile.

Monk felt foolish riding around, a prisoner. But he did not make a break.

The reason he was being meek, Monk told himself, was so he could stick around and find out what this was all about. But that big revolver was a consideration, too.

They went to a hotel. It was a remarkably fine hotel, where the minimum rate was fifteen dollars a day, American plan. The surroundings were impressive and rich.

"Be a very genteel place to be found a corpse," warned Too-Too Thomas, "if you want to try anything."

"No, thanks," Monk said. "I hope to die of old age."

Several small square envelopes had been shoved under the door of Too-Too Thomas' room. Some of the square envelopes protruded under the edge of the door, and Too-Too eyed them before he unlocked the door. He immediately picked up the envelopes.

"I telephoned a bunch of agents to rent or buy a good seaplane for me," he said. "I'll bet these are the answers from them."

He began opening the envelopes—they were the envelopes hotels use for telephone messages—and reading the contents.

"I can read with one eye and shoot with one hand," he warned Monk.

"Your modesty is giving me cold chills," Monk assured him.

Too-Too Thomas waved one of the envelopes.

"Eureka!" he cried. "Hot snakes! This guy found one for me! He says its a big new seaplane, and I can buy it." He glanced at the message again. "A hundred and twelve thousand dollars. Cheap enough. I just want it for this one trip."

Monk was quite startled.

"One trip!" he said. "That's a lot of dough to put out for one trip."

"It's a lot of trip."

A spick and span new suitcase stood on a folding baggage rack. Too-Too Thomas opened the suitcase, which held a suit of underwear and a safety razor. Packages of U. S. currency filled the remaining space in the bag.

Too-Too Thomas stowed packages of money into his pockets until he ran out of pockets.

He looked at Monk.

"I ain't got time to count out a hundred and twelve thousand, plus expense money," he said. "Here, you'll have to carry some of it."

Monk obediently loaded his own pockets with packages of greenbacks. The bills were tens, twenties, fifties and hundreds. Monk was not able to judge the total of his burden as closely as a bank cashier, but he felt it was impressive. He thought he must be packing anyway a hundred thousand.

"I feel like the mint," Monk said.

"Just so you don't get to feeling like a rabbit."

"I feel like that, too," Monk told him. "Now it would be profitable to escape."

"Yeah, maybe they could shingle your angel wings with greenbacks," Too-Too Thomas said, and sounded as if he meant it.

They got another taxicab in front of the hotel. When the cab driver heard the address, he informed them it was farther than he was allowed to drive in his zone, on his gasoline allowance. But when Too-Too Thomas showed him one of the greenbacks, he agreed to take them.

"This place is a farmhouse in the country, close to the Potomac," Too-Too Thomas explained. "We go there, and the feller shows us the plane, which is in a shed on the river."

Monk said nothing, but looked to see if the old man seemed to be telling the truth. He did, and Monk was puzzled.

There could not be any civilian plane, Monk knew, in any shed on the river. There was a government regulation

against keeping planes anywhere but on airports where
there was a guard twenty-four hours of the day. That is, it
was against the law unless the motors were taken out of
the plane. If this was a plane without motors, Monk
wanted to be around to hear Too-Too Thomas cuss.

"So you want me to run a submarine," Monk said.

"You can get me a few cases of dynamite, some caps
and fuses, too."

"What's that for?"

"To take the place of a bomb."

"What's the bomb for?"

"Now your nose is too long," said Too-Too Thomas.

The farmhouse looked deceptively innocent. The building was a long, low, pleasant structure which needed paint,
and the weeds in the yard needed cutting. If the door of
the house had not been standing open, with a man leaning
in it, Monk would have sworn the place was deserted.

"Gent's waiting for us," said Too-Too Thomas, pleased.

They walked to the door, leaving the taxi waiting at the
gate, and Too-Too Thomas asked, "You the feller with a
seaplane for sale?"

"You the guy who wants to buy one?"

"That's me."

"Come in."

They walked into the house, and there was no furniture
in the room. Not unless half a dozen men crouching
against the walls with leveled revolvers or leveled and
cocked rifles could be counted as fixtures.

"One jump makes you dead," said the man who had
been at the door. His remark seemed unnecessary.

Disturbed, Too-Too Thomas eyed them.

"Too bad I only got one gun with six shells in it," he said.
"If I had my usual two guns, I'd have enough bullets to go
around, and I would start something."

The armed men, Monk noticed, were impressed by the
old fellow. They took him with deadly seriousness. The
two who came to search him stood far from him and
reached out, acting as if they wished they had forked
sticks.

"Wow, wow, wow!" said one of the men, looking at the
money.

They kept taking money out of the old man's pockets.

"He must be stuffed with it!" one said.

"This one, too," said a man who was searching Monk.

The one who had held the door open for them and who seemed to be in charge, sank to his knees and rapidly totaled the amount of the money from the figure written on the band of paper that inclosed each package.

"Whew!" he said. "Nearly one hundred thousand dollars."

"Shucks, less than a hundred thousand," said Too-Too Thomas, surprised. "It didn't count up like I thought it would."

Unfortunately, the men were not so impressed by the money that they became careless, and Monk saw no opportunity to make a break.

Too-Too Thomas suddenly yelled and pointed at one of the men.

"Great guns, I've seen you before!" he shouted. "You're the hombre who kicked me in the ribs because I complained about the sun shining in my cell!"

"H'yah, you old buzz saw," the man said.

"So you trailed me east!" Too-Too Thomas said.

The old man's tone made Monk look at him sharply. Too-Too Thomas sounded discouraged. Abruptly he was an old man, a defeated old man.

"I wasn't so smart," he said. "You trailed me."

The man he had recognized said, "Some job it was, too. We didn't really catch up with you until about two hours ago."

Too-Too Thomas groaned. "Was there an airplane?"

"No."

"How come?"

"We just located your hotel room, and saw those little telephone envelopes sticking out from under the door. We read 'em, and found out you were after an airplane. So we put a note of our own under the door, to bring you out here."

"I must be getting old," Too-Too Thomas muttered.

"Maybe you are," the young man told him, "but you haven't shown many signs of it."

Monk now went through the motions of dusting his hands. "Well, boys, thanks, for rescuing me," he said. "Now I'll be on my way."

"What about the money?" someone asked.

"Ask old fire whiskers," Monk said indicating Too-Too

Thomas. "It was in his custody, but he didn't seem to care much for it."

"He wouldn't, considering where he got it," the man said.

Monk dusted off his hands again. "Been nice being rescued by you." He headed for the door.

At least three rifles cocked, and other weapons pointed at him. Someone said, "Take it easy, brother. That was a nice line, but you didn't hook us."

Monk stopped. He could tell by looking at them that they would shoot him if they thought it necessary. He had learned to look at men and tell when they were thinking that.

"Go tell that taxicab we're through with him, and pay him off," a man said.

One of them went out and got rid of the taxi without trouble.

Old Too-Too Thomas asked, "How did you fellows know about this farm?"

"Oh, one of us used to live in Washington, and we just drove down the road until we found an empty place close to the river. We didn't have much time to be choosy. Why, ain't the place elaborate enough for you?"

Too-Too Thomas grunted and resumed a miserable silence.

Someone pointed at Monk, and asked, "Who's this funny-lookin' bird, anyway?"

Monk, who was indignant, said, "I won't look funny to you by the time this is over."

They were not scared, and they went to a pile of his belongings on the floor and began going through them. The searcher picked up all of Monk's private money, removing it from his billfold, and pocketed it. "Commission," he explained.

The he inspected the cards in Monk's billfold. He let out a yell.

"Dammit, I knew I'd seen pictures of this homely guy somewhere!" he shouted.

"Who is he?"

"Lieutenant Colonel Andrew Blodgett Mayfair."

"Holy cats!" someone said.

The name of Mayfair apparently meant nothing at all to some of the others, one of whom asked, "What is he, half toad or something?"

"Ever hear of Doc Savage?"

The man who had made the bright remark about the toad didn't feel so funny. He swallowed with some difficulty. "Huh?"

"This guy"—the man indicated Monk—"is one of Doc Savage's five assistants."

Monk had seen the effect which Doc Savage's name had on crooks before. Usually it pleased him.

He had never, however, seen a more pronounced effect at the mention of Doc Savage, than he did now. But Monk wasn't entirely pleased.

It gave him a cold feeling when they walked off into a corner, the three who seemed to be the ring-leaders, and had a conference. Most of what they said did not reach Monk's ears, but he heard a word now and then that added up to violence and sudden death.

They came back with the verdict.

"Doc Savage has got to be caught or killed before he gets wind of this," the spokesman said. "We'll get busy on him right now."

CHAPTER III
Design for Death

The time was past, Monk realized, for any more fooling around trying to find out what was going on. He saw that he had made a mistake, a bad one.

Monk cast around in his mind, and remembered that he knew a few words of the language the Yaqui Indians spoke. He had gone to Mexico with Renny Renwick, another Doc Savage aide, on a trip Renny had taken down there to put a mine on a profitable basis.

Monk had learned just enough Yaqui to get along with the Yaqui girls. Monk being Monk, his interest in the Yaqui language was satisfied when he had learned that much. One of the Yaqui phrases Monk had learned was the equivalent of, "How about some action, baby?"

Glancing at old Too-Too Thomas, Monk—in Yaqui—said, "How about some action, baby?"

Old Too-Too Thomas started. He looked as if an angel had spoken to him.

"Yippee!" he yelled. Then he said two or three quick sentences in Yaqui.

Monk didn't understand a word of it.

Nor did Monk have long to think about it, because a man standing behind him hit him over the head with a blackjack, dropping Monk senseless.

"They were cooking something up," the blackjack wielder said. "Pop the old geezer, too, somebody."

They popped the old geezer. Two of them had to hold him while they did it, and they had to pop him more than once. A man said, "Give me your blackjack, Willis. It's heavier." But finally they knocked Too-Too Thomas out.

"Head like a rock," a man said.

The straw boss of the group said, "Tie them up, tape their mouths, shoot some cocaine in them, wrap them up in blankets and put them in the back of the delivery truck we rented."

The man then selected four men whom he named as Willis, Pet, Frederick and Bummy.

"You," he told them, "are going to help me get Doc Savage."

The four men he picked looked very unhappy.

The leader was addressed as Sam. Sam's actions showed that he was, in his special line, a competent fellow.

Back of the house, in a shed, were two delivery trucks with panel bodies. One of these bore the name of a dry-cleaning concern and the other was white and advertised a dairy. Sam and his four selected men took the dairy truck.

As they drove down the highway, he explained his reasons for using panel body trucks instead of passenger cars.

"The ban on pleasure driving has been put on again back East, I hear," he told them, "and you can't tell about the cops and these government men. They're liable to stop a passenger car, just to ask if we're on essential business, but they won't be likely to mess with a delivery job."

His four helpers were silent. They had long faces.

"Cheer up," Sam told them.

"Sure, sing and be merry," one muttered. "Like the blackbirds in the pie."

Sam said, "Savage won't eat you."

"Is that what he *don't* do to you?" the man asked sourly.

First, they had to find Doc Savage. This was a job which they tackled systematically and with some foresighted cunning.

"He has a headquarters in New York," Sam said. "We'll see what they tell us."

Sam was on the telephone about fifteen minutes, and came out of the booth minus a number of dimes and quarters as well as his confidence.

"They've had that gag pulled on 'em before," he said.

The man Willis, alarmed, demanded, "You didn't get 'em on our trail?"

"Heck, no," said Sam. "I told 'em I was General Shoozis, calling from a pay telephone, wishing to locate

Doc Savage. They told me to hold the phone for about five minutes, and they would get Doc up from downstairs."

"Oh, oh!" Willis said. "They were going to trace the call in that five minutes."

"Sure."

"We better blow."

"We are, and fast, too."

They got away from there in a hurry.

Sam, far from being thwarted, tried various war departments by telephone. This wasn't satisfactory. "I should've known the army and navy ain't givin' out any information," he complained.

"What we need," said Willis, "is something direct."

"Such as?"

"You notice that guy Monk's voice?"

"Sure. Sounds like he was twelve years old."

Willis said, "Listen." He screwed up his face and pulled in his chin and said, "You guys might use this kind of a gag, huh?"

They stared at Willis as if he was an answer to a prayer.

"Boy, that's swell!" exclaimed Sam.

"Sounded like Monk, eh?"

"Sure did!"

Willis was pleased. "Here's what I thought. Why don't we make another telephone call to New York, with me doing the calling and using Monk's voice. I tell them in New York that I'm in trouble and need help, and that I've lost track of Doc and to get hold of him and send him to help me; and I give them an address."

This delighted Sam. "That's great, Willis. Simply great. You're not as dumb as I thought you were."

"What address do we tell 'em in New York?" asked the man called Bummy.

"We'll find one," said Sam.

The man called Pet was the one who was familiar with Washington and the surrounding environs. He immediately stated that he knew just the spot they needed. The others accompanied him to look at it, and they agreed.

"Just the ticket," admitted Sam.

The building was in the active commercial part of the city. Shabby, about six stories high, with dirty windows half boarded up. It was empty.

Pet explained that the structure had been vacated and closed preparatory to demolishing it in order that a new building might be erected. But there had been a legal hitch before any wrecking had been done, so that everything was intact. Even the elevators and lights were still functioning.

"Only hitch," Pet pointed out, "is a watchman and a janitor who are on duty during the day."

"That's not such a hitch," said Sam.

They went in and slugged the watchman and janitor and tied them up in the basement.

"Make your call, Willis," directed Sam.

"To make it good, the call should come from here, huh?"

"Willis, your brain is growing, isn't it," said Sam.

Willis made the telephone call to Doc Savage's headquarters in New York, and did his imitation of Monk to perfection. Sam listened at the receiver, becoming elated.

When they hung up he said, "Yow! Swallowed it like a seal taking a fish!"

Willis said, "Mind if I make another suggestion, Sam?"

"Shoot," Sam said. "Boy, you're leaking brains today."

"What do you say we call the others. We ought to have all our crowd down here to help in this. After all, this isn't exactly a mouse-catching we're pulling."

Sam sobered. "You got something there, too."

They made two telephone calls and looked more relieved after that.

"Everybody is going to help," Sam said.

They settled down to wait, hoping the rest of their gang would show up. This was just the Washington part of their crowd and Sam said, "I wish everybody else was in town so they could help."

Willis said he wished they were, too. "I wish the two big guys could have seen my two ideas awhile ago," he said. "Might get me a bonus, huh?"

Sam, in an expansive mood, said, "It will get you a bonus anyway, because I'll recommend one. What I recommend usually goes through."

"You'll put it up to the two big guys?"

"Yeah."

"Put it up to the fat one," Willis suggested cunningly. "I

think he's more inclined to be reckless with his dough than the shriveled one. So put it up to the fat one, huh?"

"O. K." Sam agreed. "But let me give you a piece of advice. Don't ever let him hear that you called him fat. He's touchy as hell about his weight."

"Thanks," said Willis.

In about twenty minutes, there was an influx of men into the old building. They were men who had taken care to dress so that they were not too noticeable in a crowd. As far as clothing went, they were a colorless group. But none of them looked honest or at ease.

Sam took charge. He distributed the reinforcements at various points on the first floor, and in the alley, also in the street outside. They gave some thought to the men posted in the street, finally placing two of them in a greasy-spoon restaurant halfway in the block, and two more in the parked dairy truck. Another pair began to dicker for furniture they had no intention of buying in a secondhand store.

Hardly were they placed when a lookout hissed loudly.

"Coming up," he said.

Sam peered out of a window, and became a little pale. It was the first time he had seen Doc Savage in person, and he was suddenly afflicted with the wish that he was somewhere else.

Doc Savage was far from the building, at the end of the block. He seemed in no hurry, but stood there surveying the vicinity. He looked the ground over so thoroughly that Sam got the jitters.

"He's waiting to see who is hanging around suspiciously," Sam gasped. "He'll spot the guys in the dairy truck."

But the pair in the dairy saw Doc, too, and they started the truck and drove away. Sam heaved a sigh of relief. He was sweating.

"I might pick him off with a rifle from here," a man whispered.

"Too risky," Sam said. "That Monk was wearing a bulletproof vest. So Savage probably has one, too."

Doc Savage noticed the two men drive away in the small dairy truck. Milk companies did not usually put two men in trucks that small these days when help was scarce.

Two men were sitting in a greasy-spoon restaurant and

they were a little too well-dressed to be loafing in a dumpy restaurant at this time of day.

Two more men were dickering in a secondhand furniture store. The dickering was over a carpet, and this particular carpet was the only one in the front of the store, although there were others in the rear; and the traders did not go back to look at the other carpets, although the one they were looking at was in bad condition.

Doc Savage decided not to go in the front of the old building.

He had not intended to do that anyway, as he was suspicious about the call.

His aides in New York had contacted him by radio. All three of the five remaining aides were in New York. They were Renny Renwick, Long Tom Roberts and Johnny Littlejohn, engineer, electrical wizard, and archaeologist-geologist, respectively. In New York headquarters at the time they called was Patricia Savage, Doc's cousin. Pat was a young woman who liked excitement, and now that she knew something was going on, she would be in their hair.

What had made Doc Savage suspicious was the fact that there had been a previous telephone call from Washington in an effort to locate him. A call from a General Shoozis, who hadn't waited around to have the call traced.

"He skipped, so he might've been a phony," said Long Tom Roberts, who gave the information to Doc over the portable short-wave radio which they used for communication.

Doc Savage himself had said, "In this second call, someone might have imitated Monk's voice, the idea being to decoy me to some spot where they could get at me."

"Move slowly and cautiously," Long Tom had warned.

So Doc Savage was being suspicious, and he was sure he was justified.

He went around the block and, finding an alley, he entered. He did not go along the alley directly to the rear door of the old building.

Instead, he climbed to the roof of the next building. The buildings were standing side by side, one roof against the other. He grabbed the ladder of a fire escape, leaped, and pulled it down, which gave him an easy route to the roof he wanted to reach.

He took great care and crawled across the roof toward the old building.

Because he was alert and watching, he noticed that there were tracks in the dust which overlay the blacktop covering of the roof. They were the footprints of men. A quick glance around convinced him they came from the windows of the old building which was his objective.

It was obvious that at least three men were concealed on the rooftop, probably behind chimneys or skylights.

Possibly they had seen him. If so, this was no time to be reckless about sticking his head into view. He felt he was in danger.

He was taken completely by surprise when a voice, a young woman's voice, called, "Stand still if you don't want to get shot!"

He heard footsteps and the young woman came up from behind and seized Doc around the neck.

He felt something hard gouge him in the ribs, looked down, and saw that it was a gun. A blue gun about five inches long with a pearl handle, a .32-caliber. The hand that held the gun had faintly tinted fingernails.

"Stand still!" the young woman repeated.

Then she raised her voice and shouted, sounding desperate and a trifle triumphant.

"Now!" she cried. "Now! You dare bother me, and I'll put a hole in your friend!"

Doc had been right about the number of men concealed on the surrounding rooftops. There were three of them. They stepped into view. All were well-dressed and had guns.

They approached.

"Keep away!" the girl cried, "or I'll shoot your friend!"

The men kept coming.

Sounding increasingly frightened, the girl told Doc, "I was up here on the roof, and they must have seen me. They came out and were hiding around, getting ready to sneak up on me. But I'll show them."

Doc thought she was mistaken. The men had been hiding around waiting for him, not the girl. He was sure, from the expressions on their faces as they approached, that they hadn't dreamed the girl was around.

But it was also evident the men knew the girl.

"I'll shoot!" the girl cried, jabbing Doc with the gun.

"Go ahead," a man said.

"Bing him, sister, and save us the trouble," said another.

"You can't fool me!" she cried. "I'm going to shoot."

CHAPTER IV
Lena

There was no shooting, however. The girl lost her nerve. At the last moment, she released Doc, whirled and tried to run. They caught her and took the gun away from her.

Doc Savage was actually disappointed that she had not shot him. The little .32-caliber bullet from her gun would not have had much effect on his bulletproof undergarment, except that it would have given him a hard whack on the ribs.

If she had shot him, he would have had a chance to fall over and play dead, possibly getting a chance to surprise the three men. Now there was nothing to do but put up his hands, and this he did.

The man who had disarmed the girl was pale and perspiring when he finished, although it only took a moment.

Another man laughed at him. "Is she something that'll explode, Willis?" he asked.

"She's been known to," Willis said. "And when Lena doesn't explode, it's only because she's thought of something more disastrous."

"Lena?" The man pointed at the girl. "Her? Lena Carlson?"

Willis nodded.

"You're sure?"

"Would I be sweating like this if I wasn't?" Willis asked.

Doc Savage glanced at Lena Carlson with interest. He saw a tearful young woman, blue-eyed, red-headed, with an unusual quantity of good looks. But she didn't seem like a person who would make somebody like Willis burst out in a cold sweat.

Doc said, "So you are *the* Lena Carlson?"

"Yes," she said. "So you've heard of me."

"No," Doc admitted. "I haven't."

"You must have lived in a barrel all your life," Lena Carlson told him. She seemed disappointed.

Doc was a little irritated and he said, "I'm Doc Savage. Have you heard of me?"

"I would like to say I haven't, but I have, vaguely." She was not impressed, or didn't sound as if she was.

"Anyway, we are even," Doc admitted, and was amused by the fact that the girl had managed to irritate him slightly.

"What are you grinning at?" she demanded. "You're not one of them, are you? They're pointing their guns at you."

"That's right," Doc agreed.

"I thought you were," she said.

"You made a mistake."

"I did not," she said sharply. "A good idea is never a mistake. That was a good idea, grabbing you and pointing my gun at you. It just turned out that you were not what I thought you were."

Willis took whatever levity there was out of the situation by asking, "Shall we shoot them here, Sam, or what?"

"The shots would make a hell of a noise outdoors," Sam said. "Take them inside."

Doc Savage went through the motions of becoming frightened. He looked terrified and his captors would have been suspicious if it hadn't been for the impressive show he put on.

Doc's face became almost purple. A pale face would have been more effective, but it's possible to make your face purple by holding your breath and bulging your neck against your collar, whereas a pale face is difficult to fake. He trembled and his lips moved wordlessly.

He tried to speak. What he said was inarticulate, but loud, and sounded like a frightened gurgling and moaning.

"Stop that!" a man snarled. "Or we'll shoot you right here."

Doc became silent.

"What'd he say then?" Willis asked.

"Hell, nothing," said Sam. "He just blubbered from

fright. Boy, I've heard a lot of this Doc Savage. They had his nerve overrated."

Lena Carlson looked at Doc Savage thoughtfully. She did not seem convinced.

"I wonder," she said, but only with her lips.

The trick which Doc Savage had just pulled paid off as soon as they were in the old building. The trick was a simple one. The pretended fright was a cover-up for the loud gurgling, which was really a single word in the Mayan language. Mayan was a little-known tongue, and Doc and his associates used it, because of its unorthodox sound, when they wished to converse without outsiders understanding them. The tongue was ancient Mayan, and as far as they knew they were the only men in the so-called civilized world who understood it.

Ham Brooks was following Doc closely, so Doc had spoken loudly enough in Mayan for Ham to overhear.

Ham had thereupon come into the building.

The enemy had, it seemed, incautiously drawn his lookouts from the street and the lower floor of the old building, after learning that Doc Savage was captured. So Ham Brooks was free to walk up to the second floor unmolested.

Ham felt in the coat pocket in which he had placed gas grenades. He had placed gas grenades in one pocket, smokers in another, explosives in still another, and so on.

Without being aware, he got a smoke grenade instead of a gasser. The grenades all felt alike, but were different colors.

Holding the grenade aloft, Ham said, "It's all off, you guys! Nobody move! This is a grenade I've got!"

The way the men reacted told Doc Savage something about them. It told him they were not mere crooks. Common criminals would have been confused, and would have given up.

But these men had military training. It was evident from the way they acted.

Ham saw what he was up against, threw his grenade. The anaesthetic gas in the grenades was a quick-acting, odorless and colorless vapor which would bring sudden unconsciousness. Too late, Ham saw this was no gas grenade. It was a smoker.

This grenade was black and white checkered, which meant smoke. For simplicity and to avoid confusion, Doc followed the same system of marking by colors as the navy—red for gas, yellow for explosive, white for shrapnel, and so on.

The smoker popped loudly and in an instant the room was full, incredibly full of smoke. Smoke that was as black as drawing ink.

The room became full of confusion.

"Drat it!" Ham said. "I'm sorry, Doc. I didn't know that was a gas grenade."

"Have you got a gas mask?" Doc demanded.

"No!" Ham cried. "We'll all be killed!"

Actually there was no gas, unless the harmless smoke could be called a gas. But the smoke had an acrid stinging effect on the lungs and a heavy pungent odor. The smoke, in fact, smelled a great deal more like gas than most gases smelled.

Sam yelled, "Don't shoot! We'll hit each other!"

He also shouted, "Gas! Get out of here!"

The girl, Lena Carlson, thought there was gas, and she made a break for the window. Doc Savage, knowing that if she got out of the smoke she might be shot, lunged for her and caught her.

"Let go of me!" she said, taking a judo hold on his little finger, and trying to insert a thumb in his eye.

"Sh-h-h!" he warned, rescuing his little finger just before she disjointed it. "There's no gas"—this in a whisper—"and the thing to do probably is get down on the floor and stay there."

She obeyed.

The enemy rushed from all directions toward the door. No one could see where he was going, and no one wanted to stay in the room. There was no shouting, probably because they thought the place was full of poison gas and were all holding their breath.

They ran out into the hall and went thundering down the stairs.

Doc Savage, trying to capture at least one man, had no luck whatever.

Someone had kicked a packing box into the middle of the floor and he had the misfortune to stumble over that and lunge into Ham, who hit him a respectable wallop thinking he was an enemy. They got that straightened out, and charged into the hall.

There was a little smoke in the hall, but none on the stairs.

They reached the stairs, but quickly ducked back, just in time to avoid a flock of bullets which came up. The fusillade was deafening.

After the one volley, Sam's voice said, "Savage, can you hear me?"

"I can hear you," Doc answered.

"We've got Monk Mayfair and Too-Too Thomas," Sam said. "You bother us any more, and we'll kill them both."

"Aren't you a little mixed up," Doc asked, "as to who is doing the bothering?"

"Did you hear what I said?" Sam demanded.

"Yes."

"Well, think about it."

Sam and all his men then made their escape.

They all got away in the street so quickly that Ham Brooks whistled two or three times in reluctant admiration. Ham was still carrying his sword cane, which he hadn't had an opportunity to use, and he waved this angrily.

"I'll bet we discover," he said, "that those fellows have been trained in that sort of thing."

"Go telephone the police descriptions," Doc said.

Ham dashed off to find a telephone.

Doc Savage went back upstairs, suspecting the girl Lena Carlson would have fled, but she hadn't. Lena was sitting on the floor, and she was indignant.

"That was a great idea, telling me to lie on the floor," she said. "They all used me for a carpet on their way to the door."

"Things were a little confused," Doc admitted.

"I think you stepped on me yourself," she said. "There was one who weighed a ton, anyway."

Doc was irritated with her again. "You succeeded in messing things up nicely," he said.

"What's the matter, sensitive about your weight?" she asked.

Doc was not sensitive about his weight. He was not fat. He knew she was trying to rib him, and knew he should not be irritated, but he was angry anyway.

"Your interference," he told her, "wrecked our plan."

"What plan?"

"Ham Brooks was stationed outside," Doc told her, "and he was going to follow them when they left. He was going to trail them around until we found out what we thought it necessary to know, so we would be able to round them up."

"If Ham Brooks is the one who made that smoke, he wasn't in the street," she said.

"Naturally not," Doc said. He explained that he had called out a signal which had brought Ham to their aid, not telling her however that the signal was in the Mayan language or that it was even in any language at all. He just said his loud gurgling noise had been a call for aid.

"And because you grabbed me, they got away," he told her.

"I thought you were one of them."

"They didn't even know you were on the roof," Doc said.

"I guess they didn't," she admitted. "But I thought they did."

"They didn't come out on the roof because you were there. They came out to set a trap for me."

"All right, all right, I made a mistake," she said.

Ham Brooks returned. He was breathing heavily, and he looked bothered. "I called the police and gave them descriptions of all those fellows, and told them you wanted them picked up," he said.

Then Ham pointed at Lena Carlson and asked, "Is she the monkey wrench that dropped into our plans?"

Doc admitted she was.

Ham gave the girl an enraged stare.

"They've got old Monk Mayfair," he shouted angrily. "Except for you, we would have been able to rescue him."

Ham was not in the habit of shouting angrily at pretty girls. But then Ham thought a great deal of Monk, although he and Monk never spoke a civil sentence to each other if they could think of an insulting one.

The girl, for the first time, looked slightly contrite.

"Maybe," she said, "you would feel better if I told you my story."

"My name is Lena Carlson," she said.

Then she paused as if that ought to mean something, as if the whole world ought to know that name.

Ham, noticing that she thought her name would carry weight, was impressed. But Doc Savage's reaction was quite the contrary. He felt that the young woman should be spanked, shaken or otherwise relieved of self-importance.

Lena wasn't satisfied with the reaction to her name, so she said, "I trust you've heard of me."

Doc had. He had just remembered where and when. Or rather, he had concluded that she must be Madelena Smitz-Carlson.

And who hadn't heard of Madelena Smitz-Carlson? Possibly Hottentots in Africa hadn't heard of her, and perhaps some of the inhabitants of Germany and Italy where the news was censored. Because, before the war, in fact, before there was much conviction there was going to be a war, Madelena Smitz-Carlson had made headlines by offering to kidnap no one less that Herr Hitler himself, but the government and newspapers had clamped down on her hare-brained bid for publicity.

Before that, there had been other things that had put Madelena Smitz-Carlson on the front pages and made her notorious. She was a spoiled, extremely wealthy heiress who had never known a restraining hand. She had flown oceans, gotten in and out of all kinds of scrapes, and generally pursued a career of making headlines.

She was Madelena Smitz-Carlson, all right. Doc Savage listened to her as she identified herself proudly, with a touch of anger because they were not awe-stricken.

"Here," she said, "is what has happened to me."

It was simple. Somebody had tried to kill her. She didn't know who.

"Three times," she said. "The first time they drilled the exhaust stack of my plane and piped the fumes into the cabin. Carbon monoxide, you see. My mechanic found that. The second time it was poison, cyanide in a champagne cocktail in the Club Lido out West; and the last time it was simpler, just a plain shot."

She had seen who had taken the shot at her.

"So I trailed him," she said. "He was not hard to follow, because I was riding when he shot at me, riding a horse. I fell off the horse, and he thought he had killed me. So he was careless. I followed him here to Washington."

She shrugged. "To make a long story short, and to

include everything that is important, I followed him here, to this old building."

"Why did they try to kill you?" Doc asked.

"I don't know."

Doc Savage and Ham Brooks were both silent when she stopped talking and she became indignant.

"I'm not lying!" she snapped.

"You have no idea what's behind this?"

"None," she said sharply.

Doc Savage considered the situation for a while.

"Do you," he asked, "know a man named Too-Too Thomas?"

"Too-Too—oh! Oh, yes, of course," she said. "I know him, yes, of course."

"Who is Too-Too Thomas?"

"My partner," she explained. "My partner in the ownership of a ranch called the Rancho El Dirty Man, in Lower California."

"Have you seen him in Washington?"

She looked surprised. "Is he here?"

Ham told her, "Either you're a twenty-four-carat, fifty-caliber liar, or you know almost as little about this mess as we do."

CHAPTER V
Trail to Trouble

Apparently they had deflated the notable Lena Carlson somewhat. She seemed uncomfortable.

"Maybe," she said, "I did sort of wreck things."

"Amen," Ham assured her.

"Maybe you'd pick up your faces if I redeemed myself?"

"Eh?"

"I know where they have been hanging their collective hats."

Ham's jaw fell. "You know where their headquarters are?"

"That's right."

Doc Savage gripped the young woman's arm and they hurried out of the building and along the street.

"We'll have to move fast on this," Doc said. "Those fellows will guess that you've probably been watching them, and they'll change their headquarters on the chance that you know where it is."

Lena Carlson nodded. "That's right, too. From what I saw of them, they're pretty sharp."

The car which Doc and Ham were using was a borrowed one, a coach model which would have been on a junkpile if there had not been a war in progress. They got going.

"Which way?" Doc asked.

"Go north," Lena Carlson said. "It's out on the edge of town, a house in the suburbs."

Doc told Ham, "Get Long Tom, Johnny and Renny on the radio."

The radio was a portable outfit. It was so compact that it didn't look as if it had the power to reach New York, but the set would work even the Pacific coast under most conditions. Ham used the loudspeaker built into the set instead of the headphones, so that Doc could hear.

"I'll be superamalgamated," said the voice out of the radio. "We've been waiting to hear from you."

This was William Harper Johnny Littlejohn, the archaeologist-geologist and walking dictionary.

Ham asked, "Who's there with you?"

"Everybody."

"At headquarters?"

"Yes."

Ham explained, "Something has up and wrapped itself around our necks down here in Washington. This is one time we didn't go looking for trouble."

"You went down there to get into the fighting army," Johnny said.

"Well, we're in something," Ham assured him. "It's started off like a house afire, and it doesn't make the least kind of sense. But one thing is sure, we've been marked up for a killing and the gang that is after us already has Monk."

"What are they going to do about Monk?"

"We wish we knew," Ham said grimly. "They tried to kill Doc and me, so I don't like to think about Monk."

"I'll be superamalgamated!"

Ham said, "Doc has something to say."

Doc Savage, taking over the microphone, said, "Johnny, you and Renny and Long Tom get the planes' equipment ready. Get set to operate."

"Right-o," Johnny said. He sounded pleased. "You want us down there in Washington right away?"

"Yes. You had better take individual planes."

"Does that mean Pat?" Johnny asked.

"Is she there?"

"I didn't figure you would burst into song. Yes, she is."

"Tell her to go home."

"We did," Johnny explained. "You want to know what she said?"

"Never mind," Doc said. "But discourage her some way."

The bronze man switched off the radio. Lena Carlson was examining him thoughtfully. "Who is Pat? Is she by any chance Patricia Savage, who operates that beauty salon on Park Avenue?"

"That," Doc admitted ruefully, "is Pat."

"I've heard of her," Lena said, "the way you hear about electric sparks."

The house was new. It looked as if it had been built since the war. Although it was new and in a nice suburban section, the design was so standardized that one could tell at a single glance the number of rooms and the layout. Six rooms, two upstairs with two baths, attached garage, basement stairway opening off the kitchen. Even the shrubbery looked as if it had come out of a standard-lot catalogue.

Lena Carlson indicated the place.

"Now," she said, "you can see why I know so little about the gang. Show me how anyone could get close to that house without being seen. It's as exposed as a fly sitting on a billiard ball."

Doc Savage did not pass the house. "Get down," he said, as soon as it came in sight. Ham and Lena Carlson were down on the floor boards while Doc drove calmly into a driveway of a house in the same block. The garage of this house was open. He drove into it and stopped the machine.

"Ham," he said. "In the back of the car is an equipment case holding the large stuff. Get the kite out."

"Kite?" Lena said. Then she stared at the object Ham was removing from the case. "You really mean a kite, don't you?"

It was a flat kite, and there was a bridle gadget of light alloy which could be changed simply by jerking the kite string. With this, the direction of the kite could be changed somewhat; it could be flown to the right or the left. The kite string was made of a slender, strong, twisted pair of wires.

To the tip of the kite—the sticks were airplane metal tubes—Doc attached a pear-shaped gadget with a sharp spike on the end.

"Fortunately," he said, "the house has a wooden shingle roof."

Lena pointed at the pear-shaped gadget. "Mystifies me," she said.

"Contact microphone," Doc said. "Very sensitive and so sturdy you can almost hit it with a hammer. At least, it's made so that it can withstand the force with which it will strike that roof."

He put the kite in the air. There was a smart breeze, and the kite darted around. Doc maneuvered it carefully.

The fact that they had calmly driven their car into a strange garage was attracting attention. A face, a woman's face, was pressed to the window of the house to which the garage belonged. She looked alarmed.

Doc, Ham and Lena all smiled at her. But the woman did not smile back.

"I better tell her we're not after the family silver," Lena said.

She went to the door of the house and knocked, but she got no answer. The frightened woman's face did not appear again at any of the windows.

Doc Savage got the kite into position, jockeying it with skill which indicated he had done it before. He sent it point first into the roof of the house in which they were interested.*

"Turn up the amplifier, Ham," he said, "and see if we hooked anything."

There was movement in the distant house. They could hear feet stamping, apparently on a stairway, then moving through a hall, or through rooms.

"I think the noise was in here," a voice said, and there was the sound of a door opening. Then the man said, "I don't see anything, Willis."

Willis said, "What do you think that noise was, Sam?"

"It sounded as if something fell," Sam grumbled. "I thought for a minute someone was hiding up here. But I don't see anybody."

Ham clutched Doc's arm. "That's two of the men who were at the old building downtown. I know their voices." He became more excited. "I wonder if Monk is there?"

Ham got to his feet, picking up his sword cane.

"I'm going in there," he added. "I'm not going to fool around."

---

*In the old days when there was peace in the Orient (China and Japan), the art of kite fighting became a highly developed one. At one time it was almost as popular as cockfighting, and more elite. The idea was to wreck the other person's kite, and the kite strings were coated with broken glass, so one could saw an opponent's kite string in two.—Ed.

Doc agreed, "We might as well. We fooled around downtown, and were left holding the sack."

Lena Carlson looked at them unbelievingly. "How many do you think you are, anyway?" she asked. "There're only two of you. There may be fifteen men in that house. And there's something about them that makes me think they're trained fighters."

"Trained?" Doc said. "You mean army men?"

"I don't know," Lena said. "They're fighters, anyway. And there're just two of you."

"Listen," Doc said.

The others had no trouble hearing what he had heard. "Police sirens," Ham exclaimed.

Doc indicated the house to which the garage belonged. "The lady of the house must have called the police. You can't blame her."

Another police siren joined the first. This one was very close. In the same street, apparently.

"Come on!" Ham yelled. "Now's the time to close in on that house. We've got help."

Doc Savage thought so, too. Ordinarily he would have preferred to use more caution, but the arrival of the police would alarm the occupants of the house.

They went along an alley, moving fast, and headed for the house on the roof of which the kite lay. They saw a man standing in front of the house, in the yard.

The man was staring up at the roof, at the kite and the kite string. He turned around and looked at the street. He ran, jumped, got hold of the kite string and examined it.

"Wire!" he yelled. "A wire kite string. Dammit, they've got a microphone on the roof."

He ran into the house, bellowing the same information again.

The house garage was a double one, and now two delivery trucks, one the dairy truck that had been in the downtown street, popped out.

It careened into the street on two wheels. A police car was in the street, and the cops who were looking for trouble, instantly yelled and blew whistles. A man leaned out of the dairy truck and shot at a policeman. The cop jumped behind a fire hydrant, getting out his gun. From his gun came flame and noise.

The dairy truck fired back at the cops and all the policemen began shooting as they scattered for cover.

The second panel truck came out of the garage. From it also there was shooting.

In the second truck, a voice was yelling, and bellowing, making a tremendous uproar, and it was a voice which both Doc and Ham recognized.

"Monk!" Ham shouted. "Monk is in that truck!"

Ham dashed wildly into the street, hauling out an unusual weapon which he carried, a supermachine pistol of Doc Savage's design. The little gun was too complicated and delicate for military use, but when properly cared for, it could turn loose an unbelievable number of small bullets in a second. In operation, it sounded like a deep-voiced bull fiddle.

The machine pistols could be charged with different types of bullets—smokers, gas, demolition, and most often a type of "mercy" bullet which would produce unconsciousness without harming the victim a great deal.

Ham had the idea there were mercy bullets in the pistol, but instead there were smokers. The little smoke bullets made a great cloud of smoke around the truck, but the vehicle soon raced out of the pall.

Both trucks rounded a corner.

Ham expressed his feelings violently. "I'm sure having my troubles with smoke today!" he complained.

Doc Savage had wheeled back. He seized Lena Carlson, hauled her after him, and climbed into their car in the garage. As he was backing out, Ham landed on the running board. He scrambled inside.

"Chasing them is going to be a job," Doc said. "There are so many routes they can take."

Lena said, "I think I can help there. Go north three blocks, then west."

"Why?"

"They did some driving around during the time I was watching and trailing them," Lena exclaimed. "It was obvious they were spotting get-away routes in case they needed them. The one they drove over the most is the one I just told you."

Doc Savage fed the engine all the gasoline it would take. They gathered speed.

"Think of the tires," Lena said, "and cross your fingers."

The tires held. The speedometer climbed to eighty-five, which was miraculous speed for such an old car. Doc took streets which paralleled the route they were going to intercept, and finally turned into the main boulevard.

"Good guess!" Ham yelled. "There go both cars."

Then he ducked, and glass fell out of the windshield at the upper right corner. The noise a bullet had made rang in their ears.

"Either that was an accidental hit," Ham gasped, "or they've got the world's best marksman."

Lena Carlson had been riding in front. She crawled over into the back seat, and lay on the floor.

"I'm beginning to wish I had joined something peaceful, like the Commandos," she said.

CHAPTER VI
Ambush

There was some shooting, evidently quite a bit of it. They could hear the popping of the guns faintly over the noise their car engine was making. Only two bullets hit their machine, and one of these hit Ham squarely in the stomach.

When the bullet hit Ham, he barked loudly, and doubled over. First he wrapped his arms tightly around his stomach, then unlocked them and beat his stomach frantically with both fists.

Doc grabbed Ham's arms to stop the beating, and said, "If the bullet went through the vest, that isn't good for you."

Lena Carlson had gotten up in the seat. "You're shot," she said. "Here, let me take care of him." She began trying to hold Ham still.

"Get away from me, blast you!" Ham yelled, getting his breath. "And leave my shirt alone!"

But she had already wrenched open his shirt. She looked surprised, and held up a misshapen blob of lead. "You've got a bulletproof vest," she said.

"It sure wasn't kickproof," Ham said, and went off into a fit of coughing.

"Back out of sight," Doc told the girl. "Get down on the floor boards where you were. Ham, you too."

The girl got down. Ham said, "I'll be all right as soon as I get my lungs acquainted with some air again."

There was no more shooting for a while. The two trucks ahead kept together, and concentrated on speed, trying to lose their pursuers. They were not successful.

"Airport," Doc said. "They are going to an airport."

"But there is no civilian flying in the coast zone right now, because of the war," Ham objected.

Doc Savage glanced at his wrist watch.

"There is an airlines plane fueled and on the line ready for the St. Louis flight right now," the bronze man said gravely.

In the dairy truck, the man called Sam had also consulted his watch. He said, "Give it more gas, Bummy."

"She's got it all now," Bummy said. "We'll make it. There's the airport."

The other truck, a few yards ahead of them, rocketed into the airport.

"Plan two," Sam said. "Use plan two. And let's not pick any flowers."

The runways of the flying field were separated from the parking ground by a conventional factory-type steel wire fence which was closed by metal gates. The gates were closed and locked.

The lead truck slowed just enough so that nobody would be damaged by the shock, and hit the gates squarely. Both front tires blew out and the radiator caved back on the engine, but the gates burst open. The truck skewed off to one side, rocking drunkenly, and stopped.

The men in that truck piled out with their guns and began shooting at everybody in sight.

The second truck went through the gate, straight for the big airliner which stood in front of the passenger building. They did plenty of shooting from the truck, and the airline employees scattered.

The pilot made a run for his cockpit, but the truck stopped in front of the plane, so that it could not move. The pilot came out of the ship with his hands in the air.

A man removed the wheel chocks.

More men loaded Monk Mayfair and Too-Too Thomas into the airliner.

The others had flopped behind anything that was handy, and were shooting. Some shots were coming back from the armed guards around the field. But no one seemed to be hitting much.

Two men out of the truck climbed into the plane. They were fliers, experienced on big two-motored ships. They ran forward, got into the cockpit buckets, and looked over the instruments.

They started the motors and began warming them up.

The men from the other truck were now picked up by a quick trip which the first truck made back to the gate.

None of the raiders were down, although two had been hit and slightly wounded. Two airport employees were on the ground, one of them motionless, the other crying and trying to stem the flow of blood from the wounds where a bullet had gone through both his legs.

The raiders loaded into the big passenger plane. The ship had capacity for all of them, and more.

"Highball," Sam said.

The ship moved slowly, gathered speed, and went rocketing across the field, paying no attention to the runways or the frantic signals from the control tower.

It took the air, made a dangerous bank with a wingtip stabbing at the ground, and came back. Men were sticking rifles out of the windows.

Doc Savage saw the plane coming. He was still in the car with Ham and Lena Carlson, and he swerved the machine, sent it to a spot near a drainage ditch close to the factory-wire fence.

"Into the ditch," he said.

The ditch had about a foot of water, but it was narrow, and the steep sides offered shelter. They splashed into it, then crawled rapidly so that the men in the plane wouldn't know exactly where they were.

"The water is muddy," Doc said. "Submerge as much as possible, and they will not be able to spot us as well."

The big plane boomed overhead. A few bullets smacked into the ground, some driving up water spouts in the ditch. But none of them came close.

The plane went off into the distance like a cannonball and did not come back.

Ham looked around the airport, dumbfounded. "Do you realize," he asked, "that they pulled that whole thing off in not much more than a minute. Why, it must have been less than a minute."

Lena Carlson shivered. "I'm lucky, I guess!"

"I don't see anything lucky about it," Ham said. "They got away."

"I mean before," Lena said. "They tried to kill me three times, remember? As efficient as they are, it's lucky they didn't get the job done. Then where would I be?"

"They got away with Monk!" Ham said. He sounded despondent.

Doc Savage got out of the ditch, stringing water, and

went to the car. He put the short-wave radio into operation.

"Johnny," he said into the microphone. "Or Long Tom,
or Renny."

A feminine voice came from the loud-speaker. "Don't
leave me out, if you please." It was Pat Savage.

Pat's voice had some of the qualities of strength and
ability which Doc's voice had.

Doc ignored her, said, "Johnny, Long Tom, Renny!
Come in, please."

"Johnny to Doc," Johnny's voice said. "O.K. What is
it?"

"They just stole the airline plane for St. Louis," Doc
said. "They have Monk aboard." He gave them the
department numerals and a description of the plane. "Keep
your eyes open. The plane took off for the north, and was
going north when last seen."

"A fairly thick overcast extends south of Baltimore,"
Johnny said. "They are heading for that. They'll get into it
before we have a chance to overtake them."

"Try, anyway!"

"Sure, we'll try."

Doc started to put down the hand microphone, changed
his mind, and said, "Pat?"

"So you've decided to notice me," Pat said.

"Where are you? Your own plane?"

Pat sounded angry and said, "One of your helpful pals
put my personal plane on the fritz. He thought that would
keep me at home. I know who it was. It was Renny."

"What did you do?" Doc asked sourly.

"Why, I just climbed in with Renny," Pat said. "I'm
with him now. Say, is this Lena Carlson the beautiful and
notorious Madelena Smitz-Carlson? If true, you had better
watch out or you'll find yourself shopping for rings."

Doc switched off the radio without bothering to answer.

Doc Savage, Ham and Lena Carlson went back to the
house from which they had flushed the men. There was
nothing they could do at the airport, the police had taken
over, and army officers were on hand. The army had come
because there was something too precise and military in
the manner in which the plane had been stolen.

At the house, Doc Savage unearthed nothing of value.

He got plenty of fingerprints, or rather the police got them and furnished him with copies.

The house had been rented—for a startling price—three days before. The police picked up the landlord immediately for violating the rent ceiling edicts, filing the technical charge of suspected complicity in the crime of attempted murder. None of the police had been killed when the men burst out of the house, but some had been wounded.

Doc Savage told Ham, "You might get the ultraviolet projector."

This ultraviolet projector was a strong source of light rays outside the visible spectrum, equipped with a good filter lens. Doc switched it on, and pulled down the curtains in the various rooms in the house.

Then the bronze man began going over the floor, over the lower walls and the furniture with the ultraviolet light.

Ham knew the object of the search, but Lena Carlson and the police were puzzled.

It had been a practice of Doc Savage and his aides for a long time to have at least one button on their clothing which was composed of a chemical plastic. When used as a pencil for writing, on almost any surface, it would leave a mark that was invisible to the naked eye, but which would fluoresce under ultraviolet light.

"What's the idea of the lantern, Diogenes?" Lena Carlson asked.

Ham Brooks explained about the invisible writing which would fluoresce under the black light.

"What's fluoresce?" Lena countered.

"I can see keeping you posted scientifically is going to be quite a chore," Ham said. "Let's leave out the details and just say that when something fluoresces, it glows under the effect of black light."

"Oh, like a firefly, you mean?"

"Could be," Ham admitted. "As I understand it, they don't know exactly what makes a firefly shine, though."

Doc Savage made an unexpected small trilling sound which was low and exotic, strangely musical and yet completely tuneless. It was a small, unconscious thing which the bronze man did in moments of astonishment.

"What's that?" Lena asked.

"It's Doc's substitute for a grunt of astonishment," Ham said. "But don't ever kid him about it. He learned it from an old mentalist and master of mental control in India a long time ago, and Doc has never been able to get rid of the habit."

Lena Carlson hurried forward to see what Doc had found that provoked the trilling sound.

The message had been written on the new varnished hardwood floor of the house. The fluorescence was very faint until Ham went into another room and got a blanket and came back and made the room considerably darker than it had been. Then the scratching on the floor was more decipherable.

It said:

THEY HAVE TWO BOSSES, NAMED DER HASE AND DAS SEEHUND. Submarine involved. Is big business. Monkey business, too. Am keeping big ears fanned out but learning little except couple of new cusswords. Learned those when they found out Doc was on their trail. They are keeping me around because of mysterious order from boss named Der Hase to do so. Glad to know I am such a worthy character to this Der Hase. Am well and hope you are the same.

Ham Brooks read the message, and he chuckled. His chuckle was so relieved that it almost held tears.

"That's old Monk," he said. "Old Monk wrote that."

"How can you tell?" Lena asked.

"Nobody but Monk would write a silly message like that."

"Is it his handwriting?" Lena asked, amazed.

"That toad-scratching aspect of the writing," Ham explained, "was probably caused by Monk's hands being tied behind him. The chemical-plastic button he used for the writing was doubtless one of the suspender buttons off his trousers, in the back. He could get to that button, with his hands tied."

"He certainly wrote a long message and said very little," Lena said.

"That's Monk. He must have had plenty of time, and not much to say."

Lena frowned. "Der Hase and Das Seehund. Who are they?"

"Was about to ask you the same thing," Ham said.

"I never heard of them. Why should you think I had?"

Ham shrugged.

Lena said sharply, "I don't know why I'm involved in this. I have no idea what it's about."

Ham shrugged again, more elaborately.

Doc Savage was examining the note written on the varnished floor with invisible chemical script. "Der Hase and Das Seehund," the bronze man said. "The words are German. They mean the Hare and the Seal."

"Nicknames," Ham said.

"Obviously."

"Ever hear of them?"

Doc evidently had not. The bronze man was silent for a while.

"Ham," he said, "go down to the war department and borrow a couple of enemy prisoners. Borrow a couple who have seen the light, and have been willing to talk to the American military authorities."

"Where do you find such an article in Washington?" Ham asked.

"The War Department will tell you."

As soon as Ham had departed, Doc Savage got in touch with the airport by telephone and asked whether his aides had landed as yet. They were just coming in, he was told. "Put one of them on the wire," Doc requested.

It was Renny who came to the telephone. Renny Renwick was an eminent engineer with a voice which habitually shook the surrounding scenery, and a pair of fists like suitcases, nearly.

"Holy cow, Doc," he said. "We didn't see fuzz nor feathers of that plane that carried Monk off."

"Is there much excitement at the airport?" Doc asked.

"There is still quite a bit."

"Inquire around and look over the situation," Doc said. "It might be that someone recognized one of the raiders, or one of them might have dropped something that would be a clue."

"Right," Renny said.

"Call me back by radio."

"Right."

"Are Long Tom and Johnny in yet?"

"No. They got started a little later, and their ship is not as fast as mine," Renny explained. "They'll be showing up soon."

"Good," Doc said.

"Wait, don't hang up," Renny said. "Doc, Pat came down with me. She just barged in, and when I told her we didn't want her mixed up in this, she said go to the devil. What do I do?"

Doc sighed wearily.

"Try telling the police or the Army Intelligence she is a notorious international spy, a regular Mata Hari," Doc suggested. "Maybe they will lock her up and keep her out of our hair."

"That won't work. All the cops know Pat by sight."

"If they did not, she would probably smile at them and hypnotize them," Doc said wearily. "Think of something."

"I've got a headache from thinking," Renny said.

"It is probably nothing to the headache we will have if you don't think of something that will work," Doc assured him.

Renny Renwick, at the airport, hung up the telephone receiver, looked at the telephone and complained, "That was a lot of help." Finally he grinned at himself.

Pat was in their hair, all right. And all of them knew, Doc as well as the others, that there was not much they could do about it.

As a matter of fact, Pat wasn't quite the calamity they pretended she was. There were times when she had been a considerable help, but there were other times when she had complicated matters.

Renny was thinking of that when the man in the white coveralls accosted him.

"They told me you were a Doc Savage associate," the man said. "I'm Reeves. I'm a mechanic, a grease monkey here at the field."

Renny eyed him. "What have you got on your mind?" Renny was not too impressed by the man, and he did not want to be bothered by somebody who just wanted the distinction of having talked to a Doc Savage associate.

"Found this," the man said. He fumbled in a pocket. "It help you any?"

It was a folded bit of yellow paper.

"Where'd you find this?" Renny asked.

"Over by where they smashed through the gate in the car, them guys who stole the plane," the man said. "They tumbled out of their car after it was wrecked by hitting the gate, as you may know. I happened to be standing where I could watch them. I saw this fly out of one of their coat pockets, but I didn't think much about it at the time. There was so much going on that I don't think I hardly noticed it."

It was a telegram.

Renny glanced over it.

"Holy cow!" he said. He looked up. "Why didn't you give this to the police?"

"I just remembered about it, and went out there and found it where some dust had been scuffed over it," the man said. "To tell the truth, I was looking around for a cop when I saw you, and I thought I'd show it to you."

"Good," Renny said. "What did you say your name was, Reeves?"

"That's right."

Renny beckoned to an airport executive who was passing a man in the mechanical end. He indicated Reeves, asked, "You know this fellow."

"Yes," the airport man said. "Hello, Reeves."

"He work here?"

"Sure," said the airport official. "What's wrong? He done something?"

"Not at all, he's been helping me," Renny said. "I just wanted to check on his identification. Thank you. And thank you, Reeves."

Renny headed for his plane. He encountered Pat Savage on the way.

"Come on, Pat," he said. "We're taking off."

"What's up?"

"I hear a hen cackling," Renny said, "and I'm pretty anxious to get there before she lays the egg."

They took off in Renny's private plane. Renny went through the business of getting a clearance and filing a flight plan after he was in the air, a matter that kept him busy and red-faced for some minutes.

"Dang the official red tape," he complained. Then he switched on the private short-wave radio, and began trying to raise Doc Savage. He got Doc without much trouble.

"Doc," he said, "something came up. I am heading for the Arizona desert country."

"What on earth?" Doc said, sounding surprised for once.

"One of those raiders dropped a telegram," Renny explained.

He got out the telegram, which read:

> TANK TRUCK AVIATION GAS BE AT LIGHTNING FLATS FOR USE ANY TIME. LIGHTNING FLATS IN ARIZONA. SIGNAL BLINKING RED LIGHT RAPIDLY.
>
> H. I. JACK.

Renny read the telegram to Doc, and added, "Holy cow, I couldn't take a chance. With that big plane, or with any plane the way it is in wartime, they've got to land at some out of the way place for gas. Maybe this is the tip-off."

"Where are you?"

"In the air headed for Arizona and the place."

"We will join you," Doc said.

"Good. Here is where I got the message." Renny explained about the man at the airport, the fellow who had found the telegram.

Doc Savage made no comment on that, except to check on the man's name. Then Doc asked, "Pat with you?"

"Yeah. What am I going to do with her?"

"Put a parachute on her," Doc said, "and drop her over a nice wilderness somewhere."

Renny chuckled, and the radio conversation ended.

"I'm very popular, am I not?" Pat said. "My own cousin, dropping me in a wilderness. Nice stuff."

Renny said, "We'll have to drop off in Kansas City and pick up an Arizona chart. I don't know where this Lightning Flats is in Arizona."

"It sounds interesting, anyway," Pat said.

Renny was fiddling with the radio. "Holy cow!" he said.

"What's the matter?"

"Blamed radio," Renny said. "Seems to have gone on the fritz."

"That's strange," Pat said.

CHAPTER VII
Lightning Flats

Doc Savage, in Washington, told Ham Brooks, Johnny Littlejohn and Long Tom Roberts, "The trouble with investigating is that it takes time."

Lena Carlson looked a little irritated, but the others did not take it as criticism.

Ham said, "The guy had been working at the airport about four months. His record wasn't too good. About borderline, I would say, not bad enough to be fired and not good enough to make them think much of him."

"Four months," Doc Savage said. "When Renny asked, and found out the man had been employed there that long, he would not be suspicious."

Long Tom Roberts, the electrical wizard, was a thin man with an atrocious complexion. His sallow coloring didn't mean a thing as to his health, but he could stand alongside a mushroom and make the mushroom seem rosy-cheeked.

Long Tom said, "I had a heck of a time with the telegraph companies. They wanted a special edict from the president, and a personal threat from Hitler, apparently. Anyway, they finally got busy and put a currycomb through their files."

"And?" Doc asked.

"No messages from Arizona," Long Tom said. "They checked by wire with the Arizona relay offices, and the Arizona point of origination, and there was no such message sent."

"Trap," Doc said.

"It doesn't look good," Long Tom admitted.

Doc turned to Lena Carlson and asked, "What about your contribution?"

"Well, all I can say is if you're not satisfied with the

time I made, you should have seen the amount of work I did," Lena Carlson said.

"What did you find out?"

"You asked me to learn where these men could get a truckload of high-test gas," Lena reminded him. "I was supposed to check the whole country in no time at all, comparatively speaking. Anyway, I got the job done after a fashion. I will say that your name worked wonders with the government people I talked to."

"Did you get any results?" Doc asked patiently.

"Sure. A truckload of high-test aviation gas was high-jacked in Arizona, but in eastern Arizona, which is no-where near this Lightning Flats."

"What happened to the truckload of gas?"

"They're hunting for it. The thieves got away with truck and gas, both."

"I'll be superamalgamated!" Johnny said. "That makes it look as if they're going to refuel in Arizona, anyway."

Doc turned to Johnny. "Any contact with Renny and Pat on the radio yet?"

"None," Johnny said.

"We had better get out to the airport," Doc said, "and talk it over with that fellow who said he found the telegram."

The man who had found the telegram was in the locker room, getting out of his work clothes. It was not quitting time, and he looked uneasy when he saw them.

"I wasn't feeling so good," he told them. "I guess it was the excitement got my nerves. I'm taking off the rest of the day."

He was a somewhat flabby looking man, and his uneasiness grew.

Doc Savage took the man by the arm.

"Want to tell us all about it?" Doc asked.

The man jerked wildly to get away. "What're you talking about?" he gasped.

Doc said, "Ham, the truth serum. We might as well give it to him here and now and have it over with."

Ham then produced an impressive hypo needle. As a matter of fact it was one of the huge needles used by veterinaries to treat horses and cows. The mechanic took one look at it and bleated uneasily.

"Truth serum!" he yelled. "What you mean?"

"Makes you talk," Ham assured him. "Sometimes it is such a shock to your system that it kills you, but we've got to use it anyway. We haven't time to fool around prying information out of you."

The man did some struggling, some bouncing around, some sweating. Ham knew by the signs that he was weakening, so Ham clicked the needle noisily, and filled it with orange pop from a bottle which he had thoughtfully provided with an impressive skull and crossbones label.

Words began coming out of the frightened man.

"They told me it was a gag," he whined. "I didn't know it was anything like it was."

"Who told you?"

"Them guys. They paid me to give the telegram to one of your gang and say I had found it. I was to give it to Savage or one of the others. They told me it was a joke."

Long Tom said ominously, "Now look, brother, let's cut out the lying right now. You know danged well that shooting wasn't a joke, and you gave the telegram to Renny after the shooting, so let's not have any more joke talk. You knew it wasn't any rib."

The man grew pale.

"They paid me so much money to do it!" he mumbled.

"The telegram was a phony?"

"Yes. But I didn't realize—"

"Who were the men who hired you? What do you know about them?"

"Nothing," the mechanic said, and he sounded sincere.

Just to make sure that he was not lying, however, they worked the fellow over thoroughly with words, and Ham did some more impressive flourishing with his prop hypo needle. In the end there was no doubt but that the mechanic had told them all the facts in his possession.

"I didn't realize it was wrong!" he kept wailing.

"The only thing you didn't realize," Ham told him grimly, "was that you'd get caught."

Long Tom growled, "Let's try to overtake Renny and Pat. We'll do our best to intercept them by radio. They may have to set down for fuel somewhere."

In the meantime, Renny Renwick and Pat Savage had decided to make a nonstop high altitude jump to Lightning Flats, in Arizona.

Pat had gone through the chart case in the plane. She flourished a chart triumphantly.

"Why don't you clean out your chart box now and then?" she asked. "Look here. A map which shows Lightning Flats."

Renny examined the map. He found that Lightning Flats was a desert section which apparently had no distinction other than being flat, arid, and as hot as the hinges of that place, probably.

It was then that Renny decided on the nonstop flight.

"I've got the fuel," he said. "And old Monk is in that other plane. So we'll not waste any time."

He took the plane up above thirty thousand where the air currents were favorable enough to add another hundred miles an hour to the near pursuit-plane speed of his craft, and they unrolled miles for a few hours.

Pat pried into the radio to see what was wrong with it.

"Look here," she said, indicating a soft black mess of stuff in the radio mechanism.

"What is it?"

"It's wax," Pat said, "mixed with graphite dust apparently, to make it a conductor of electricity. A lump of it was put in the radio, and the heat of the radio tubes melted it a few minutes after the radio was switched on."

"Hey, that's sabotage!" Renny rumbled. "When the radio was switched on for a test on the ground, it would test O. K., then go out a while after it was in the air, after it had been on for a time."

"That," Pat said, "is the hole the polecat came out of."

"What do you figure it means?" Renny asked.

"I don't know," Pat said. "But to me, it means I'm going to keep at least one eye open."

Renny scratched his head and finally muttered that he didn't know when the dirty work had been done, although it might have been done in Washington while they were refueling the plane.

"We got something else to think about," he added. "Down there is Lightning Flats."

He upended the plane, sent it boring down in a steep

dive until about five thousand feet, close enough to the earth so that they could distinguish the general contour of objects.

It was a flat place in the desert, nothing more interesting than that. The desert itself wasn't particularly picturesque, for it had few of the colorful qualities of the Painted Desert. There were hills. They didn't seem to be much as hills seen from this height, but Renny knew they were large hills.

It was dusk, too, nearly dark, and in that light in this clear air, measuring distance with the eye could lead you astray.

"Looks peaceful," Renny said.

"So does a stick of dynamite," Pat said. "Sometimes one looks just like a harmless candle."

"See anybody?"

"No."

"They couldn't hide a plane down there," Renny said.

"True," Pat admitted. "But trouble doesn't always come in planes."

Renny dropped the plane lower, examined the place some more, and finally said, "I think I see a hump of dirt that is either a Navaho hodag, or a structure of some kind."

"Hodags are round," Pat said. "This one isn't round."

"Give me the flashlight," Renny told her. "We were supposed to signal with a blinking red light. Isn't that what the telegram says?"

Pat found a flashlight. "It doesn't have any red lens."

"I thought of that," Renny said. "I have one of those card holders in my billfold, and it is made of red celluloid. I'll just hold a sheet of it over the flash lens."

While Pat handled the plane controls, Renny tried out his idea.

"Holy cow!" he said immediately. "I got a bite. Look! Down there by that structure I noticed."

It was another red light, also blinking rapidly.

"All's well in sneaky town," Renny said, chuckling. "Now we land and have a surprise party."

Pat said, "I don't like this."

"What don't you like? They don't know we are enemies, and we'll be right up on them before anything goes wrong, before they know there isn't any butter on their bread."

Pat shook her head.

"It's too open and shut," she said. "I keep thinking about the doctored radio."

Renny was enthusiastic for a fight. "When we get down there, we'll doctor somebody," he said.

"You're getting as bad as Monk where a fight is involved," Pat told him. "You'd better stop, look, listen, and whistle at the crossroads."

"Maybe," Renny said, "you'd like to cancel your ticket for this trip."

"Eh?" said Pat.

"You weren't invited, you know."

"You," Pat said, "get my goat at times."

"I can remember the times," Renny told her, "that you've brought out a cold sweat on me, too."

Pleased with himself, he put the plane into its landing bank, the usual triangular approach which he used. He straightened out for the landing glide.

A noise, a rush of air, made him turn his head.

"Hey!" he bellowed. "Holy cow!"

"I think I'll check out," Pat said, "and watch from the side line."

She jumped, the parachute pack dangling on its straps, her hand on the ripcord.

Renny twisted his head around and watched to make sure she landed safely. By that time, he had overshot his landing, so he hauled up the nose and went around again. That time he set the plane down without trouble.

Lightning Flats apparently was an old lake bed which had dried as smooth as a concrete highway. Because of its high speed, the plane which Renny handled landed hot, and he nursed it along, sending it toward the end of the lake where the light signal had been returned.

He would, he decided, sit in the plane with a gun and take the enemy by surprise. The plane cockpit was armored.

By the time he reached the other end of the field, Renny had his machine pistol ready, and had opened the cockpit windows. He opened the windows only a slit, enough to shove the machine pistol barrel through, because the windows were also bulletproof.

Straining his eyes, separating objects in the rapidly increasing dusk, he saw that the structure he had seen from the air was not a hodag, nor one of those round structures of logs covered with sod which the Navahos sometimes used for a winter house.

This was a tank truck, a big transport truck covered with a camouflage of sagebrush and tumbleweeds.

The refueling truck, Renny thought. This is where they were going to refuel, all right.

He knew enough about the speed of his plane to be quite sure that he had beaten the stolen air transport to the spot.

Renny rolled his plane up to the concealed truck, stopped it.

Men walked out from under the truck camouflage cover. One of them waved sociably. They did not seem to be armed.

Renny shut off his motor.

"This the spot?" he called.

The men stopped.

"Hell!" one of them said. "That guy ain't one of the outfit."

Renny laughed loudly, gleefully. He shoved the snout of his machine pistol through the window slit.

"You bet I ain't," he said. "I'm a wolf in sheep's clothing, that's what I am."

They stared at him in horror.

"You boys," Penny added, "had better jump for a star. Come on! Try to grab one!"

There was an explosion, a very loud one. Sand, fire in a sheet, came from under Renny's plane. The plane itself gave a big jump straight up and changed its shape somewhat. The plane fell back to earth.

The men dashed forward and hauled Renny out of the wreckage.

The man who had thrown the big grenade approached also. He had been concealed cleverly under the ground, in a shallow pit scooped out and then covered over with paper which was the same color as the dried lake bed.

Other men had been concealed in the same fashion in the earth in the neighborhood. They were shouting questions, demanding to know if their help was needed. Evidently it was quite a job to conceal them, and they were not breaking out unless they were needed.

"Is he dead?" the grenade thrower asked, staring at Renny.

"Probably just overcome by surprise," a man said, chuckling.

Renny was affected by something more substantial than surprise. His head had banged against the side of the plane cabin. But it was not serious.

He was tied hand and foot, and was kicked in the ribs when he regained consciousness.

"Who used the parachute?" they demanded. "Who jumped just before you landed. And why?"

Renny thought: Pat wasn't smart—she couldn't have known this was a booby trap. She was just lucky. And how lucky! From now on, she'll be hard to hold. I won't be able to tell her a thing, without her pointing to what happened this evening and laughing in my face.

A man kicked Renny again and repeated, "Who used the parachute?"

"My personal gremlin," Renny said. "And brother, that's closer to the truth than you think."

This wisecrack brought him another kick in the ribs. But they did not get more information from Renny. He just howled indignantly and mentioned specific parts of anatomy, such as ears and arms, which he was going to snatch off his captors individually before this thing was finished.

The captors sent off an expedition of four men to search for whoever had used the parachute.

They came back empty-handed and uneasy.

"Too dark to find anybody out there," they said.

"The thing to do," a man decided, "is get out of here."

"What about our plane from Washington?"

"Get on the radio. See about it."

They used a portable radio—it was a very modern and efficient set operating on various wave lengths to which it was switched in succession by a synchronized clockwork arrangement, which was the latest method of defeating eavesdropping and the use of a direction-finder in locating a radio transmitter.

"Plane's only about fifty miles away," the man said. "They're going to land, refuel, and we'll all pull out."

Before long, Renny was watching the stolen transport plane from Washington drop down on the dry lake bed.

He watched the ship pull up close, and the gasoline truck roll to the craft and refuel it.

Then Renny, still tied hand and foot, was tossed into the cabin of the airways craft.

He found Monk Mayfair there.

"How are you?" he asked Monk.

"Indignant," Monk said.

"How come they haven't shot you?"

"They got orders not to."

"Yeah? Who from?"

"Somebody," said Monk, "called Der Hase. That's German talk for the Hare, or the Rabbit."

"Where is this Der Hase?"

"At the place we're heading for."

"Where's that?"

"You now know," Monk said, "as much as I know about it."

Renny looked around, and saw another figure, that of a leathery, weather-beaten, elderly man who looked as if he had reached old age on a diet of cactus and sage.

"Who's Methuselah, here?" Renny asked.

"You big-fisted, sad-faced lump of gristle," said the old man sourly. "I'm twice your age and twice as active right now. When you're my age, I'll be six times as active."

"Who's he?" Renny asked Monk.

"Name's Too-Too Thomas," Monk explained. "And he's the key that unlocked all of this for us. He's the match that fell in the gasoline barrel."

"Old-timer, where they taking us?" Renny asked.

"If you fellers had talked sense to me in Washington," Too-Too Thomas muttered, "you wouldn't be asking silly questions now."

A man walked back into the cabin. He had a short automatic.

"All this talk is getting tiresome," he said. "Give us a rest, huh?"

CHAPTER VIII
Sea Trail

Patricia Savage lay flattened out in a desert gully and listened to the motors of the big plane warming up again. The engines had been shut off during the refueling, so now she knew that the refueling had been completed.

Pat smiled grimly. She lifted her head to watch. The night was dark, but they were using flashlights around the plane, so that she could tell what was going on. They were getting aboard the plane.

With clenched fists, Pat waited. It was hard waiting, but she could think of no way of disabling the plane, so there did not seem to be much to do but wait.

She watched the plane go hiking across the flat dry lake bed, pick up its tail and lift heavily into the night sky. The pilot did not fool around the vicinity, but went droning out over the desert.

Now Pat crawled closer to the gasoline transport truck. It was not where it had been—the covered spot where the truck had been camouflaged earlier was much easier to reach. But the truck had been rolled out to refuel the plane.

The plane had left three men behind. They were talking. Their voices came plainly to Pat.

She listened for a while, then relaxed. There was no sense in making an effort to capture these men, when such an attempt would be a long chance anyway. Because these men knew nothing of value, obviously.

The trio had been hired to steal the truckload of aviation gas. They were talking about that now. They mentioned the amount of money they had been paid, speaking in tones of awe. They discussed the division of the payment, and one man seemed to think he was entitled to an extra share. He was voted down immediately.

The men had a small car concealed under the camou-flaging. They got in it, and drove away. Pat let them go.

She hadn't like the looks of the men. The old-fashioned bad man, who wouldn't harm a woman, was a thing of the past in the West, she was afraid. There was too much at stake to take chances.

She sat and waited. She wished she had a radio, but the one in Renny's plane had been smashed. The smashing job was an expert one.

However, Pat did find Renny's flashlight, and the bit of red celluloid from his card case which he had put over the lens of the light. She got this.

Gratefully soon—not more than twenty minutes later—she heard the drone of a plane engine. The craft circled the field.

Pat used her red light, signaled rapidly. She got an answer. She listened for the sound of the motors of the big plane, and decided they had enough distinction for her to recognize them. It was Doc's plane.

Pat, with the white light, signaled, "Get down here, Doc. This is Pat."

She sent the signals in a phonetic spelling of Mayan, partly, so there would be no delay while Doc made sure she was Pat. Doc would know that few persons other than his aides knew Mayan, so he would take it automatically as identification.

Doc landed. Ham, Long Tom, Johnny and Lena Carlson were with him.

Pat told them what had happened.

"Now don't tell me I'm a nuisance any more," she said. "If I hadn't jumped, both Renny and I would be prisoners, and you fellows would be looking for a needle in a haystack."

"Your modesty becomes you," Doc said dryly. "Why did you jump? Feminine contrariness?"

Pat laughed. "My particular brand of it," she said. "But it turned out all right."

"How do you figure it turned out all right?" Doc asked. "They got Renny."

"Oh, yes," Pat said triumphantly. "But I fixed it so we could trail them."

"Eh?"

"That's right," Pat said.

Lena Carlson had been standing by listening, and now she entered the conversation.

"That," she said, "is ridiculous. Trailing a plane is ridiculous, unless they have a radio transmitter switched on in the craft, or something."

"Ridiculous, eh?" Pat said.

"Certainly. I've done enough flying to know."

Pat eyed Lena Carlson. Apparently the two young women weren't going to get along too well together.

"You've done too much talking in your time probably, too," Pat said.

Turning to Doc Savage, Pat asked, "You have infrared filters for the landing lights?"

Doc Savage was astonished. So were Ham, Long Tom and Johnny. "I'll be superamalgamated!" Johnny said.

Doc asked, with frank admiration, "How did you get the stuff into their gasoline?"

"I took it with me when I jumped from Renny's plane," Pat explained. "That was why I jumped, and why I took the stuff along—there had been mention before, you know, of high-test gasoline, and that meant refueling their plane. So I took this stuff along—Renny had a supply of it as part of the equipment in his plane—when I jumped."

Doc said, "How did you get it into their gas, though?"

"I didn't put it into their gas. I put it into the truck tank, and they filled their tanks from the truck, so everything is hunky-dory."

"Gosh, I hope they use the gas out of the refilled tank right away," Long Tom said. "Otherwise, if they filled a tank that isn't feeding for a while, we'll play heck picking up the trail."

Pat said, "Flying this distance, from Washington here, in a commercial plane, their fuel supply would be pretty well exhausted. I thought of that, and watched. They filled all the plane tanks."

Doc Savage said, "Come on. Get in the air, and fast."

They piled into the big ship—the plane was about the size of a B26 army job, but since it was an experimental job, it had many bizarre features—and got off the ground.

Doc Savage turned the controls over to Ham Brooks. "Switch on the special filaments in the lights," he said.

Ham obeyed—with the result that the wingtip lights seemed to become extinguished.

"What's the matter, the lights burned out?" demanded Lena Carlson.

"Keep your bustle straight," Pat said. "And watch."

Doc asked, "Pat, which route did the plane take."

"I lined it," Pat said, "as making directly for that tall rock over on the horizon."

Ham laughed, said, "That tall rock just happens to be one of the biggest mountains in Arizona."

"Well, if it's Adam's beard, what's the difference," Pat snapped. "Try lining up and flying toward it. I would say an altitude of about five hundred here, and a climb of about five thousand feet to the mile."

Ham nodded. The plane began to swing from side to side as it climbed, making S turns slowly.

Lena Carlson said, "This is a silly business. If you're going to chase them, why not chase them."

Nobody answered her. Doc said sharply, "There! We went through it!"

Ham nodded. He had seen. He banked back cautiously.

A luminous green material as nebulous as the tail of a comet appeared in their path. It came out of nothingness, and it stretched ahead in a powdery stream that had a few waves in it.

Pat turned to Lena Carlson. "I put a chemical in the gasoline of the other plane," Pat said. "The chemical, when burned in the motors, leaves an exhaust trail which is ordinarily invisible, but fluoresces in the presence of infrared light. Our infrared projectors are in the wings."

Astonishment held Lena Carlson silent for a while.

"That's marvelous," she said finally. "Why doesn't our army and navy use it—why don't they have spies get the stuff in the enemy gasoline supply?"

Pat shrugged. "It was tried. The trouble is, the enemy only has to add a tiny amount of a counteractive agent to their gasoline, and the thing is worthless."

"Everybody get busy," Ham called. "Following this trail in the sky isn't the cinch it would seem to be."

Lena Carlson nodded. "I can see that. The varying air currents will push it all out of shape in a little while."

They were exhausted when, an hour and a half before the official sunrise time, they came to the end of the air trail. They had not, somewhat to their surprise, headed toward the Dirty Man Ranch for the last hour.

Lena Carlson had been positive the Dirty Man was their destination.

It turned out, however, to be nothing of the kind. Not just now.

Lena had explained, "It would all tie up. Old Too-Too Thomas has been managing the Dirty Man spread for years. He built it up from nothing, on capital furnished by my father, and by myself."

"I thought you were his partner?" Long Tom said.

"I am, legally."

"What kind of a place is Dirty Man?"

"It's the kind of a place Too-Too Thomas would like. You saw him."

"A hard country, eh?"

"Made of trouble and glory, if you get what I mean," the girl said. "It's big. Hundreds of square miles of mountains and range around, inhabited by the toughest kind of Yaqui Indians, who are all afraid of Too-Too Thomas. But the Indians aren't afraid of anybody else, and they run strangers out of the country so fast it isn't funny. I don't think anyone but Too-Too Thomas could operate Rancho El Dirty Man for any length of time. He has the Indian sign on the Yaquis, you might say."

"You think," Long Tom asked, "because Too-Too Thomas is half owner of the Dirty Man, that the trouble centers around the ranch."

"Don't you think it's obvious?"

But as they got into Lower California, then turned sharply out to sea, she wasn't so positive.

"Why are we flying out to sea?" she kept asking. "Could it be that the air currents have swept the trail way out here?"

"No. There is hardly any wind. Look at the sea."

The sea, as they all could observe, was calm. It was amazingly calm even for the Pacific, which is a tranquil cow among oceans. There was hardly a swell at all, and in the bright moonlight the water looked as slick as if greased.

They saw the plane easily.

The trail of fluorescent particles led down to it. The plane had apparently sought to land on a narrow strip of reef, hitting the water first and then side-slipping onto the bit of land to keep from sinking.

"Look!" Ham yelled, pointing at the plane. "Doc, you want to land?"

"Circle a few times," Doc suggested. "These fellows have shown themselves to be tricky."

Their big ship cannoned over the surface of the sea, and they saw that the airliner had landed on a reef. The surrounding ocean was miraculously calm.

Figures stood on the wings, waving at them.

"Only three," Long Tom said, counting them. "I wonder where the others are?"

"Did one of those look like Monk?" Ham demanded anxiously.

Long Tom said, "The way you worry about Monk, nobody would think you two have been acting as if you were about to decapitate each other for years."

Ham, his nerves driving him into a sudden rage, snarled, "Did you see Monk, I asked you!"

"Take it easy," Long Tom muttered. "No, I didn't see Monk."

They circled back, and the figures on the airliner windmilled their arms, signaling for help.

"Wait a minute," Pat said. "I think one of them is signaling by semaphore with his arms."

Doc Savage kept the plane in a slow circle in which it held its altitude not far above the sea, and watched the man signaling.

Pat cried, "He says the others are unconscious or injured inside the plane. Says gas failed."

Doc Savage said, "We will have to land, regardless of the possibilities of trouble. They might not be lying."

"What makes you think they are lying?" Lena Carlson asked skeptically. "It looks strictly O. K. to me."

Doc made no comment. He brought the plane in slowly, set it on the surface—the plane was an amphibian suitable for operation from either land or water, so taking off again from the surface of the sea should present no complications, as calm as the water was. He gunned the motors, first one then the other, to guide the plane more readily, and sailed up to the other plane on the reef.

"How are they?" Doc asked.

"Pretty bad," the man called from the top of the plane, "they are inside."

Doc Savage, Johnny and Long Tom were on the wing of their own plane, along with Lena Carlson. Ham Brooks was handling the controls, jockeying the ship closer to the beached plane.

Then, unexpectedly, Pat Savage cried out in horror. She pointed at the water.

Lena Carlson saw, gasped, "A shark! A big shark!"

"Made of steel," Doc Savage said grimly, and tried to reach the cabin of their plane.

He was too late, because the submarine was coming up under them fast. It had been lying down there, concealed by the blackness of the water, lurking, waiting.

Now the submarine came up. It hit the plane hull; hit it hard.

It came up so that the forward mounted deck gun hit the ship, and impaled it. And as the submarine rushed out of the water, snorting, bubbling, compressed air whistling and spurting, the plane was lifted partly out of the sea and held there as if it was a duck which had been seized by a shark that had a mouth in the middle of its body.

Doc Savage and Ham were both thrown into the sea. The others managed to stick with the plane, except Pat, who fell off on to the deck of the submarine, where she managed to land without too much of a shock.

Pat, as soon as she hit the submarine deck, got up and worked frantically with the deck gun, a piece of about five-inch caliber, in hopes of getting it ready to operate, and pointed at the deck of the submarine.

But men came out of the sub hatches, and seized her. There were many men, all efficient. They showed Doc Savage and Ham Brooks, who were in the sea, some grenades.

"Kommen," a man said. "Kommen Sie os bald wie moglich, bitte."

"Hey, they're Hitler's boys," Long Tom called.

CHAPTER IX
The Unexpected Herr Schwartz

Ham Brooks whispered to Doc Savage, but Doc couldn't hear the whisper, so Ham remembered that he could use Mayan. Ham spoke in that, and asked, "Any chance of disabling this fish? Maybe get one of our explosive grenades against the hull?"

. Doc, also in Mayan, said, "Our pocket grenades would not discourage that submarine hull. It is built to withstand depth bombs. Three hundred pounds of TNT has to explode within fifty feet of it to crush it."

The man on the submarine with the hand grenade said, "Are your chappies saying your prayers, or are you going to climb aboard?"

"We are feeling very meek," Doc told him.

The bronze man and Ham Brooks got aboard the submarine. They were tossed lines.

The others were unloaded off the impaled plane.

Pat and Lena Carlson created quite an impression.

"Ah, *Fräuleins*," one man said as he straightened his necktie.

Some moments were spent in an admiring inspection of Pat and Lena. Then a walrus, or what could have passed for the head of one, put its head out of the side hatch of the conning tower and spoke pointedly in accented English. The words were American, but the accent was definitely Teutonic.

"Vot is it, a tea party?" the walrus head asked. "Do you want to get below, or shall we submerge and you swim?"

"What," asked Long Tom, "was that?"

"According to its hat," Ham told him, "it is the commander of the submarine."

"I thought sub commanders were all Prussian ramrods with acid for blood," Long Tom said. "This guy looks like something out of a funny paper."

The walrus head advanced from the conning tower hatch. It was followed by a body equally as comic, round and jovial, but probably quite muscular and efficient.

"Get down below," the skipper said, "or somebody gets der pants kicked."

From the way the sailors behaved, they evidently got their pants kicked now and then. None of them seemed to think the comical-looking old gentleman was fooling.

Doc Savage and all the others were hurried below decks, being efficiently searched as they passed, one at a time, down a hatch.

Several sailors showed great interest in the project of frisking Pat and Lena.

"Nix, nix," said the walrus-faced skipper. "Vun or two of us are gentlemans, regardless of what the rest of the world thinks."

He confronted Pat and Lena and bowed. "In my cabin," he said, "are two silk bathing suits. I purchased them for my two daughters, bought them in Japan. I guess there is noddings to do but contribute them to this good cause. You vill put on der bathing suits. Then I vill feel safe about you hiding veppons." He chuckled. "My cholly boys will enjoy dot, eh?"

The grins on the faces of his jolly boys showed that they would enjoy it immensely.

The submarine, Doc Savage noted, was one of the late type of U-boats, a craft built for efficiency and strength rather than impressive size and cruising ability. In the present war, it had been discovered by the enemy that smaller submarines took less material, were more compact, and could be maneuvered more readily under circumstances where maneuverability was the answer to whether the crew got back home or not.

The craft was evidently quite new. Long Tom noted this, and said, "We're evidently sinking their U-boats so fast that they're putting them in the water while the rivets are still hot."

The walrus-faced sub commander snorted. "You do pretty goot, at dot," he said.

They were escorted into a forward compartment, squeezing through the cramped quarters of the submarine, bending often to get under pipes and machinery.

In the compartment, there were about fifteen people. Monk and Renny and Too-Too Thomas were among them. The others were the men who had been in the airlines plane.

Ham stared at Monk.

"You all right, you homely bassoon?" he asked.

Monk sneered at him. "What've you done, joined up with the Nazis? You couldn't be just a common captive. Not with that great legal brain you're always bragging about."

Ham made his voice disappointed and said, "I guess they haven't beat any sense into you."

Lena Carlson and Too-Too Thomas looked uneasy, distressed by the soured meeting between the pair.

Doc Savage and the others were impressed also, but only by the fact that Monk and Ham's meeting had lacked fire. Usually they managed some really original insults, and enough thunder and lightning to make a bystander think a mutual murder was imminent.

Now one of the submarine crew, who had been guarding the prisoners, shouted and waved his arms.

"Ich nein kenne diesen Mann!" he yelled. *"Nein!"*

"Was ist?" blurted the sub commander.

There was a rapid exchange of German.

Doc Savage and his men, who understood the German language, listened with much interest. The word exchange was enlightening.

The sailor who had spoken was an informant.

He had, it seemed, been a spy on two men called Der Hase and Das Seehund. He had put the finger on the prisoners, the men who had seized the airways plane, for the submarine commander. He was responsible for the capture of the other plane.

But, pointing again at Doc and his associates, and at Lena Carlson, the sailor shouted that they were strangers. They didn't belong.

Moreover, the man insisted, the big bronze man was the American scientist, Doc Savage.

"Herr Doktor Savage," he said excitedly.

"Is dot right," said the walrus, examining Doc. "Well, well, I caught me a whale, seems as if."

He turned then, and gave an order in German. Separate the prisoners, he commanded. Put Doc and his group in another compartment.

He pointed at old Too-Too Thomas and ordered, "Put him in with them."

The submarine compartment in which Doc's group was locked was smaller, not at all comfortable, and the air had that typical heaviness of grease, electricity and machinery. It was air to which they would soon become accustomed, however.

"Sorry dot you have no carpets," the commander said. He waved to indicate the cell. "Herr Hitler's private suite," he said.

Monk grinned at him, said, "If they had you back in Berlin, they would hang you up by one leg for saying that."

The sub commander chuckled. "Dot they have tried, two or three times," he said. "They find old Adolph Schwartz does not hang so well."

Doc Savage asked, "You are Schwartz?"

"Herr Oberleutenant Adolph von Schwartz," the man said.

When he said that, he popped his heels, and a snap and an impression of iron attention came into his stocky body. For that moment he was a different man, not a genial old German naval officer who made gags about the Nazis.

In that moment, Schwartz was an iron-fisted old-line Prussian with the soul of a rifle barrel and the backbone of one.

It was impressive, the change.

Having identified himself, Schwartz made a little speech.

"It is unfortunate—for you—that I happened to catch you in the net with the rest of my blackbirds," he said. "For that I am sorry."

He looked at Doc Savage and chuckled. "No, I am not sorry at all. It will be good for Germany, having a man like Doc Savage out of the war." He leered at them like a comic strip character. "Undt now I say *aufwiedersen*."

He left them. The door was fastened from the outside. They were alone.

Monk sighed when the skipper had gone.

"If you ask me," Monk said, "that old gaffer is something to watch out for. Something you don't want to find in your breakfast dish."

"One sure thing," Long Tom Roberts agreed, "he isn't the hooligan he pretends to be. Notice his accent? He must have read that in the Sunday papers. He puts it on and takes it off at will."

Old Too-Too Thomas cleared his throat.

"If that's the Schwartz," he said, "that Der Hase and Das Seehund have talked about, he is hell on wheels."

Monk turned to old Too-Too Thomas.

"Pop, you can tell us what this is all about," Monk said. "Would do?"

"Sonny," said Too-Too Thomas disapprovingly, "you keep on calling me pop, and I'll breathe on you and bake you to a crisp."

"You resent it, eh?"

"You ain't fooling."

"If I apologize," said Monk, "would you tell us all the little details?"

"Might be."

"I apologize," Monk said.

"Here," said Too-Too Thomas, "are all the little details."

CHAPTER X
The Dark Turn

Too-Too Thomas took his time, ignored interruption and demands that he get at the heart of the mystery at once, and gave them a brief resume of Rancho El Dirty Man, in Mexico.

"Maybe you would just call it a big ranch," he said. "But me, to me it's something special. She's a big place and we've got our own dock and warehouse down in the cove where we ship our beef out by sea. Our own packing plant, too, where we process our own beef, before we ship it out." He nodded at Lena Carlson, "Remember, Lena is a partner in the Dirty Man."

"Get to the point," Monk said.

Too-Too Thomas ignored that and said, "No other civilization within many a mile. Get that. In this day of airplanes we are probably as isolated as any part of the world except the Arctic. We're isolated because down there there's no place for a plane to be heading, much, that would take it over our neck of the woods.

"Now," he continued, "here's a general idea of who this Der Hase and Das Seehund are. They are both big-timers in the enemy set-up that's caused all the trouble in Europe. This Der Hase has been sort of public hypnotizer for the mob since it began. He decides what they'll tell the public, what they'll feed the suckers. He's the twisted mind behind their publicity. Not the figurehead, mind, but the real brains.

"Das Seehund is the fellow who set up the submarine campaign for the enemy. You've seen his pictures—a great, fat guy. Enormously fat, and covered with medals. In a different uniform and a different big car every time."

"I know the guy you mean," Monk said.

"All right, they're scramming out of Europe," Too-Too Thomas said.

"Leaving Europe? Der Hase and Das Seehund, you mean?"

"That's right."

"Rats," Renny said, "and the sinking ship. Holy cow!"

Too-Too Thomas grinned. "You said it."

"The war must be closer to the finish than we figured," Renny remarked.

The older man shrugged. "Anyway, the two are beating it out of Europe."

"How?"

"By submarine," Too-Too Thomas explained. "What they did was get a bunch of guys who could be bought, or who were ready to get out anyway, and a submarine, and they began moving out, and bringing their money."

"Money?" Ham Brooks said. "Listen, that German money is not going to be worth much after this is over. Nor the other Axis money, either."

"Gold," said Too-Too, "ain't gone out of fashion."

"Where would they get gold?"

"Plenty of it in Europe. Not all in Fort Knox, you know."

"I guess those two cookies could get their hands on it, too."

"They have."

"Eh?" Ham stared at him. "You mean that they've already moved in?"

"Couple of months ago."

"Where?" Ham yelled.

"The Dirty Man Ranch in Mexico," Too-Too Thomas said. "That's what all the whirling around is about."

Big-fisted Renny Renwick rumbled, "Holy cow!"

Leathery, frowning old Too-Too Thomas became long-winded again. He spoke rapidly, sourly, giving a clear picture. "Two months ago they moved in on the Dirty Man," he said. "They already had the place planted with some of their men. I had taken these birds on thinking they were all right. They spoke English better than I did, and most of them spoke Spanish, too, with the accent of an American."

He waved an arm to indicate the crew of the submarine.

"You take these guys on this tin fish, now. Notice how all or most of them look and sound like Americans? Well, they're picked men, men picked because they speak English and look American, and probably most all of them have spent some time in America one time or another.

"Der Hase and Das Seehund," he continued, "picked their men the same way. You got acquainted with some of them in Washington."

"You mean those fellows were all Europeans?" Monk demanded.

"That's right."

"Why'd they chase you to New York?"

Too-Too Thomas said, "I got away from them. They had me a prisoner in Mexico on the Rancho El Dirty Man, and I got away. I scrammed right out of there. I did it in a plane. You could not tell it to look at an old cuss like me that I can fly a plane, but I can. I got to Los Angeles in my plane, and they were right after me. I could see the plane in which they were following me in the air to the south. If they'd had machine guns, they would have shot me down before. There was an airliner ready to take off for the East, and I got on that. It was headed for Washington, so I stayed on. I got to Washington. I was trying to get to somebody important to tell my story confidential, when I met you fellows."

Doc Savage had taken no part in the questioning, but now, after Too-Too Thomas became silent, the bronze man asked, "How did it happen that the men were well established in Washington? They did not get that well established in a few hours—the few hours which elapsed after you got to Washington, and before you met us."

"That wasn't over a couple of hours," Too-Too Thomas said. "But the way I figure it now, they were planted there for Lena."

"For me?" Lena Carlson said. "Gracious, why?"

"Hadn't they tried to get rid of you?"

"Yes."

"I thought so," said Too-Too.

"But why?" demanded Lena Carlson. "Why would they do that?"

"If they killed you, the ranch would go to me according to your will," Too-Too Thomas explained. "And they already had me, or had until I got away. What could be simpler."

"But if you had the ranch entirely for yourself," Lena said, "how would that help them?"

"Oh, they were going to whittle on me until I deeded over the place to them, all legal and everything."

At this point, there was an outburst of noise in other parts of the submarine. It began with animal howls, angry yells, profanity in English and German, and shots. There was plenty of shooting.

The fight outside developed, became furious. They could hear men dashing back and forth in the narrow steel-walled corridor outside, and the submarine tilted sharply upward with the ballast tanks blowing.

Doc Savage and Monk were instantly working at the steel bulkhead door. It was too tough for their barehanded efforts, however.

Monk listened to the fight, said, "Brothers, that sounds like something I hate to miss."

"What do you suppose has happened?" Pat asked in alarm. "We were running submerged, so it can't be an attack by American naval forces—they would use depth bombs."

"Consarned thing sounds like a family row to me," Too-Too Thomas said.

The fight died away. There was some more profanity, a few blows, and finally one shot.

Then the bulkhead door into their compartment was undogged from the outside, thrown open and they were ordered back.

"Holy cow!" said Renny, looking at the man who gave the orders.

It was the man called Sam, who had straw-bossed the group which had first seized Monk and Too-Too Thomas in Washington.

"I feel sort of triumphant," Sam told them. "So I might have the courage to shoot the first one of you who bats an eye at me."

No one batted an eye, probably.

"Throw old faithful in with them," Sam ordered. "Safest place for him."

The walrus of a submarine commander, Schwartz, was pitched headlong into the compartment. The place was so crowded that Schwartz, Renny and Ham, tangled up were on the floor.

Schwartz was apparently in a mood to fight anything that moved, so he immediately began slugging Renny and Ham, who were in the same mood and lost no time slugging back. While this was going on, Sam slammed the steel door and his men dogged it on the outside.

Schwartz and Renny and Ham hammered each other with vigor, nobody doing much harm, but venting plenty of steam.

"Let me in on that!" Monk said eagerly. "I want to hit somebody, too!"

Doc Savage said, "This may not be a time to entertain yourself."

He got busy and stopped the slugging.

Commander Schwartz sat up indignantly. *"Es ist wirklich argerlich!"* he said.

"What'd he say?" Too-Too Thomas asked.

"He remarked that it was rather annoying," Pat translated.

"He's got a good choice of words," Too-Too Thomas said.

Commander Schwartz composed himself. He did this by waving his arms violently and calling on Davy Jones to witness a fine mess. He shouted, *"Heil, der Fuehrer!"* But this last he didn't say as if he meant it at all. He said it the way a man would say, after falling on his face and bruising himself, "That's what I get for eating my spinach."

That was apparently the wind-up of his rage, and intended to be humorous, because he leaned back against the bulkhead, mopped his walrus face on a sleeve, and grinned sheepishly.

"The path of a patriot has its thorns," he said.

"What happened?" Monk asked.

"One of my goot men," said Schwartz, remembering to use his comic accent, "vas so careless as to bend over mit a pistol sticking out of his hip pocket. Vun of der prisoners got hold of it."

"Can you," Monk asked him, "speak the English without all the vuns and ders and mits?"

"Vots wrong, isn't dot goot Cherman accent?" asked the skipper.

"Suit yourself," Monk said. "It might make us laugh, and bless us, we need some entertainment."

"Goot," said Schwartz. "When you feel depressed, say

so and I will talk some of the funny accent for you. I like to do it. I used to get your comic papers and study it, perfecting myself."

Monk eyed him. "You're quite a guy," Monk said thoughtfully. "But you don't fool me. You're a good guy to watch out for, aren't you?"

"There are those who say so. And if I'm not, I have wasted a lot of time acting fierce."

"What happened?"

Schwartz surprised them by talking readily and telling what was obviously, from the sound of his voice and from what they knew of the situation thus far, the truth.

"Ever hear of Der Hase and Das Seehund?" he asked by way of beginning.

"We were just talking about them," Monk admitted.

"Good. Then you know they are leaving the ship like rats."

"Leaving the sinking ship like rats," Monk agreed. "We used the same words."

"The ship isn't sunk yet," said Schwartz, and there was a flash of the ramrod-backed Prussian in him for a moment.

"O. K.," Monk said. "But the point is becoming less and less a basis for argument. Go on. What happened?"

Schwartz scowled at his own thoughts.

"This fellow, Das Seehund," he said, "has corrupted some of the men of our underseas division. Word got to me that something strange was going on. So I investigated."

Commander Schwartz paused and spat to show how he felt. "For investigating, I got a good bust on the shoulder straps. I was reduced in rank from a vice admiral with a good swivel-chair job to going to sea again as commander of a submarine. I was supposed to keep my nose clean, as I believe you would express it."

"But you didn't stop investigating?" Monk surmised.

"I certainly kept right at it. And that is why I am here with my submarine. I planted a spy with the group working for Der Hase and Das Seehund. By devious means, I got the spy, who was piloting that commercial plane, to land on the sea where I could capture them. Then I was going to the hide-out, get Der Hase and Das Seehund, take them back to the fatherland, and turn them over to Der Fuehrer."

He grimaced. "To Der Fuehrer, I wouldn't give a dog that had bitten me. But I was going to give him Der Hase and Das Seehund."

"What would have happened to Der Hase and Das Seehund then?" Monk asked curiously.

The skipper made a cutting gesture across his throat with a forefinger.

"Geek!" he said.

CHAPTER XI
Rabbit and Seal

The mystery of why Doc Savage and his aides were being kept alive was explained when they were taken ashore at Mexico to the Dirty Man.

The mystery had been bothering walruslike Oberleutenant Schwartz, too. He did quite a bit of snorting and muttering during the course of the night, and when Monk asked him if he was nervous, he disclaimed it much too violently.

Pat and Lena Carlson had a quarrel. This fracas began when Lena mentioned the extremely highbrow and expensive beautification and body-reducing establishment which Pat conducted on Park Avenue. Lena called the place, "that gold-plated thieves' roost you run." Pat resented that, although it was a fact that she unmercifully overcharged clients who could afford it.

"That's a very pretty feather-lined head you have, dear," Pat said. "Didn't it occur to you to ask the police for help when these first attempts were made to kill you?"

"I thought of it," Lena said.

"Then why didn't you?"

Lena glanced at old Too-Too Thomas, and said, "I might as well tell it. I got the idea that these men who were trying to kill me had been at Dirty Man. And I was afraid Too-Too was mixed up in something that might get him in trouble if the police knew about it."

Too-Too Thomas grinned at her.

"I'm sorry, Too-Too," Lena said.

"You apologizing for thinkin' I might be a crook?" Too-Too asked.

"Yes."

"That's so durned nice of you," Too-Too said, "that it moves me to return the favor."

Lena stared at him. "Eh?"

"You heard how, when I first approached Doc Savage and his men in Washington, I wouldn't tell them what was going on?" Too-Too said.

"Yes."

"Well, that was because I thought *you* might be mixed up in the crooked mess," Too-Too told her. "I knew that if we could get a plane and a bomb and sink the submarine—not *this* submarine, but the one Der Hase and Das Seehund use—it would stop the affair without involving you. I figured if that happened, you would get scared out."

Lena Carlson was startled.

"So you thought I was a crook?"

"Sort of was led to believe it," Too-Too said, "by them two lads, Der Hase and Das Seehund."

"Well," said Lena sharply, "I never in my heart, not once, really believed you were a crook."

"Same here," said Too-Too, "about you."

"You're probably both lying," Pat said.

The submarine traveled on the surface the rest of that night, but submerged during the day, which cut down its speed somewhat, and then it laid offshore with motors barely turning for a considerable time.

"We're probably lying outside the cove of Dirty Man," Too-Too Thomas surmised, "waiting for it to get dark so we can go inside."

This was obviously what they were waiting for.

Later the motors picked up, and the U-boat surfaced. They could hear the hatches clang open, and heard men tramping around on deck.

The craft bumped against something gently, and stopped.

"That's the dock," Too-Too Thomas said. "They let the sub lie on the surface during the night, and on the bottom during the daytime."

"Do you suppose they'll take us ashore?" Pat asked.

"What I can't understand," Too-Too said, "is why they don't just tie rocks to us."

Eventually the bulkhead door was opened. The prisoners were at once shown a formidable array of submachine guns and other weapons, for the purpose of intimidating them.

Sam said, "This is Mexico. You wouldn't want to die in a foreign country, would you?"

He was obviously very pleased with himself.

They were carefully shepherded out on deck, in groups of three. Pat and Lena were the last to go, and purely by accident, Lena slipped and fell off the side of the sub. As Pat grasped her hand, some of the guards stepped forward, guns ready. But it was purely accidental, and nothing worse than a wetting of the silk bathing suit came of it.

All got onto the dock. The dock was a most substantial affair. On the other side of it lay a second submarine, somewhat larger than Schwartz's charge.

Schwartz groaned disgustedly when he saw this other submersible. "Lying around here," he muttered, "when it should be out sinking Allied ships."

"March," ordered Sam. "Up the hill."

The hill was more of a cliff, with stone steps, slowly angling back and forth, overhung by vines. It was a pleasant spot, and lighted by plenty of hand flashes, so that there was no chance for a break.

The ranch house, or houses, were at the top, at the foot of another cliff, sitting on a wide tableland that probably included four or five hundred acres. The tableland extended along the seashore, and it was its narrowest here, with a cliff coming in from the mountains behind to stand close to the buildings.

The moonlight was bright, putting a pleasant silver sheen over everything.

"Not bad-looking," Monk said.

"You should see in the daytime," Too-Too Thomas said. "The packing plant and the loading corrals are down on the shore of the cove, a quarter of a mile from the dock where the submarines are lying."

They came to the ranchhouse, apparently the main building of several structures. Ham eyed the walls, saying, "They built a fort, didn't they?"

The walls were ponderous, thick, and the building itself a vast affair of cool interiors. The rugs and carpets were thick, and the ornaments on the walls, the pictures and the armor, the silver-mounted saddles, the inlaid revolvers and swords, were all good pieces.

Sam sent a messenger away, instructing him, "Tell them that I made a clean sweep. All prisoners are here."

Sam sounded as if he was about to burst with self-esteem.

The messenger came back and said, "Der Hase will see Herr Savage, *alone*."

Sam frowned. "But did you tell Das Seehund—"

"Der Hase will see Doc Savage alone," the man repeated meaningfully. He also spread his hands in a gesture that said he shouldn't be blamed.

Sam told four men to take Doc Savage to Der Hase. Sam also added, to the messenger, "I ought to kick a window in your anatomy. I told you to tell Das Seehund we were here, and that you needn't tell the other."

"The other one caught me first," the man complained. "What could I do?"

Doc Savage was a little puzzled at the evidence of dissension between the higher-ups.

The bronze man was soon straightened out on what was what, however. Almost the first thing Der Hase said did that.

Der Hase turned out to be pretty typical of the pictures of him which had been published in the American newspapers.

Der Hase was a small, emaciated man, but not crippled in one leg as had been claimed. He moved forward with ease and agility, although his gait had a twisted swing to it due to some difficulty with his hip rather than his leg. The story of deformity probably had arisen from the nature of his face, which wasn't deformed; but was a face with such unusual mobility, such powers of expression and flexibility, that it seemed unnatural. The man had a deep voice which was artificial, a voice that he had painstakingly trained in an effort to use his voice as a mob-swaying device. He had failed. He had bright eyes, bad teeth, a bad breath which he seemed to be able to blow several feet as he talked.

Der Hase said, "You are yourself proof of what can be done with a master race system, Herr Savage, so I think we will have no misunderstandings."

Doc Savage did not comment.

Looking at the man, Doc suddenly realized he had seen the fellow once before. He had known Der Hase briefly, some years ago when Doc was undergoing the course of specialized scientific training to which his father had subjected him beginning in childhood.

Der Hase then had been a student, as was Doc, at a

Vienna University. His name was not Der Hase, but Vogel Plattenheber; but he had been called Der Hase, it suddenly came to Doc's mind, even in those days. He was called the Hare, or the Rabbit, because of his timidity and fear. Looking at him now, Doc saw that the man still had the fear, but that he had turned it into an artificial superiority complex that was a honey. That, if you wanted to get tangled in psychology, was what had put this Master Race stuff in the man's head.

Der Hase frowned at Doc.

"I could use many words," he said.

"You have, on occasion," Doc said.

"All the words would just express more fully, what I wish to say." Except for a slight stiffness in phrasing, the man's English was good. "It is obvious now that we have made mistakes in Europe. But the noble experiment must not be allowed to fail. That is why I have retreated to this out of the way place to form a nucleus for a new effort and plans for the new effort."

The man wheeled and walked to a desk. The room in which they stood was enormous, and sitting on a dais at the far end of the room was a tremendous desk. Not only was the desk high, but the light was very bright in the eyes of anyone sitting or standing in front of the desk. Der Hase made good use of all the conventional tricks to make an interviewer feel uncomfortable.

"I could use an intelligence such as yours in making the new plan," he told Doc.

Doc Savage did not ask questions. There was no need for questions, for everything was perfectly understandable. This man they called Der Hase—Doc wondered if anyone called him that to his face and decided that Der Hase would encourage it in his perverse way—had the ability to make things perfectly clear with a few words.

The man was a fanatic. He was sincere in what he was doing; he believed in it. He had not come here to Dirty Man Ranch in Mexico, had not come those thousands of miles from Europe, with any idea of escape. He was not a rat leaving a sinking ship. He was more of a rat in a corner fighting. He had fought, and he was going to fight again.

Doc said, "Why are you keeping us alive?" He knew, but he asked the question anyway.

Der Hase pointed at his own forehead.

"You can see the way the thing is going in Europe," he said. "We are getting licked. All of our ideals will be smashed by this vandalism called democracy and equality."

He indicated his head again and added, "The trouble is with the thinking that was behind it in the beginning. Mistakes were made. The master race idea is sound, but its execution was not properly thought out."

He had something there, Doc reflected.

"What makes you believe," Doc asked, "that some thinking ahead of time wouldn't have convinced you that the whole thing is barbaric?"

"Barbaric?"

"As barbaric," Doc said, "as the tribes of primitive people who used to go out and take another tribe and make slaves out of them."

"That is childish talk."

"It is simple talk, easy to understand, I will admit," Doc said. "And logical."

"I take it you refuse?"

"You should have known I would," Doc said.

Der Hase looked at him unsmilingly. "You will," he said, "get twelve hours in which to reconsider."

CHAPTER XII
Bad Break

The other man, the one they called Das Seehund, came in then. He made his entrance grandly, with his feet banging the floor as if he were goose-stepping.

Doc Savage looked at him, and kept a straight face.

Das Seehund was wearing a new kind of uniform, a cowboy outfit. The motif was Mexican caballero and Cheyenne frontier days, the loudest of each, and there was probably no louder raiment than these two. His hat was the biggest, his pants the tightest, and there was more color and silverware on him than Doc had ever seen on a cowboy, dude or otherwise.

He wasn't happy, though.

He said to Der Hase, *"Was nun?* Did you have to make a speech before the execution?"

"An execution," said Der Hase, "may not be necessary, if he sees things our way."

"The execution should have been done at sea," growled the enormously fat man in the flamboyant outfit. "They should never have been brought here. That Oberleutenant Schwartz, or any of them."

"Schwartz will be executed," Der Hase said.

The fat man indicated Doc. "What about this one? Don't you know he is probably as dangerous a man as we could have caught? Every minute he is around here, we are fooling around dynamite with a lighted match."

"I admire his brain," Der Hase said.

"Ach!" Das Seehund shrugged. "Me, I admire my own neck."

"If this man Savage would help us, sincerely help us," said Der Hase, "it would be a marvelous thing."

"He will not help."

Der Hase glanced at Doc, seemed grimly stubborn. "Savage is a product of scientific training. He is a living example of what men can do with themselves. He knows this. What we want to do, what the master race wishes to do, is handle men on a cold basis of scientific fact, not sentiment."

The fat man said, "It is a dream."

Doc Savage, watching them, was suddenly sure of a point. They were not in sympathy, did not have a common aim. They only pretended to have the same object.

Dipping a little bit into his memory, Doc got a general idea of the situation. The fat man, Das Seehund, had always been a fellow who sampled life. He wasn't a dreamer, and he had no high ideals and he carried the sword for no particular cause, other than himself. He was a man who liked his steaks thick and rich. Nothing else described him better than that.

Das Seehund wasn't a man who would travel along with Der Hase on any idea of making another attempt to inflict a super race on the world—not if it meant any trouble and risk on his part.

Doc decided what had happened. Der Hase had come here with what wealth he could get, to prepare for another great effort to change the world. Das Seehund had come along, with the wealth, just to escape the consequences of what was going to happen to the Axis leaders in Europe.

Each man knew the other's ideas. They were too clever not to know that much about each other.

"Lock him up," Der Hase ordered a guard, indicating Doc Savage.

Das Seehund looked uneasy as he watched Doc being led out.

The prisoners—the men—had been confined to one large cell. Pat and Lena Carlson were locked up in another room across the hall. Both rooms had stout steel doors, and old Too-Too Thomas was busy explaining how there happened to be iron doors.

"I tell you, they put 'em in since they came here," he said.

"I halfway suspect," Monk told him, "that you had jail cells here in the ranchhouse all along."

Too-Too Thomas snorted indignantly. "When we caught a Yaqui, we didn't use a jail cell on him. And the same went for any of us the Yaquis caught."

"Where are your ranch hands?"

"Locked up," Too-Too said grimly, "down at the settlement where the ranch hands live. It's a kind of fort down by the cove edge. Built by the Spaniards four or five hundred years ago."

Doc Savage was shoved into the prison room at this point, and old Too-Too Thomas took the opportunity to yell loudly at one of the guards, demanding to know whether his Mexican ranch employees were safe.

"We still have them," the guard said. Then he added frankly, "But they are not safe."

"What are you going to do with them?"

"Unless they listen to reason," said the guard, "we shall have to have a wholesale execution."

Too-Too Thomas, beginning suddenly to perspire, said, "None of my men will go over to your rascality, you lizard! They're good citizens of Mexico."

The guard slammed the door and locked it. The lock was a small modern one, a padlock, which fitted into a standard hasp that had been welded to the sheet steel of the door.

Monk came close to Doc Savage.

"Careful, Doc," he whispered. "There's a microphone hidden behind the picture on that wall over there. We just found it, but let on we didn't. So don't say anything you don't want them to overhear."

The bronze man glanced sharply at the picture.

And he made, for a moment, the low trilling sound which was his unconscious habit in moments of excitement. The trilling, which had the fantastic quality of a wind in a wilderness of arctic ice spires, caught the attention of the others. Doc shook his head quietly, and Monk and the others understood.

But Too-Too Thomas was puzzled. He demanded, "What the dickens was that noise?"

"Must be the wind," Monk told him.

"Ain't no wind in here. They got the air conditioner turned off."

A bit later, Monk got Doc aside, and with his fingers—using the sign language of the deaf and dumb, in which he could stumble along after a fashion—he asked, "You get an idea, Doc?"

Doc Savage indicated he had one.

The bronze man also gave the others orders in the sign language, instructing them, "Keep your eyes open and let me know if you see Der Hase at some moment when you are sure he is not with his partner, Das Seehund, and cannot be seen by Das Seehund."

They agreed.

Too-Too Thomas, puzzled, demanded, "What are you fiddling your fingers at each other for?"

"Oh, we do that for exercise," Monk told him.

They didn't need anyone to point out to them that the situation was serious. Old Too-Too Thomas took it on himself to do this, however.

He launched into a description of how isolated Dirty Man Ranch was, and how iron-fisted were their captors. "These two guys, the fat one and the rat-faced dreamer," he said, "have been mixed up in that mess in Europe and they've seen millions of people killed. At first there were only a few killed, people they had to knock off because they stood in their way. But it got worse and worse until finally they started the war and millions have gotten killed. They belong to the greatest gang of mass murderers in history. Those are the kind of guys who have us. Do you think they'll let us live? No. Certainly not."

Monk groaned disapprovingly.

"We know there is a dead cat," he said, "without you dragging it out and waving it around in front of us that way."

The leathery old man snorted. "I'm scaring myself."

"You're scaring us, too," Monk said. "And we don't need any scaring. We're scared already. Why scare yourself?"

"Well, it's this way," Too-Too confessed. "When I'm in a tight spot, I always scare myself good. It seems to help me to think up a way out."

Monk advised, "Cut it out. It just paralyzes me."

Too-Too Thomas grinned thinly. "You seem to be holding up all right."

It was late in the afternoon when Renny Renwick, who had been leaning against the barred window looking out sourly at the mountain landscape and the red glow of the evening sun, made a grunting sound, and said in Mayan, "Come here, Doc."

Doc Savage went over to the window.

Renny had discovered the scrawny dreamer, Der Hase.

The man was evidently taking a walk, a constitutional. He had his head back, had pushed out what did him for a chest, and was walking rapidly with his skipping gait that came from the condition of his leg or hip muscles.

Der Hase disappeared in a thicket, following a path.

Renny whispered, in Mayan, "I figured he would go out of sight. You wanted to know if he left without the fat man."

Doc Savage nodded. He said, also in Mayan, "Gather around, all of you. We are going to start a little civil war."

Monk and the others approached. They were puzzled. Then, when Doc used an excellent imitation of Der Hase's voice, they understood.

Imitating Der Hase's studied oratorical delivery, Doc said, "I thought this would be a good time for an exchange of opinions."

Doc, in his normal voice, said, "We had the idea the thing was fairly well settled."

At this point, Too-Too Thomas, not getting the idea, hurried over and demanded, "Say, what's going on here! If there's any funny business—"

Monk hit him. He didn't hit the old fellow very hard, with the result that Too-Too Thomas wasn't more than jarred, and immediately swung a return blow that almost knocked Monk's head off his shoulders. Monk hit him again, this time without so much politeness. Too-Too Thomas collapsed.

They waited tensely for the guard outside the door to investigate, but the fellow paid no attention. Evidently the thick doors shut out most sounds.

Doc Savage used the fantastic methods he did, his assistants long ago had realized, because he had such unusual tools. His methods worked only because he was good at them. And he was good because of the training which he had received from childhood on. That, and the fact that he kept practicing and exercising continually, an average of about two hours daily, which was a lot of daily exercising when one thought about it.

The bronze man's voice imitations, for instance, were excellent. They weren't letter-perfect, not as remarkable as they somehow seemed, but the fact that he could listen to a man speak a few words, then do the man's voice and delivery so well that no one would notice unless he was expecting something of the kind, was a very convenient trick. He used it often.

As a matter of fact, though, Doc was quite familiar with the voice of Der Hase. The man was one of the louder Axis orators over the radio, and had been for years, so that Doc had heard him often over the air. And Doc used radio voices in the exercises which he employed to keep in trim with his voice imitations. He had practiced Der Hase before. So he did particularly well with Der Hase now.

Der Hase: "Have you changed your mind?"

Doc (his own voice): "About getting rid of Das Seehund?"

Der Hase: "If you must state it so bluntly, yes."

Doc: "It is an interesting offer, but it goes against our conscience."

Der Hase: "Do it, and I will free you—providing I have your word of honor that you will forget all about me and this hide-out."

Doc: "You put a lot of trust in my word."

Der Hase: "Your word is good."

Doc: "There is one reason why we will not do it."

Der Hase: "It is a reason that is none of your business."

Doc: "We think otherwise."

Der Hase: "You mean, you would refuse just because you do not want me to proceed with my plan of starting another new world order, another project of establishing a master race to cure the ills of the world?"

Doc: "Right."

Monk and the others were tensely silent. They saw now what was going on.

The microphone behind the picture was only a few feet, not more than an arm's length, from where Doc Savage was carrying on the conversation with himself. There was no question but that it could pick up what was being said.

Too, there was no doubt but that there was either a listener, or a recording apparatus, connected to the microphone.

The outcome depended on whether Das Seehund listened to the thing first, or Der Hase, or the two together. There were two chances out of three to get results.

Doc continued his deception.

Doc: "Aren't you afraid Das Seehund will find out that you want him killed?"

Der Hase: "That fat oaf! *Ach!* He does not think."

Doc: "But you will let us go if we kill him for you."

Der Hase: *"Ja."*

Doc: "But we have to give our word not to interfere with your plan for another new order attempt?"

Der Hase: *"Ja."*

Doc: "How do you plan to go about this New Order attempt the second time?"

Der Hase: "Use the money we have brought here, and wait until things are quiet again after the war, then start in and get power pretty much as before."

Doc: "You want to use Das Seehund's money, as well?"

Der Hase: *"Ja.* To put it bluntly, I do."

Doc: "Which might possibly be why you want us to wipe him out?"

Der Hase: "Are all these questions necessary?"

Doc: "Interesting, anyway."

Der Hase: "Are we going to get together?"

Doc: "Why don't you take care of Das Seehund yourself?"

Der Hase: "That might be inconvenient. He has many friends. The men here like him, some of them. I would rather an outsider did it."

Doc: "You figure we could do it and escape?"

Der Hase: "I would aid you."

Doc: "You want to know something?"

Der Hase: "What?"

Doc: "This would be a more appetizing proposition if Das Seehund was making it."

Doc made the Der Hase voice splutter with rage, and growl, "You have not many hours to make up your mind!"

Doc then stepped back, and in German, said, "Guard, I have finished talking. Unlock the door."

To make it a little more realistic, he tried an imitation of the guard's voice also, and said, "Yes, sir."

Old Too-Too Thomas had been watching them with much interest, as had Oberleutenant Schwartz. The latter understood the German language where it had been spoken, and knew the set-up, and what was happening.

Too-Too, on the other hand, had not recovered from Monk's punch in time to get a full understanding. But Too-Too was silent.

Schwartz winked one walrus eye at Doc Savage. He seemed pleased.

"Dot vas goot," Schwartz said with his best trick German accent. "So goot I could donce und sing."

"I'll bet that would be a spectacle," Monk told him unkindly.

CHAPTER XIII
The Fat Fish

There was an unscheduled guard change shortly after midnight.

The fat man, Das Seehund, made it, and he said, "I want men I can trust doing this guarding." He said this to the guards Der Hase had posted at the door. There was nothing subtle about the fat man. But he got his guards substituted for those the other partner had placed.

Monk whispered, "It looks like the fat fish got the bait."

Doc Savage was uneasy. It was a long chance he had taken, not so long in risks as in possibilities that it would succeed.

Der Hase and Das Seehund were men who were naturally suspicious of their partners. They had seen too many murders for convenience in the rise of their fortunes in Europe to be otherwise. On that fertile ground, Doc had planted seed. The change of guards probably meant it was sprouting, but he could not tell yet in which direction it would grow.

It grew the way he had hoped.

Das Seehund opened the cell door an hour later. He had a needle-snouted automatic.

"We wish to talk," he told Doc Savage, having trouble with his accent.

Doc stood very still. He had no definite plan beyond splitting the two factions. But now he saw what might be one. It meant immediate action.

Doc held his lips motionless, or as motionless as possible. He used Der Hase's artificial voice.

"I guess I will have to shoot him myself, Herr Savage," Doc said in the imitated voice.

It was good voice simulation and good ventriloquism.

Ventriloquism is not the art of throwing the voice, as it pretends, but of speaking in a voice which sounds as if it came from somewhere else, then indicating a spot from which the hearer will logically think that it came.

The only logical spot this voice could come from was the door behind Das Seehund.

He whirled.

Doc lunged forward, came on the fat man from behind, got hold of the thin-snouted pistol. The pistol began gobbling, because the safety was off. Two guards stood in the door at the moment, and they both fell down, both shot through the same leg by the same bullet.

Pat, in the cell across the hall, cried out, "Don't go off and leave me!"

Which was optimistic, considering that the fight had hardly started.

Doc Savage, in his own voice and loudly, cried, "Run, Der Hase! Run! I will take care of this fat one."

He said it in German, so that there would be no question of the fat man understanding.

It was Doc's idea that it wouldn't hurt if Das Seehund thought Der Hase had actually been in the hall, and had ducked back out of sight.

Doc Savage got the long-nosed pistol. He rapped Das Seehund over the ear with it, and the fat man became limp and astonishingly heavy.

Monk gouged Too-Too Thomas in the ribs.

"Come on," Monk said. "Show us how you fight Indians, pop."

There proved to be five more guards in the hall, which made seven in all, quite a number. They had been standing at attention, however, as was the custom when one of the leaders was around. It took them a little time to get organized, because nobody was giving orders.

Doc helped the confusion out a little by saying loudly, in Der Hase's voice, "Do not shoot Savage! Hold your fire!" He said that also in their native language.

Monk and Too-Too Thomas and the others piled into the hall, shoving each other in their haste. They got on to the guards, in a flying melee. Out of the mess came two rifle shots, an agonized howl, much grunting and scraping of feet and solid fist sounds.

"Here!" Pat cried. "Don't forget us!"

Oberleutenant Schwartz responded gallantly. A valorous expression on his walrus face, he took a run and a jump feetfirst against the cell door.

The door was a steel plate which looked as if it was armor plate, solid enough to hold back a five-inch deckgun shell. But its looks were somewhat deceptive, because it caved enough for the lock to tear out of its fastening.

The steel door burst open, much to the astonishment of everyone but Schwartz.

Schwartz picked himself up, said, "I thought I recognized the metal of which the doors are made. It came from one of our Italian factories. I think the factory formerly made cheese, and forgot to change their formula."

Pat said, "Good for them!" and came out with Lena Carlson.

Monk and Ham had a guard down on the corridor floor, and were pushing at each other, trying to decide who would have the privilege of knocking him senseless. The matter was settled by another guard, who kicked Monk as hard as he could where the kicking was best, sending Monk galloping down the hall on hands and knees, involuntarily. Ham administered the finishing touch, then got up and went to work on the man who had kicked Monk.

Ham got the fellow out on his feet just as Monk came galloping back, bellowing.

"You kicked me!" Monk howled, misunderstanding what had happened.

"Get away from me," Ham said, "or I'll kick you again."

Big-fisted Renny had downed a third guard with a blow from one of his enormous fists.

Too-Too Thomas, with the idea of trying to live up to the reputation he had been giving himself with words, endeavored to take the two survivors for himself. Unfortunately, one of his choices knew a great deal about jujitsu, and got a hold on Too-Too. The result was that Too-Too Thomas ended up on the floor against one wall, gasping and squeaking, with the foe on top of him, preparing to remove an arm.

Long Tom Roberts went over and rescued Too-Too.

"So that's the way you fought Indians," Long Tom said unkindly, after he had slugged the guard who knew judo.

Old Too-Too Thomas scrambled to his feet, tripped and fell down again.

"You hurt?" Long Tom asked.

"I'm too mad to stand up," Too-Too said malevolently.

Johnny Littlejohn had his incredibly long thin arms and legs around the surviving guard. He squeezed. There was a cracking sound, and the guard screamed and fell on the floor, where he groveled and held to his leg.

"I'll be superamalgamated!" Johnny said, and kicked him on the temple.

Pat and Lena Carlson were out of the other cell. Everyone was in the hall. The guards were all out. But from other parts of the big ranchhouse, there was anxious bellowing, the men yelling to other men to get their guns.

Doc grasped Too-Too Thomas, asked, "How many men, usually, on the submarines at night?"

"One," Too-Too said. "One, usually. There'll probably be one on each."

Doc said, "We will try to get aboard one submarine, and disable the other one."

Oberleutenant Schwartz put back his head.

"*Achtung!*" he roared. "*Wohin sind sie gegangen?*"

He was so excited he was mixed up. He had asked, in German, where they had gone, which obviously wasn't what he meant. However, it served.

He got an answer, an excited shout.

"*Beeilen sie sich!*" a voice replied excitedly.

It was down the hall some distance, behind a door.

"My men!" Schwartz told Doc Savage excitedly. "They are imprisoned down there!"

Without more words, he struck out at a lumbering run down the hall toward his men.

Monk pounced on one of the pistols which the guards had dropped, and lifted it. Doc got the gun pushed down.

"Let him go," Doc said.

"That old geezer," Monk said, "is all for the Axis. If he gets the upper hand, we'll be no better off than we were."

Doc reminded, "He is not exactly friendly toward Der Hase. We can use his help."

"O. K.," Monk said.

At the far end of the hall, Schwartz tackled a door with the same tactics he had used on the prison of Pat and Lena Carlson. A run and jump. That door also smashed in.

Doc said, "Come on. Bring the fat man."

Monk and Too-Too Thomas were first to reach the prone, senseless form of Das Seehund. They picked him up, grunted in amazement at the fat man's weight. "Made of bricks!" Monk gasped. "Here, somebody help with this tonnage."

No one heard Monk, however. He and Too-Too wrestled with the burden.

Doc Savage found a room that wasn't a prison cell, and smashed open the window in the room. It led to a flagstone terrace, pleasant in the moonlight.

"Come on," the bronze man said.

He stepped out into the terrace, but got back inside again in haste, as a machine gun began filling the terrace with lead. The gun apparently was on the roof, and the gunner believed in burning powder.

They tried the corridor, and the other side of the ranchhouse. They were glad they did, because they found the gold.

Wealth was probably the thing they least needed at the moment. But they were human enough to get a boot out of it. There wasn't a roomful of it, not quite. But then it was a big room.

It was not all gold. There were jewels, good jewels cut and uncut, and bars of platinum, and even two cases of the most expensive of European cameras. Tiny cameras, miniatures worth two or three hundred dollars apiece in packing cases. There were valuable paintings also.

Evidently some kind of an inventory had been in progress, because everything was spread around on tables, or open on the floor, and there were long ledger sheets and adding machines on other tables.

Ham stared at some of the uncrated paintings, said grimly, "I thought they claimed they didn't steal anything from the Louvre!"

Finding all the wealth in that room did them no good, except to give them pleasure in seeing so much wealth in one spot.

There were no windows.

They went back. Now there was more shooting in the ranchhouse.

Monk and Too-Too Thomas labored along with the fat man. "Find a way outa here!" Monk gasped. "We're gettin' tired carryin' this tub!"

Doc found a door. There was a roof over it. He went outside, saw there were bushes, beckoned the others.

They got into the shade of the bushes, the moon shade that was intensely dark, and began moving cautiously.

But the machine gunner on the roof heard them, and cut loose freely with his weapon. He had mistaken their location, or was indefinite, because he began riddling one bush after another.

Monk watched carefully, fired the pistol he had picked up, shooting only once. The machine gun went silent.

Ham said angrily, "You know Doc's rule against shooting, particularly shooting to kill."

"Oh, I just barked him, like you bark a squirrel," Monk said. "Probably just tapped his scalp gently."

It was dark on the roof, too dark for Monk to have seen anything but the muzzle flare of the machine gun which had been shooting at them.

"Here, help us carry the fat boy," Monk urged.

Ham ignored him.

It appeared now that the way to safety down at the submarine lying to the wharf was moderately clear. There was some shouting from down at the cove, but there were only two voices, and both were demanding to know what had happened, and what they should do.

Renny Renwick, who spoke good German, bellowed, "Just wait until we get there, boys!" to them. Then he muttered, "Brother, just wait!"

The pair at the cove seemed to think a friend had addressed them. They asked if the submarine should be made ready for flight.

"*Ja, bitte,*" Renny rumbled at them.

They should have known that such a voice belonged to no one they'd ever met on a friendly basis, but the echoes from the sides of the cove fooled them.

Doc Savage, with Renny and the others, was descending the long flight of zigzagging steps cut in the cove side. The going was slow, for the steps were steep.

Monk and Ham, burdened with Das Seehund, had

dropped far behind. So far back that they did not dare shout for aid.

"Blazes, what do they stuff these fellows with?" Monk asked finally.

Too-Too Thomas dropped the end he was carrying, the lighter end. "I'm puffed out," he said. "Can't carry this carcass another step."

"He is a very important prize," Monk said. "The American government would like to get him and ask him some questions about his playmates at home."

"You carry him, then," said Too-Too Thomas. "I don't figure you could 'a' been carryin' your share anyway."

"Blast it, pop, I've been carrying him and you, too," Monk said with conviction.

There was a volley of shots. The echoes whooped and gobbled. It was evident that Oberleutenant Schwartz had gotten his crew into action.

Monk and Too-Too Thomas sat down and puffed for breath.

"We could sit on him and use him for a sled," Monk suggested, "and slide down on him."

"Skin him up some," said Too-Too. "But it ain't a bad idea."

At this point, their fat burden came to life. They had been having too much trouble carrying him to realize that Das Seehund had revived. But he had, then had remained doggo until he got his wits organized.

The fat man, lashing out with both legs, managed to kick Monk and Too-Too Thomas simultaneously, upsetting them and tumbling them down the steps. It was quite dark, the steps were steep, and they did some uncomfortable bouncing before they got stopped.

They scrambled back. But the fat man was gone. He was going up the steps with the agility of a freshly awakened mountain goat.

Monk and Too-Too Thomas were too tired to catch him.

"If you had carried your share," Too-Too said, "we wouldn't've had to lay him down."

Down at the cove edge, on the submarines, there was a sudden uproar. Automatic rifles and machine guns put down a barrage which had the volume of a battle.

"Two guys ain't doing all that shooting," Monk said uneasily. "The crews must be aboard the submarines."

"Podner, we're in kind of a pickle," said Too-Too Thomas. "If they're on the submarines, they've got the foot of the path blocked. A fly couldn't go up or down this cliff except on the path. And seems I recollect we left some unfriendly fellows up above."

CHAPTER XIV
Geek!

Too-Too Thomas reached the foot of the path ahead of Monk, which disgusted Monk somewhat with his own agility.

Doc Savage and the others were there. They had taken shelter on the steps, which were cut into the stone at this point deeply enough to give cover.

Ham asked, "Monk, where's Das Seehund?"

"He kicked us down the steps," Monk said truthfully, "and went the other way."

"That's a big help," Ham said.

The gun cut loose from the submarine. It rattled and gobbled, and knocked rock off the cliff. The gun had put in a drum of tracers, and these bounced around in the night looking like straight red strings from one point to another.

Doc Savage said, "Get back up the path."

"It's blocked at the top by now," Too-Too Thomas said.

"There is one point," Doc said, "where the whole group of us can step off the path." The bronze man began moving. "Quick," he added. "Before they limber up a searchlight on that submarine."

The others followed him. They went as silently as possible whenever the machine gun on the submarine was not gobbling. The spot where Doc was bound was not high.

"Here," Doc said.

It was a kind of shelf, a niche between an outthrust thumb of stone, and the path. Here they were not only off the path, but they were concealed from bullets and searchlights used off the sub.

Doc made sure everyone was under cover, then said,

"They will be coming down the path from above, or up from the bottom. Whichever group passes us first, drop in with them. The path is dark enough so that they will not recognize us. That will give most of us a chance to reach the top or the bottom, then make a break."

No one said anything.

From the top of the path, around the ranchhouse, there was steady shooting. A great deal of it. Some of it was hollow thumping inside the house, but more and more of it was getting outdoors.

From the sub, fifty or sixty bullets.

"*Halten!*" a voice roared from the ranchhouse. The voice added that it meant the submarine.

No more shots from the submarine.

"Use a searchlight on that path," the voice ordered. It was Der Hase.

The searchlight sprang out, hot and white in the night, somehow unexpected in spite of the fact that they had known it would appear. It began searching the path.

The beam passed over Doc and his group without disclosing their presence.

From the submarine: "All clear. We see no one on the path."

From the house: "We are coming down. Shut off the damned light so that Schwartz's men can not see us."

The path became dark.

They could hear the men coming down the path. Der Hase and Das Seehund were in the lead, and they were having violent words.

Monk listened, chuckled, and said, "They've joined forces, but they're still suspicious of each other."

The two Europeans, the thin fanatic and the fat one, were arguing as they passed Doc's group.

"You were a fool to fall for such a trick," Der Hase was saying. "Where are your brains?"

Das Seehund snorted. His snort said that he still suspected the whole thing.

As they filed past, the leaders first, then their men, Doc Savage stepped out and joined them. The others did likewise, one at a time, as silently as possible.

If the enemy group had been descending the cliff under ordinary conditions, it would have been impossible for Doc and the others to have joined them. Theoretically it would have been feasible, but an actual impossibility. They would have been discovered.

But they were under fire from above. Oberleutenant Schwartz and his men were firing from above, trying to search out the path. The walrus-faced Schwartz, shouting commands, sounded exactly like a walrus barking, as the echoes mixed up his words.

Doc and his group joined the retreat without being discovered.

They got to the foot of the cliff.

"Keep that light off!" Das Seehund called to the submarines.

Someone—Doc Savage could not tell who it was, but the individual was close behind him—threw a rock. Doc heard the rock whistle past his ear. He heard it hit its target, which was Das Seehund. It knocked the fat man down.

Das Seehund got up, wheeled, thumbed on a flashlight, and planted the beam on Der Hase.

The fat man shot Der Hase four times, seeming to put all four bullets between Der Hase's small eyes.

Der Hase dropped.

The fat man switched out his light, and changed position rapidly.

"Now I am in command here," he said in his native tongue.

No one said anything.

"Get on our submarine," said the fat man. "We will get outside the cove, and shell the ranchhouse from out of rifle range. We can blow them to bits."

No one said anything still.

"The man I just shot was a traitor!" Das Seehund said. "Get moving, quick!"

They walked toward the submarines meekly.

Doc Savage, knowing what to expect, knew that his aides were ducking off into the darkness. Shadow lay over this part of the cove, over the submarines, due to the height of the cliff.

Doc kept with the group. He marched out on the dock with them, until he found which submarine they were taking.

Doc got aboard the other sub. He got aboard fast. There was one man on the grille walk, and he struck that fellow, knocking him overboard.

The bronze man was able to reach the conning tower, went inside. This one hatch would be the only one that was open. And if the others were open, there was a mechanical means of closing them that operated instantly when the controls were thrown into crash dive position.

Doc yanked the conning hatch shut, went down into the control room, and worked frantically with the valve controls.

The submarine, with no headway to make the diving rudders effective, submerged slowly. But it went down as water poured into the ballast tanks.

The mooring lines held the craft for a while. Then they snapped, and the ship sank quickly, grounded on the rock bottom, and lay there.

The bronze man looked around for the listening apparatus. He got hold of a new type of apparatus for underwater communication which at first confused him. Then he found the listener.

He heard the other submarine back out of the cove.

Doc brought the submarine back to the surface, not without difficulty, for that many controls were never intended to be operated by one man.

"Come aboard!" he shouted from the hatch. "Monk, the rest of you."

They arrived, running, grimly silent, and scrambled aboard. Pat had been aboard a submarine before. Lena Carlson and Too-Too Thomas apparently had never been in one. They stood back gingerly, fearful of touching anything.

"Cast off," Doc said. "Renny, you and Long Tom in the engine room."

They operated under electric power until Renny got the Diesels going. By that time, they were out of the cove. Doc let the sub idle there.

"Man the deck gun," he said.

Monk and Ham did that. Johnny got ammunition ready. They fooled around with the piece, learning its peculiarities.

Monk said, "Ham."

"Yes?"

"Somebody hit Das Seehund with a rock, and it made him mad, and he shot Der Hase," Monk said.

"Yes."

"Nice work."

"Just like you, praising yourself," Ham said.

"Wait a minute, I didn't do it!" Monk exploded. "You did it!"

"I never!" Ham yelled. "Don't try to lay it on to me. Whoever did it knew that the fat man would kill the other one, thinking an attempt had been made on his life."

"Don't you bellow at me!" Monk roared back. "And stop trying to lay it on to me."

Old Too-Too Thomas cleared his throat modestly.

"You gents needn't get all hot," he said. "I'm the culprit."

"You threw that rock?" Monk asked Too-Too.

"Yep. One of my old Indian fighting tricks."

Monk and Ham both chuckled.

"You murdering old scamp," Monk said. "Come over here, pop, and let me shake your hand."

"If I come over there, I'll kick you overboard," said Too-Too Thomas indignantly. "Quit calling me pop!"

Out to sea about a mile, there was a gunflash. The shell screamed overhead, hit the cliff and exploded. It had missed the house about two hundred yards.

"Got it," Johnny said, and called out range numbers, getting confused somewhat, finally saying, "I'll be super-amalgamated! Guess we'll have to wait for the next shot."

The next shot came.

Instantly, their own gun barked. The shell was fused to explode when it hit almost anything, and it bloomed out to sea.

They had missed the submarine by an embarrassing margin.

"As a gun pointer," Monk told Johnny, "you are a good archaeologist."

But the other sub did not fire again.

They waited ten minutes, suspiciously on edge, cautiously changing the position of their own craft, then lying silent, so the other vessel could not locate them with its listeners.

Nothing happened.

Long Tom put his head out of the conning tower. "I've been on our listener," he said. "That other sub is beating it. Full speed out to sea. Want to chase him? We couldn't catch him, because from the looks of the two subs, that one was faster."

"Let it go," Doc said. "Put about, get in position, and let go a few shells at our friends on land."

"You'll blow up my ranchhouse!" Too-Too Thomas shouted.

"Miss the house," Doc said.

They fired about twenty rounds at the cliff, generally banging up the scenery. At first, machine-gun fire answered them. Then there was no response.

Doc said, "We will put into the cove. Where are your men imprisoned, Too-Too?"

Too-Too told him where, and they ran to the spot, carefully beached the sub with its bow high, but not so high but that they could get it higher and back off the beach if necessary. Then they went ashore.

There were four guards in the little village inhabited by the ranch hands. These fled after some shouting and scattered shooting.

Too-Too released his men.

"Get these boys some guns," Too-Too said. "They're old Indian chasers, too."

A few weapons were located.

But the advance on the ranchhouse was without excitement. The birds had flown.

"Go after 'em, caballeros," Too-Too Thomas told his men.

Too-Too Thomas and his ranch hands returned about four hours after daylight. Considering their bag of prisoners, they should have been happy. But their faces were long.

"One got away," said Too-Too Thomas sourly. "It was that walrus-faced hombre, Schwartz. He stole one of the best saddle horses in the country, and there ain't a chance of overhauling him."

"Let him go," Doc said.

"I can have my Yaquis put out a signal, and maybe round him up."

"Let him go," Doc said. "Do not try to catch him."

After Doc had gone, Too-Too Thomas scratched his head and said, "I don't get that. I think maybe my Yaquis could catch that Schwartz."

Monk said, "I thought you got your before-breakfast exercise scrapping with the Yaquis."

"Oh, me and them Yaquis has been brothers for years. This is the first good fight I've had in about seven coon ages."

"Well, forget Schwartz. Doc wants him to get away."

"The fellow may have some of that gold on him."

"No, it's still there," Monk said. "Somebody slammed the door and locked it when we went out. It's all there."

"Then why—"

"Doc," Monk said, "wants that Oberleutenant Schwartz to get back to Europe."

"He does! Why's that?"

Monk said, "Can you imagine what will happen to Das Seehund when Schwartz gets back and tells the Fuehrer the story."

Too-Too Thomas grinned. He felt of his throat.

"Geek!" he said.

THE LOST GIANT

I

He had gone to much trouble to get where he was going. He had used great care, and some of the things he had done were peculiar.

The theater ticket, for instance. It was a single ticket to the play *Oklahoma*, the hit play; and times were so screwball that it was known to be a major venture into diplomacy to try for a ticket to *Oklahoma*.

But he had gotten one, and then he hadn't used it. That is, he hadn't used it to see the show. He had used it for the purposes for which he had bought it: to create a commotion buying the ticket, making it appear certain that he was going to attend the show. Too, to make anyone who might be following him think that he was in the show from curtain rise, eight-forty, until after eleven.

There was no certainty in his mind that anyone was following him, but he was not taking chances. It was important not to be followed. So vital, in fact, that merely thinking about it during the afternoon had made him physically ill. He had not even dared make the usual moves to find out whether he was being watched.

He entered the theater. He was recognized, although he would rather not have been. Being recognized was something that could not be helped, because of his conspicuous size and his reputation; and he sat there patiently in the seat he had made such a point of getting, knowing he was being stared at and whispered about. He kept a sour expression on his face—that was easy since he was so worried—and this probably discouraged anyone from trying to talk to him. At least no one did.

Fortunately a war hero came in, almost stoop-shouldered under the weight of his medals and looking self-conscious about it, and distracted some of the attention. The war hero was a nice-looking young guy. The Army was using him in bond drives, but apparently he would have been happier flying the P38 with which he'd downed so many Fritzes.

The lights went down before the curtain rise. Instantly, he was out of his seat. It was a side seat, close to the side hallway, and he was in the hallway in two steps.

"All right, take my seat," he told the man waiting there.

"I don't look too much like you," the man said.

He didn't, either. He was as wide, but not as tall. And he was homely. But he was wearing the same kind of a suit, had deeply tanned makeup on his face, and had worked a bronze hue into his hair with dye. But he was shorter, very much shorter. The first man was a lithe giant, naturally proportioned so that he seemed only about five feet ten and of normal build until one got close to him and realized his bigness.

"You bring a cushion to sit on, Monk?" the big man asked.

"Sure," said the one who had waited in the side hall. "It'll raise me up. But what about intermissions?"

"Get your face in a program, and keep it there. You can handle it all right."

"Okay," Monk said. "Seen any sign of anybody trailing you?"

"No."

"Good luck."

"The same to you, Monk."

Monk said, "I'm not the one who needs it," and meant it.

He got out of the theater by way of a rear door, not the stage entrance but a door that was less likely to be watched, as unobtrusively as possible. He took off his coat and rolled up his sleeves and got a very light-colored felt hat out of his pocket and straightened it out and yanked its shapeless brim over his eyes. Going down the side street, he looked very different.

He rode a cab uptown. He changed and rode a cab downtown. He went across town on one subway train and came back on another and used all the tricks he knew. He walked down a long dark street, down a series of long dark streets, and finally it seemed impossible that he could be followed. So he went to an apartment on Fifty-fifth Street east of Madison Avenue.

He rang an apartment bell. A pleasant lady answered. He said, "I have an appointment to see Mr. House."

"Are you Mr. Seems?"

"I used that name."

"Will you come this way. Mr. House is waiting. I am Mrs. House." Then she looked at him intently for a moment. "Your name isn't Seems, is it?"

"No."

"Aren't you—"

"Mr. Seems, if you please," he said, and smiled. His smile was amiable, confidence-winning, and one would have to know him well to realize how much tension was behind it.

The pleasant lady suddenly looked a little frightened. "My husband is waiting," she repeated hastily.

House was a small man like a mouse. A man with a little voice, as smooth as culture could make it and very gentle. His eyes were large, his mouth large, his forehead oversize, and one got the impression that the rest of his face was nothing much.

He became bug-eyed with astonishment.

"Good God!" he said. "I was expecting somebody named Grimes or Chimes or Seems or something."

"How are you?" the big bronze man said. He extended a cordial hand, then wondered if he was going to be able to keep the hand from trembling while he shook hands with House. "I am sorry about the misleading names. It was better not to use my own name to make the appointment with you."

"Oh now, that's all right," House said. "Just ease my curiosity by explaining why I am honored, and I'll be very happy."

"You already know why I came."

"I do?"

"You were told when the appointment was made."

"Oh, you—" House blinked, and for a few seconds was silently, mentally chewing on his thoughts. He asked, "You really came here to consult me about changing your appearance?"

"Yes."

House stared at the big bronze man, and he started laughing, his laugh large, hearty, full of this-is-ridiculous robustness. "You!" he said. "You coming to me for such a job. You, with your ability along those lines."

The bronze man's composure slipped for a moment, his quiet smile going, and a little of his inner tension rising to twist and draw his face muscles. It was as if a fierce, tormented animal had come out of a cave.

"I'm sorry," House said. "I am very sorry. I don't know why I laughed when you said you had come to me to have your appearance changed. I guess maybe I was very flattered. Maybe that is why I laughed."

"Can we go to work right now?"

"Oh. You are in a hurry?"

"Very."

"What is—"

"You are not to ask questions."

"I don't understand?"

"It is very simple. No questions. Or, at least, don't expect answers."

House frowned. He was Jonas House, and he was very good in spite of his modesty a minute ago. There might have been greater masters of make-up than Jonas House, but they were neither known nor recognized as such.

Jonas House was of Hollywood, naturally. Make-up exists as an advanced art practically nowhere else, if one excludes the cosmeticians' branch of it. Certainly without Hollywood, a man like Jonas House couldn't have developed. He was in New York for the winter, and currently making one of his sporadic efforts to retire from the picture business. In a few months, by spring at the latest, he would be back on the coast. He always went back.

The man was not to be taken lightly. He didn't just smear on greasepaints and apply hair dyes and make rubber fillers for the cheeks, although he could do that sort of thing, too.

House had been examining the bronze man thoughtfully. He shook his head suddenly.

"Look," he said. "To do a job on you, I've got to know things. I've got to know such facts as whether you're going to be out in the weather, on a boat at sea, or in a coal mine. For instance, salt from sea water will bleach out some dyes, and in a coal mine you've got the chemicals in the coal and the soap you wash the coal grime off with."

"I'll give you enough information."

"For example?"

"Snow, wind, cold. Probably more than forty below

zero. Out in the snow quite a lot. Then exposure to warmth of open fireplaces. In contact with the hands such things as skiing wax, campfire smoke, ice water, and possibly a sled dog might be licking my hand. That help?"

"It's a start."

"It's about all you're going to get."

House nodded soberly. He didn't insist. "This is important, isn't it?" he said knowingly, bluntly.

"More than you probably imagine."

House smiled a thin smile and said, "Having heard of you by reputation, my imagination is probably much more active than you think."

"Can you get going?"

"How much time have you?"

"None at all."

"This will take two days."

"More than four hours is absolutely impossible," the bronze man said.

"My God!" House walked to the door and opened it. "Momma! Momma! You better help me on this job," he called. "Hurry."

He was big and blond. He was still big, because even Jonas House couldn't shrink a man. But now he looked soft. Before there had been a corded litheness in his every movement, the tight spring and the corded smoothness of a man who had abnormal strength. Now he looked soft and lazy and comfortable. He was no longer a panther walking, he was a lazy, well-fed young fellow at whom people would look and wonder, why isn't that bird in the army?

The miracuolus thing about the change in him was that no part of him was actually changed to any extent. Slight changes here and there, but no effort anywhere to alter him completely.

"That's the best I can do on short notice," Jonas House said.

They shook hands in the hall.

He left the House apartment, and standing in the elevator riding down to the lobby, he examined himself intently in the mirror.

Looking at himself, he got a queer feeling and a creepy one; for a moment he was positive he wasn't himself. He was very pleased, but shocked also, because it was unnerving to discover that another man could work such wizardry with you. These were strange feelings for him to be having. I'm upset, he thought, and that isn't good.

He left the apartment house, and two nice-looking young men came out of the shadows and joined him. They didn't say anything, but they walked beside him.

He stopped. He mentally seized all his fears and anxiety and shoved them back into his mind where they wouldn't interfere. At least, he thought, gratefully, I am still able to do that.

"All right," he said. "What is this?"

"Do you have a cigarette?" one of the young men asked.

He said, "Never mind playing around with words. Who are you? What do you want?"

He was tense, clear-headed, and already he had decided just where he would hit these young men with his fists and how, if it was necessary. He didn't think it would be needed. He thought he knew who they were.

"We got off a northbound train," one of the young men said.

"Train?"

"Bus, I mean," the young man said. "And I'm afraid we're lost."

"You are not lost."

The young men were relieved. They hadn't seemed too tense, but they must have been, because they acted as if an electric current had been going through their bodies, and now it had been shut off.

"Jonathan Wister is waiting around the corner," one said. "He wishes to speak to you."

He went with the two young men.

He was startled at the change in Jonathan Wister, at the way terror had laid hold of Wister.

It shocked him especially because he had known Jonathan Wister a long time and had genuine respect for the man's judgment, calmness and directness of thinking. He had believed that nothing was big enough to shock Wister the way he was shocked now, to drive him into a tailspin of terror.

Jonathan Wister was entirely unknown to at least a hundred million citizens of the United States. Yet his picture had appeared in the newspapers often, in a semi-anonymous way, in pictures where Wister was one of a photographed group of the internationally notable, groups with the President, the Prime Minister, Stalin. Wister was the man in the background, the man whose name wasn't in the cutlines printed with the picture.

Wister was a career diplomat. The head of his department took the credit for Wister's good work, and took the blame for Wister's mistakes. Wister made mistakes. And his kind of mistakes could cost lives, maybe many lives, because they could start wars.

Wister was a good man. The State Department handed him their delicate negotiating, their egg-handling. They gave him their tense, terrible jobs that scared the hell out of everybody in Washington who knew what was going on.

Wister said, "Is this a northbound street, or is it even a one-way street?"

"Street?"

"Avenue, I mean."

"You're all right."

Wister said, and his nerves crawled out and got in his voice, "What are you doing? My God, what are you doing?"

He got in the car with Wister He was angry, startled, impatient. He said to Wister, "Look here, Wister. I told you fellows to drop me, to stay away from me entirely, not to interfere or try to help me in any way."

"We're not," Wister said.

"How did you find me here?"

"My men learned it. They have your telephone tapped and have covered you completely."

"What do you call that?"

"Which? Why, efficient work by my agents, I suppose. They are good men."

"I don't mean that."

Wister hesitated, then complained, "Oh, I suppose you are complaining that we are hampering you."

"I told you to leave me alone. You're not doing it."

"No, no, you misunderstand. This is a protective cover we have placed around you, a guarantee of your personal safety and—"

"Take them off."

"Eh?"

"Call them off. Every last man of them."

"Oh."

He waited for Wister to think it over. He had expected this trouble with Wister. Wister was accustomed to working with a large and complicated organization, and the man thought in such terms. Wister was certain to feel a little the way the operator of a thundering pile-driver might feel about seeing another man tackle a baffling job with no tool but a tack hammer.

He told Wister, "Get away from me—all of you, every last one."

He made his voice heavy with firmness, solid with conviction, and gave it a little bite of anger, or rather he could not keep the anger out.

Wister moved uncomfortably. "All the help possible —"

"Will make as much commotion as a herd of stampeding elephants," he told Wister. "I am going to do this my own way. That was the understanding."

"But it's so big—" Wister suddenly sounded sick.

"Want some advice?"

"Yes, of course!"

"Go home and sleep. Relax."

"Sleep, my God!" Wister muttered. "Since this broke, I haven't even been able to feel the ground under my feet, and I can't taste my food."

He was silent, scowling, because Wister's terrorized anxiety was taking hold of him also. Something like that, he knew, would wreck him. When terror laid hold of you, you could do just one thing—fight like a wildcat. You couldn't plot, connive, check move with counter-move, scheme and devise. You could strike blows and take blows, was all.

He told Wister again, violently, "Take your agents off me! I've got to work alone!"

Wister shivered.

"All right," Wister agreed. "Whatever you say."

"Fair enough," he told Wister. "Now, what about this girl?"

"Didn't your man Ham Brooks tell you she was taking the Lake Placid train?"

"So your agents are around her like a swarm of locusts, too?"

"Well, we—"

"You were supposed to leave me alone, and leave her alone."

"We—"

"Wister," he said quietly, "I appreciate the strain you are under, but on the other hand I assure you that it is grinding me down also. But you must leave this thing alone. Take your hands off."

Wister gave way, saying in a low, wild voice, "I wish they'd never put such an incredibly vital job in the hands of one man!"

"I wish they hadn't either," he told Wister, and he sounded a little ill himself.

He got out of the car.

II

Ham Brooks met him at Grand Central Station.

"She's in a Pullman," Ham said. He passed over an envelope. "Your reservation is in the same section. You have the upper, she has the lower."

"Good work."

Ham Brooks smirked. "She's a dish."

Alarmed, he demanded, "You haven't been talking to her?"

"No, but it took will power."

He imagined it had, because Ham Brooks had a weakness for blondes. Ham Brooks was Brigadier General Theodore Marley Brooks, and a General was supposed to have some dignity, even when he was on the inactive list, as Ham—against his wishes—was. Ham was also an eminent lawyer. But he was still like an eighteen-year-old sailor when a pretty girl went by.

"Has she noticed you by any chance?" he asked anxiously.

"Nope."

"Sure?"

"Positive."

"All right. You and Monk stick at headquarters and wait for orders. Better sleep by the telephone."

Ham said, "With a thing like this, I don't feel much like sleeping."

He left Ham and walked down the long sloping ramp to the train, carrying his skiis, and wondering if Ham had really kept out of the girl's sight. Ham was one of his assistants. Monk, who had taken his place in the theater seat, was another associate. But both of them had an eye for an ankle, and he had learned not to depend implicitly on them where legs were involved.

This girl surely had ankles. She was showing one of

them, and very much something it was, as he came down the aisle, seat check in one hand, suitcase in the other.

He consulted his seat check, put his hat on the seat, then walked to the other end of the car and stowed his skiis in the space which was used for that purpose.

He got, at the mirror in the end of the car, another start, because for a moment he did not recognize the lazy looking, soft young man as himself. Walking back to his seat, he was fully appreciative of the job Jonas House had done with his appearance.

With the picture of how he looked fresh in his mind, he conducted himself as he thought such a fellow would behave.

"My name is Joe Powell," he said. "I hope you don't mind getting acquainted."

"I'm Doris," she said.

Which wasn't the truth. Her name was Edith Halcyon. He didn't know much else about her, but he knew that.

"I'm an orchestra leader," he said.

"That sounds quite essential," she said.

"Meaning why I am not in the army?"

"That's right."

"Since you want to know, I'll tell you."

"I don't."

He said, "I don't think we're going to get along very well together, Doris."

"You caught on quickly," she said, and picked up a book and began looking at it.

He laughed and stretched out and hoped he looked quite comfortable. He felt silly, sitting there wearing ski pants and a loud woolly sweater and a trick ski jacket and big ski boots. There were others on the train dressed the same way, it was true, but he was not comfortable. This was not a snow train; the railroads weren't operating snow trains any more. But a lot of skiers still used the trains wearing their ski clothes, even if there was a war and death and fright and destruction around the world.

Frequently in times like these, he thought, it is embarrassing to wear civilian clothes. And to be on a train dressed for frivolity in a ski outfit was, it struck him suddenly, something to be ashamed of.

Suddenly he looked at the girl. Why, darn him if she

hadn't gotten under his skin about that being the army crack. That was why he'd started being ashamed of being in ski clothes.

He watched the girl, wondering what such a young no-good as he was pretending to be, would do to reopen the conversation. He couldn't think of anything, which must be evidence that he was inexperienced, or possibly that she had upset him. He realized that the train was moving, having started with hardly a perceptible jolt.

He said, "It's what you deserve, getting it flattened."

He thought she wasn't going to answer, but she was only keeping her eyes on the book while she tried to puzzle out what he meant.

"What?" she asked, curiosity getting the best of her.

"Your nose is little and kind of flat on the end," he explained. "It probably got that way from people pushing against it to keep it out of their business."

"Whose nose in what business?" she demanded.

"Yours into mine, in this case."

"You must have misunderstood me. I don't care in the least whether you have fur or feathers."

He said, "Then why jerk open the door of my hidden room? Meaning my room where I keep the secret of why I'm not in the army?"

"I like," she said, "to kick tin cans when I pass them."

"You could scuff your shoe."

"They clank and make hollow, empty noises. The cans, I mean."

He grinned, and eyed her speculatively. She wasn't a show girl, probably, because she didn't have quite something that show girls usually have. Something in manner, in attitude, voice. She didn't have that. But she had the looks.

She was tall and quite blonde and on the spectacular side. The sailor across the aisle was looking at her a great deal, and a soldier and a fat man had both had three drinks apiece at the near-by water cooler.

He sneered at her. "You're going to cause a traffic problem."

"I hope you get trampled in the rush," she said.

"If you keep on showing such a bawdy amount of leg," he said, "I might."

She looked uncomfortable.

The train was out of the tunnel and around the curve at Kill Van Kull, and rolling northward toward Harmon, where the electric locomotive would be taken off and the steam one put on. Their seat was on the left side of the train. They could look out over the Hudson, partly visible in the evening murk.

A little snow lay in the sheltered places, thin and granular. But the river was not frozen over, and there was not much float ice.

He was thinking about the girl, drawing conclusions and making guesses. He wished he knew more about her, as did various other people. In that category one would include the American, British, Russian and Chinese governments, and perhaps some others. He reflected that it sounded pretty dramatic when you thought of it that way, but it still seemed like an understatement. If ever big events hung by a thin thread, they were hanging from one now, and this girl was the thread.

She could have looked more like a Mata Hari, he thought. She could at least have been hard. He would have felt more at ease if he could get the conviction he was dealing with a bad lot.

This lovely, though, was the wrong type. A very pretty blonde who was a little sassy and probably somewhat spoiled because she was so pretty. He wasn't sure about the spoiled part, either. She had chopped away at him pretty sharply, but then he had put his neck a long way out, asking for it.

And he liked the way she had blushed when he mentioned her leg.

He liked the blush. But it frightened him. It was a girlishly innocent thing to do. And if this girl was as important as they thought she was, she wasn't likely to be girlishly innocent. Or was she?

Was she? Who had made the rule that women who lived dangerously had to be tigers in skirts? Possibly story books had started that. Probably there was nothing to it. He knew some nice, gentle and very moral young men who lived so dangerously that it would put your teeth on edge. It might be the same with a woman. He hoped not.

But was she the key they thought she was? Suddenly fears began to pick at his nerves. Suppose there had been a mistake? It could be. He hadn't gotten the information about her himself; that had been passed to him by Wister and the State Department, and they could have dug up a bum lead.

It would be horrible if this was a wild goose chase.

He was aware that she was staring at him. She asked abruptly, "Are you ill?"

He realized he must be showing his terrors.

"Look, Doris," he said. "Give that sailor two seats back half a chance. Or let's have a truce and a meal on me."

She put her book aside.

"It might be a pleasure to chisel you out of a dinner," she said.

He learned one thing in the diner. He found out they were being followed. Either she was, or he was, or they both were. He couldn't tell which.

The follower was a lean, gray-haired elderly man who didn't look in the least as if he would be following anybody.

The diner meal was not too good. Even for wartime, it was not too good. The gray-haired man went on through to the club car. He came back later, took a seat in the diner and ordered coffee and a sandwich. He insisted on paying when he was served, which was a give-away. He was arranging so that he could get up and leave in a hurry, if they went anywhere.

"Joe, what is the name of your orchestra?" the girl asked.

"Powell's Tune Rangers," he said.

"I never heard of them."

"A few others haven't, too."

"In radio?"

"Not as much as we'd like. But a little."

He wondered if the girl knew the gray-haired man was attached to them. She gave no sign, absolutely none, of being aware.

She asked, "How far are you going?"

"Lake Placid."

"Ever been there?"

He had. He thought he had better admit it, for that would be safer. "A time or two," he said.

"How are you on skiis?"

"I'm pretty hot," he said. He was, too, and he believed

he'd better say so, because it was hard for a ski expert to act like a greenhorn.

"Skating is my dish," she said.

When they were back in their pullman, she showed him the book she had been reading. "It's Figure and Fancy Skating, by George Meagher," she explained. "It's fifty years old, a first edition. George Meagher was the World Champion in his day, and the book has a foreword by the Earl of Derby. In the end papers there are some very interesting old advertisements of road skates with pneumatic tires. The advertisement states that France, Russia, Sweden, Japan, and so forth, have ordered samples of the road skates with the idea of equipping their armies with them. Isn't that quaint?"

He decided to admit that he could skate.

"I can do a few school figures," he said. "Eights and grapevines and a Double Salchow that's on the ragged side."

"You're not exactly a dub, then," she said.

They talked freely about skating for quite a while. He admitted once having met Salchow, who had improved on the star figure invented by Englemann, the star of four crosses, forward rocker, back loop, back counter. She talked about the great women skaters, Maribel Vinson, Freda Whitaker, Sonja Henie, Madame De Linge, and their styles. She talked brackets, Mohawks, Choctaws.

She knew more about skating than he did, that was sure.

He decided he'd waylay the man who was following them, as quickly as possible.

III

The snow was good at Lake Placid, and the resort still had some of the winter color which had made it so nice before the war. The dog teams were still at the station, offering a picturesque taxi service.

The girl took a dog team taxi. He got her bags for her, two of them, and stowed them in the dog sled. He heard what he was hanging around to hear.

"Stripe Lodge," she told the driver.

He didn't exactly go cold at that. But it was a shock. Stripe Lodge was the place she would go if she was as important as they thought she was.

"Maybe I'll see you," she said.

"If it's not too much of a strain on either of us, you might," he told her.

He watched her go sliding away, the dog driver shouting, "Mush!" and putting on an impressive show.

He got his own skiis, climbed into a more conventional taxicab, and said, "I'll have to find a good lodge. Know of one?"

"You want one on Mirror Lake?"

"That would be all right. Are the places crowded?"

"Not very," the driver said. "We'll try a couple."

They found a nice lodge. He rebelled a little at the price, twelve dollars a day, but checked in.

When he turned around from signing the register, the gray-haired man, the shadow from the train, was standing there. Not three feet away. The man looked at him, but showed by no sign that he was looking at anyone he had ever seen before.

He walked over and stood in front of a big fireplace with a moose head above it, watching the gray-haired man get a room. The man did not go up to his room either, but went over and began looking at the skiing pictures on the south wall.

The fellow is practically stepping on my shoe laces, he thought.

He went up to his room, and got his climbing skins and wax out of his bag. Coming downstairs again, he met some skiers, red-faced from the cold, coming in. He asked them how the snow was.

"There's just the right amount of powder snow," he was told.

He went into the ski shack, actually a part of the basement, with great plate glass windows on three sides, pulled a couple of horses out onto the floor, and waxed his skis. He put on blue wax, corking it and polishing it with his palm, then rubbed in some orange under the bindings, to help in climbing where the skins wouldn't be needed.

There was a practice slope outside. He snapped the bindings tight, took a run down the practice slope, stemming, stem-turning, doing a christy or two. He was a little rusty, he decided.

The gray-haired man came out of the ski shack with a pair of boards, which he put on. The gray-haired man was good. He did a practice run, then went on, herring-boning up the hill toward the tow.

He was thinking that the gray-haired man doubtless expected him to go over and use the ski tow, which was the fellow's reason for going off in that direction. And he was considering double-crossing the clumsy shadow by taking some other direction. This was in his mind when a lithe, dark-skinned tall man came flying down the slope on a pair of narrow-bladed *langlauf* skis and did a beautiful telemark turn.

The tall newcomer went off in the direction taken by the gray-haired man.

Did the shadow have a shadow? He was suddenly chilled with concern.

He decided to use the tow after all. He climbed the hill, and because his leg muscles weren't used to the business of herring-boning, they began to ache a little.

The tow was chugging away. He bought a seven-day tow ticket, and the man wire-stapled it to his jacket lapel. The tow hook caught him with a jolt, and he looked around as he carried upward. He didn't see the gray-haired man immediately, then discovered him as he reached the top.

The view was nice. There had evidently been a heavy powder snow during the night, since the snow hung heavily and pleasantly on the evergreens, and the whole world had a draped and glittering beauty. The mountains were not too impressive as mountains, not like the Alps in Switzerland or the Tyrol, but they had some ski runs that were hard to beat anywhere.

He made two runs down the number two run, then one down the advanced run. That time, he nearly took the bark off a tree. Better stay away from hot skiing, he decided grimly, while he was so concerned.

He rode the tow up again, and by now he had decided on a course of action. He took the ski trail this time, swinging down the other side of the mountain in a long meandering course which would eventually bring him past a lake and a small stream.

He went fairly slowly, looking back whenever he could conveniently do so. The white-haired man was following him.

He put on more speed when he was out of sight of the gray-haired man, dropping down a sharp slope in a whistling schuss, then braking with a stem, and christying in sharply around an overhang.

Here was a trail hut, a small cabin with an enormous fireplace and a stock of firewood, on the bank of a rushing little green-colored stream. The stream was frozen over, but in places the ice was thin, and here and there the green water showed in swirling violence.

He hurriedly scooped up a long stick of the fireplace wood, a heavy stick, and backtracked to the point where he was concealed behind the overhang. He waited, hefting the stick, estimating how hard he had better pitch it.

He heard a skier coming, heard the thumping of the man's boards as they rounded a sharp rough turn, heard the fellow grunt with the effort of making a stem christy. The man was a serious skier.

He threw the log as soon as the man popped around the rock. It was the gray-haired man, and the log caught him about at the knees, knocked him off balance. The man went down, flopped head over heels.

He was out and on the gray-haired man before the latter stopped rolling. The man was trying to get at something in a pocket, and he blocked the man's hand, got at the pocket with his hands and felt a gun under the clothing. He slugged the man without delay.

The blow didn't quite knock the fellow out. But the man was dazed, too dazed to more than kick feebly as he was dragged bodily into the trail shack.

He straddled the man menacingly.

"Don't!" the man said. "I'm from Wister's office!"

He stood over the man for a moment, putting down his anger, which took effort. With a situation this tense, the thought that Wister would put such a clumsy operative on him poured rage through him.

When the flame of his rage had died a little, he told the man what he thought about it. He did not swear, but he used words that told very clearly how he felt.

He ended, "Wister is going to ruin everything if he doesn't keep his hands off. I only took this thing when it was agreed I should handle it my own way, and with my own assistants."

The gray-haired man said uncomfortably, "My name is Kelly. I think you have the wrong idea about my assignment."

"You were following me."

"My orders were to do so," Kelly said. "And the purpose was to give you protection."

"Your so-called protection can be about the most dangerous thing that could happen to me."

Kelly said, "You are thinking of the dark man who is also following us?"

"You spotted him?"

"Yes."

"Who is he?"

"One of them, possibly. I have no idea."

"Could he be another one of Wister's bright ideas?"

"No. I am positive he is not."

"Could he be a Russian, an English or a Chinese agent?"

"I am positive he is not."

"All right, Kelly. You get out of here. Leave Lake Placid."

"Wister won't like that."

He said grimly, "When I get hold of Wister again, there will be some other things he won't like."

Kelly got to his feet. He grimaced, and sat down again suddenly. "My knee!"

"Sprained?"

"No, I can make it."

Now he made an angry gesture, anger at himself. His brains, he thought, must be on a vacation. Because now he had an idea, the kind of an idea he should have had minutes ago.

"Wait here, Kelly," he said. "And give me your cap."

He went outside with Kelly's cap. He went down, wearing his skiis, to the stream, and moved along the ice to one of the potholes where the water was boiling and green as it poured past. He made many tracks going down. He made others coming back.

He re-entered the shack again.

There was no place inside that would hide a man.

"You will have to get into a snowdrift," he said.

They went outside. There were plenty of snowdrifts, and he picked one that had filled a ditch. He gave Kelly his gun. "You may not have to use it, but if you do—don't fool around," he said. "My advice would be to stay in the drift until night, then walk to the railway station and get a train out of town. Do not go back to the hotel."

Kelly stared at the snow, apparently thinking of the hours until darkness. "It'll be cold."

"Not as bad as you think."

He picked Kelly up bodily and tossed him, feet first, into the snow-filled ditch. The crust under the powder snow broke, and Kelly shot down out of sight.

He used one of Kelly's skiis to rake powder snow into a pile, to knock it over the spot where he had thrown Kelly. When he had finished, it looked as if skiers, doing quick christy turns on the trail beside the ditch, had knocked loose powder snow flying. That was all. No visible evidence that Kelly had disappeared there. Under the snow, Kelly could breathe all right.

He carried Kelly's skiis down to the creek, to the hole where the dark green water rushed and gurgled, and poked them, with the ski poles, under the ice. Two of the ski poles and one ski were whisked away, but the other pole wedged under the ice. The handle loops of the pole were visible through the thin ledge of ice. He poked at the pole, trying to free it.

The rushing water was making some noise, but he knew that a skier had appeared on the creek bank. He kept poking at the pole.

Then he looked around. He pretended to become aware the man was on the bank.

He froze. He hoped he looked shocked, but cold, competent, in possession of himself.

He went back to poking at the ski pole.

The man on the bank was the lithe dark-skinned tall man who had been trailing Kelly.

"See a fish under there?" the tall dark man asked.

"That's right."

The tall dark man went away and came back with a long dry stick. "You might do better with this." The stick came sailing down and landed on the ice.

The stick was longer. With it, he got the ski pole dislodged, and the rushing green current whisked it away under the ice that covered the stream wherever it did not run so swiftly.

He climbed back up the bank.

"Fish get away?" the dark man asked.

"Yes."

The dark man looked around for a while. When he showed emotion, he did it deliberately, like an actor putting across a definite mood, feeling. The thing he put across was that he knew that there had been no fish under the ice, but a ski pole, and before it, the body of a man.

You are a murderer, the dark man's expression said. I just caught you disposing of the body. But I'm not saying anything about it, you see.

He was pleased, because that was what he had hoped the dark man would think. But he didn't look pleased. He looked grim.

"Sheck is my name," the dark man said. "Robert Sheck."

"Joe Powell," he said. "I just got in today."

"I know."

"Oh."

"Where are you staying, Powell?"

"A place on Mirror Lake. Nice place, but the price sort of knocked my hat off. Twelve bucks a day."

Sheck laughed. "They hang it on you."

"They sure do."

Sheck said, "Why don't you try Stripe Lodge?"

"Don't you have to be a member to get in there?"

"I could take care of that. They're not too strict."

"You really think you could get me in?"

"Sure."

"I'll take you up."

All the way back to town, and to the Mirror Lake place where he collected his stuff and had an argument over getting a refund of his first day's room rent, a fact kept jumping into his thoughts. It was the lie Sheck had told about Stripe Lodge, about them not being too strict there. They were strict. They were absolutely exclusive, and it was an ominous kind of exclusiveness.

It wasn't good to have a membership in Stripe Lodge, the way the State Department felt about the place right now. The F.B.I., too.

Stripe Lodge knocked his eye out, because he had as much appreciation as any other man for fine worldly things. He sat in the big bearskin upholstered chair in the main lounge and examined the logs, concluding they must have been imported from Norway. The rock in the big fireplace had come from all over; he saw rose quartz from the Black Hills and fool's gold from Columbia and Galena from Missouri.

There was a swimming pool with a wall of plate glass around it, and the steam-heated water gave off swirling quantities of fog so that it looked as if it was boiling.

He got up and walked to another window, and found himself gazing at the skating rink. It was a fine rink with electrically shaved ice.

Two skaters were on the rink. One was Doris—or Edith Halcyon, as he knew her name to be. The other was a man.

The man was good. He was a lithe man with lots of shoulder and the legs of an athlete. He was doing school figures; he launched out in a series of bracket eights, rocker eights, and Choctaws. He was poetry on steel runners. He did a beautiful sitting pirouette, came out of it with lunging strokes and did a double Salchow that was a very tough thing to do.

The man glided to the near side of the rink, and his face was discernible. It had wrinkles. It wasn't the face of a young man.

Edith Halcyon applauded. She said something, but he couldn't hear her words through the window.

The man made a gesture, and music began coming from a loudspeaker; he and the girl did some pair-skating, some echelons, some exhibition stuff.

They were experts, he reflected, and you could see they loved skating.

Sheck came and stood beside him at the window.

"That's Doris," Sheck said.

"Nice."

"The man is Thaddeus Fay."

"He has more wrinkles than an alligator."

"He has other resemblances to an alligator, too," Sheck said.

"Yes?"

"He's a great fisherman, too," Sheck said in an emotionless tone. "He likes to fish under the ice, also."

Sheck walked off, leaving that statement standing for whatever it meant.

IV

By dinnertime he was aware of a tension in the lodge. He had become aware of the feeling slowly, at first thinking it might be his imagination, then growing more and more certain it wasn't, and becoming amazed that such a tension could exist so subtly. It was a the-fuse-is-lit-when-will-it-go-off kind of thing.

Yet the feeling was hard to identify definitely. Nobody was going around with cocked pistols and knives under their coats. There was no face-making, and no nervous starting at noises. The tension, as you became more and more aware of it, was much worse because it was under cover.

He was interested in the guests at Stripe Lodge, and spent his idle time before dinner indexing them, examining them and putting them into the classifications where he thought they belonged. When he was done, he realized he had practically everyone in the same classification.

If you would write a classification heading for them, he thought, you'd write something like: *Industrial Diamonds With Flaws*. He thought of them as industrial diamonds because they were interesting to look at and frequently beautiful, but there was an impression without definite proof that they were hard enough to cut almost anything. The flaw part was more vague. There was just a feeling that something was wrong with each one of them. He had nothing to base it on.

The funny thing was that the servants went into the same drawer. He got the feeling a time or two that they weren't even servants at all, but men or women of ability that equalled or exceeded the guests. They were much too exquisitely efficient to be real. And again, he warned himself, this might be his imagination.

He met Thaddeus Fay at dinner. Sheck introduced him.

"This is Joe Powell, whose specialty is fishing through the ice," Sheck said.

Thaddeus Fay shook hands. He had a grip like a handful of iron snakes.

"Sheck told me about your ice-fishing," Thaddeus Fay said.

Showing just a little emotion, he told Fay, "That one got away."

"Yes, under the ice, I heard," Fay said.

It was a strange way to talk about murder, which was the kind of talk it was. Sheck was sure that Kelly, the State Department agent, had been murdered, and it was plain he had passed his information along to Fay. Their double-talk was casual. It was hair-raising.

"Won't you join me in a grouse?" Thaddeus Fay asked.

The grouse was good. Fay explained that it was shipped in from a farm which raised grouse and other game exclusively for Stripe Lodge.

The meal was without more talk of murder. Thaddeus Fay had quite a bit to say about politics, the war, the post-war problems, and his ideas were original, not the sort of thing he had gotten out of the newspapers. Fay was—at least in his talk—a combination of conservative and radical; a man who believed strongly in individualistic rights, but who also had extreme notions about the government sugar-nursing everybody. The two views were inconsistent.

"Join me for coffee?" Thaddeus Fay invited. "I'd like to show you my skating trophies. Everyone here has seen them so often they're bored. Do come look at them. It's one of the things you have to do to be initiated into Stripe Lodge."

They went up to Fay's private suite, which had as much grandeur as the public parts of the lodge. The suite could almost have been a lodge by itself.

Thaddeus Fay seemed to forget he had mentioned skating trophies. He sank cross-legged, like a small boy, on a Polar bearskin rug in front of a fireplace in which a blaze whispered.

"Do tell me, where is Chester Wilson?" Fay said.

If the room had blown to smithereens around him without warning, he could not have been more startled.

Chester Wilson was absolutely the last name he expected to hear mentioned. What talking the State Department had done about Chester Wilson had been in whispers, and no one else had breathed the name.

He was stunned. He took hold of himself in a hurry with mental hands of steel and tried to hold his emotions still.

"Who?" he said.

Fay laughed. "I did hope we could talk freely, but that is up to you. Need I remind you that both Sheck and I are aware that you killed a man—Kelly of the State Department staff—and pushed his body under the ice of a brook. Sheck is aware of this because of what he saw, and I because Sheck told me."

"And that is the whole story, told in your own merry way?"

Thaddeus Fay frowned. "You don't like me?"

"What would that have to do with it?"

Fay laughed. "I guess we could go on without love."

"Need we go on?"

"We'd better."

"Just who do you think I am, Fay?"

Fay smiled and said, "Now that's a subject I can speak freely on. My initial surmise was that you were an agent of that grand old lady in hobble-skirts, the United States State Department. But I was unable to find you in the State Department file—mind you, I am speaking of my own file of State Department men, not any official records in Washington. I didn't find you there. That indicated you weren't a State Department man. Then you killed Kelly, who obviously was a State Department sleuth, and so that put you in a different category."

"Which would be?"

"The same as myself."

"Eh?"

"I imagine we have identical aims."

"It's doubtful."

Thaddeus Fay leaned forward. He was excited, but it was a controlled excitement. He was like a panther. He acted as if he was on skates and whizzing across the ice, all set to do a difficult piece of figure work, one of his Salchows or something like that.

"Let's not tiddledy-wink around with each other," Fay said. "You're not one of my men. You're not one of

McGillicuddy's men. Now, those are the only two groups of men involved in this, and you're not one of them, so who are you? Presto! You're your own man."

"You think so?"

Fay leaned forward. "Right now—tonight—I'm in a hell of a pickle. I'm caught short. Nobody but myself and Sheck are here at Stripe Lodge, none of my men are here. And we've got a job. It may be more than the two of us can handle."

"Yes?"

Fay smiled, but with absolutely no humor. "As you will realize in a minute, if you haven't already—I wouldn't ask you to help if I wasn't in a jam. I need help. I need another man. So will you help me?"

"Help you what?"

"Get Chester Wilson," Fay said.

When Fay said Chester Wilson to him, it made his skin crawl the way it had a few moments ago. It was an explosion again, a shock, a jolt that almost hurt him in the marrow of his bones.

He was also confused, which didn't help any. He did not know who Thaddeus Fay was, nor who Sheck was, nor what their game was. McGillicuddy? The name of McGillicuddy had been mentioned. He didn't know who McGillicuddy could be. He had a hunch that McGillicuddy was a nickname for somebody, but he wasn't sure. He wasn't sure about anything—except that he was getting so excited he wouldn't be surprised if it made him sick.

Because he did know a man named Chester Wilson had vanished and it was his job to find that man.

The thing was more than just finding a missing flier. So very much more, that it was frightening. Although he'd been told just what the situation was, he still had difficulty grasping the magnitude of the matter, and the consequences if Chester Wilson wasn't found, and quick.

Yesterday the telephone in his office rang. It was Wister of the State Department saying he'd like to drop in for a talk immediately. He knew Wister, so he knew from Wister's voice that something was on fire. But he hadn't dreamed it could be of such magnitude. He only found out when Wister sat, face the color of a dead fish, across the desk from him and unburdened. Or rather, handed him the job of finding Chester Wilson.

Wilson, Chester Rice. Age 28, brown hair, blue eyes, 73 inches. Identifying marks, nicked left ear lobe, old glass-cut scar on instep left foot. Finger print classification, special code Roget forty-two, Mary, Zero, nine.

Wister had become nearly inarticulate trying to impress him with the monstrous consequences of the situation, and one thing Wister had babbled was that every soldier and every sailor in the Allied forces would without hesitation be ordered to drop whatever he was doing right now and hunt for Chester Wilson. If it would do any good. It wouldn't.

No, it wouldn't do any good, and it was a melodramatic way for Wister to try to paint the size of the problem; such words sounded ridiculous. Wister should merely have told it quietly and normally, and it would have been just as fearsome.

Chester Wilson, seized by persons unknown. A girl named Edith Halcyon had telephoned Chester Wilson before he vanished. The text of the telephone call was as yet unknown, but it might have been made to lead Chester Wilson into the hands of whoever had seized him. Edith Halcyon was making a hurry-up trip to Lake Placid, now that Chester Wilson had disappeared.

He had decided to go to Lake Placid with Edith Halcyon. He was here.

Stripe Lodge? The place hadn't entered the picture until he heard Edith Halcyon tell the dog sled-taxi driver at the station to take her to Stripe Lodge. But Stripe Lodge was down in the little black books of the State Department and the F.B.I. as one of those places where there might be devils, very big and sly.

He shut off his thoughts—they were useless anyway—as he would close a water faucet.

"You have Chester Wilson?" he demanded.

"No," Thaddeus Fay said. "No, I wouldn't be sitting here on a volcano if I had him."

"You want to get Wilson, then?"

"Oh, brother!"

"Why?"

Fay leaned back and closed his eyes, and keeping his eyes shut, said with more force than it seemed possible a man could get into his voice, "Can you imagine what it would mean to have Chester Wilson? Can you imagine the infinite possibilities of such a thing?"

He could see what Fay meant. He wondered if his hair was standing on end.

The rest of the deal was short and simple.

"I guess we're in this for the same thing," he said. "I'll take you up."

Fay said, "I just knew you had to be after Chester Wilson yourself. Are you working alone?"

"No. I have a couple of friends."

"Two? Where are they? Can you get them here to help us in an hour?"

"No. They are in New York."

"A damned poor place for them to be," Fay said. "A damned poor place. But you and Sheck and I can do it ourselves, I hope to God."

"How much time have we got?"

"About two hours."

"We'd better get on it."

Fay shook his head. "We'll let it stack up, then we'll shoot the works all at once. We'll pick you up, Sheck and I."

"What do I do?"

"We'll pick you up, I said. Stick around the Lodge and take it easy. But be easy to find. Stay in the public rooms. Stay in plain sight." Fay indicated the door. "You better get out of here now. We'll be seeing you."

He nodded. He went to the door, put a hand on the knob, took it away and turned slowly. "We haven't said anything about a division," he said.

"What do you want?"

"Half."

"That's damned robbery!" Fay said in a low voice that filled with anger.

"The time to rob a man is when he's in a corner, isn't it?" he said. "Would a third make you any happier?"

"A little," Fay said, but the anger still crawled in his voice. "A third. All right."

He had a hot chocolate by the window which overlooked the skating rink. When he lifted the cup off the saucer, there was a small clattering, his hand shook so. He scowled at the hand, realizing that he had not been so nervous in years. Nervous? Just a little. About like a man who had fallen out of an airplane without a parachute.

On the skating rink, a slender shape whirled out on the ice and made a fast flashing circle with quick cutting strokes. He could hear the faint sound of the skate blades on the ice, like knives whetting together.

It was Edith Halcyon. Doris, she had called herself. But she was Edith Halcyon, and she was a mystery. She sailed around the rink, leaning forward, on one skate, doing a pretty glide. She was as graceful as a kite. A kite, he thought, was a pretty good simile. A kite, and he had grabbed its tail, and it had yanked him into this thing. Yanked him high.

Suddenly he knew he couldn't sit here. It wasn't like him to be so nervous, and that frightened him. He had always taken pride in his amazing self-control.

But he couldn't sit here. For once, he was about to fly apart.

He arose and went up to Thaddeus Fay's suite. Fay wasn't there. At least, no one answered. He went downstairs again, glanced at the ice, and saw Fay.

Thaddeus Fay and Edith Halcyon were skating pairs. They were doing it to soft music, and with the kind of skill that makes a thing look ridiculously easy. He watched them. They were wonderful. They were poetry. Laughing, they straightened up in the old-fashioned English style of skating, and did some "valsing" that was as Victorian as bustles and button shoes. They did echelons and serpentines and circulars and they were a delight. And their laughter was as pleasant as candy, as hearty as hamburgers with onions, and it wasn't at all like skeletons rattling, which was what it should have been like.

Thaddeus Fay skated over to a bench, and watched the girl whirling on the ice.

He went to Thaddeus Fay, sat beside him, and said in a low voice, "Who is she? That girl?"

"A wonderful skater."

"But who is she?"

Thaddeus Fay turned his head. He seemed alarmed. "What are you doing, kidding me?"

"All right, all right, but I want to make certain of something. Who is she?"

"She belongs to McGillicuddy."

"Not with us?"

"Not with us," Thaddeus Fay said. "And that's a shame, too. Because she can think about as well as she can skate, which makes her a female Einstein, or a female whoever-your-favorite-thinker-is: I wish I could have her around to skate with and look at." Fay grinned at him. "You couldn't charm her away from McGillicuddy, could you? No, I guess not. You won't have time. You better get away from me. Somebody might start thinking."

He left Thaddeus Fay and went back to his hot chocolate by the window. He wished that he hadn't talked to Fay about the girl, because he had seen that Fay had thought he'd known all about her.

For a moment there, Fay'd had a grisly suspicion that he'd made a mistake. That wasn't good.

He sipped his chocolate and waited. He didn't know whether he was going to be able to wait it out or not. It was such a horribly difficult job, waiting. It wasn't just the grind on his own nerves; he could have taken that. It was, as much as anything, knowing what a tremendous thing was involved, and knowing there wasn't any time to lose, and then having to sit here and fritter it away drinking chocolate and with his brain sweating icicles.

He couldn't take it. Suddenly he got up. He went to a telephone. He got the long-distance operator, and called a New York number.

Monk Mayfair, his associate, answered.

He said to Monk, "This is Joe Powell."

"Good evening, Mr. Powell," Monk said. "What can I do for you?"

"I'm sorry to bother you at this time of night, but I'm up here at Lake Placid and the skating is wonderful and I've got the fever, but no good figure skates. I wonder if you have a pair in stock, which you could box tonight and rush up here."

Monk said, "I remember you were interested in two pairs of skates when you were in the shop. Would you like me to send one of those?"

"Say, why don't you send both pairs—the figure skates and the speed skates. Maybe I could use both pairs."

"Sure, sure, Mr. Powell. I'll get them out tonight. Where'll I send them?"

"Stripe Lodge, Lake Placid. Mark the package rush."

"You bet I will. We're very glad to get your business, Mr. Powell."

"Bye."

"Goodbye."

He hung up and he knew the operator at the Lodge switchboard had listened in, because he had seen her writing furiously. She must have taken it down in shorthand. He saw her reach into a cabinet and get a telephone book. It was a New York directory, but a cross-numbered one, not a regular directory. In it, you looked up the numbers first, and opposite them was the name and address of the firm or individual to whom the phone was listed.

The operator, he surmised, was looking up the number he had called in New York. That was all right. The number was listed as a sporting goods house. It was actually one of the telephones at his headquarters, though.

He saw the telephone operator call the desk clerk. She gave the clerk a note she'd scribbled. The clerk went away with the note. He wished he could follow the clerk. He didn't dare.

He went back to his chocolate, another cup of it. His nerves were all knots, and his brain was beginning to make his head hurt on top, from the strain.

The two skaters left the ice. They were laughing. But suddenly he knew there was no mirth in their laughter; it had a sick sound, a frightened, tense, this-is-about-the-end quality. They were acting, Thaddeus Fay and Edith Halcyon, and they were very good actors, but they were about at the end of their ropes.

Thaddeus Fay came past. "The chocolate good?"

"Nice."

"About two minutes," Thaddeus Fay said. "About two or three minutes. Then breathe your prayer to the devil, because it's going to be tough."

"I just telephoned my two friends in New York."

"That was a fool thing to do."

"No. I ordered two pairs of skates. You could investigate until the hot place gets an ice crust, and you couldn't prove I didn't order a pair of skates."

"How long will it take them to get here?"

"Couple of hours. They will come by plane."

"That'll be too late."

"Couldn't we hold this up?"

"No."

"Well, my two friends will be here, in case there are any pieces left to pick up."

"There won't be any pieces. Either we'll have the bull in our pockets, or there won't be a grease smear left of us."

"That's nice and cheerful."

Fay's face was getting pale. He was losing color, and his frightened heart was kicking a big visible pulse in his throat. The sinews in the backs of his hands were beginning to stand out.

"Another minute or two," he said. "And don't forget to ask the devil for his influence."

V

A man came over and took a chair by the front door, on the right side of the front door, and in a moment another man sauntered over and took a chair on the other side of the door. Both of them had overcoats across their arms which they did not remove when they sat down.

He watched them, and in a moment he made out the dark blue muzzle of a gun under one of the overcoats. He lifted his chocolate cup, and drinking, let his eyes move over the place.

Tension had crawled into the room as if it was visible, like a fog, and violently noticeable, like a prowling lion. There had been tension before, but it was under cover. Now the curtain was peeling back. The raw state of affairs was being unwrapped.

The clerk was standing tight behind his desk, a silly figure in a ski suit, a silly looking scared man. Two waiters from the dining room, dressed in Tyrolean gear for atmosphere, came and stood spike-legged at the dining-room door. In the right uniforms, they would have looked as if they might have been standing on the concrete blocks where the two sentries used to stand at the Brandenburg Gate, on Unter den Linden.

A fat man did the most obvious thing of any of them. He got up and took a good hunting rifle, a rifle with a telescope sight, off a wall rack. He sat down in the chair where he had been, holding the rifle, pretending to examine it. He hauled the bolt back, just a little, and the brass of a cartridge gleamed in the receiver. The gun was loaded.

Thaddeus Fay had gone out of the room. Fay came back now, with a little of his aplomb missing and a slight perspiration on the back of his neck, so that his skin looked as if it had been greased. He was scared and his

144

nerves were as tight as fiddlestrings. But Fay had everything under control except his sweat glands.

Sheck sauntered in next. Sheck had a skier's rucksack in one hand and a length of rawhide cord and a knife in the other and he obviously was hoping it would look as if he was going to repair the rucksack. The sack had something in it.

Everyone in the big lobby looked at Sheck at least once in the next twenty seconds. Sheck whistled off key and went over to the big fireplace, with his rucksack.

Now Edith Halcyon came in. She still wore her skating costume, a brief and eye-catching affair of brown tweed and beaver fur. Very good cheesecake. She was a pretty girl. She had a good form. She took your breath.

She came over and said, "Hi, Joe Powell, orchestra leader."

He said, "Go away. You don't like me."

"That's right," she said. "I saw you skiing this afternoon, and you still impress me as a healthy young man who should be fighting for his country."

"What did you think of my ice-fishing?" he asked.

"What do you mean?"

"Didn't you see me?"

"See you what?"

"Ice-fishing?"

"I saw you skiing," she said. "I saw you come down the tough run, and you can ski."

"I told you on the train I could ski."

"What about this ice-fishing?" she asked.

She didn't know about the man he was supposed to have murdered and shoved under the ice, the State Department sleuth he was supposed to have killed. He was positive she didn't know.

"Nothing about it," he said. "Skip it."

Whatever was going to happen at Stripe Lodge was about ready to happen.

Everyone in this room, he decided, knows that something is going to pop. But not the girl. She doesn't know. Fay knew, and Sheck, and the desk clerk, the two waiters, the fat man with the rifle. They all had their mental fingers in their ears, waiting for the explosion.

But Edith Halcyon did not know a thing about it. And

that, he thought, is a joke on me. He had followed Edith Halcyon here because he thought she would know what was what.

Suddenly he wished she would get out of the lobby. If she was an innocent bystander, she had no business there. He wished she wouldn't stand there and smile at him the way she was doing now, a smile that had some friendliness in it.

"Listen," he said. "Will you do a draft-dodging orchestra man a favor?"

"What is it?"

"Go away," he said. "Just go away."

"You're so nasty I'm beginning to like you." She pulled a nearby chair around so that it half faced him and sat down. "Do you really want to fight, Joe?"

He shook his head and asked, "Know why I want you to go away?"

"Why?"

"Because I came over here to Stripe because you're here, and now I'm ashamed of myself. So scram, will you. It would be better for my self-respect."

She watched him intently for a moment. "That was nice, even if you did say it that way. I'm glad you said it because—"

"I'm not trying to be nice. God forbid."

"Wait, let me finish," she said.

And then she went silent, a little embarrassed. "I don't know how to put this," she said.

He waited for her to think of a way to put it. And he watched Fay and Sheck and the fat man with the rifle, the two waiters, the clerk. They were motionless, frozen. They were waiting for something. They had suddenly shed all pretense of being casual, of acting naturally. They must have heard or seen something. He wondered what it was they had heard or seen. He wished he knew. He was scared.

"Let me put it this way, Joe," the girl said. "I want you to help me."

"Uh-huh," he said, wishing she wouldn't distract him, that she would go away.

"Listen to me," she said. "I'm in trouble. I'm afraid I am in the strange predicament of not being able to leave here if I wanted to."

Shock hit him as if it was a solid blow. "Eh?"

"I'm frightened," she said. "Joe, help me, please! I think I'm actually a prisoner here."

On top of everything else, he thought with horror, now something like this. He wished he knew women. He wished to God he knew more about the feminine half of the human race. He wished he could look at their pretty faces and tell just one little thing about them.

Because this girl was frightened, but he hadn't known it until now. She had looked natural and sounded natural.

Mostly, his emotion was anger. She was a Trojan horse; and he hadn't thought anything was wrong.

he hadn't known she was terrified, and he blamed her because he hadn't known it. Damn women and the way they could deceive him!

He didn't know what to say or to do. But his emotion, his feeling about it, was terrific. His feelings must have shown on his face, and they must have looked like fear to the girl. Actually his emotions were mostly fear, too.

She said, "For God's sake, don't look so scared. I don't want them to know I'm asking you for help." She leaned forward. "Wipe that wild look off your face!" she said frantically.

He wiped it off. Or hoped he had. And now he was hearing a sound, the sound of an automobile, and he knew it was what had electrified Fay, Sheck, the other men in the lobby.

She said, "I came up here because I was told I could find a man here. The man is a flier. He is my brother-in-law. He is married to my sister."

The automobile was coming closer.

She was speaking more rapidly. "Something mysterious has happened to him. I was told that, if I came here, I would find him. I was told he wanted to see me. You see, I talked to him, and he told me a little, enough to alarm me. That was before he—he disappeared mysteriously. And then, when I was told that if I would come here and talk to him, it would be what he wanted, I thought that was the thing to do. So I came. And now he isn't here, and I am afraid I won't be allowed to leave."

He saw the tall graceful evergreen trees light up with gray ghostly light as the car turned into the drive.

She said frantically, "I'm scared, Joe! I just talked to a man and he said I can't leave. He said almost everyone in this lodge is mixed up in it."

"Why pick on me?" he demanded.

"Because of the way the man acted," she said. "I asked him if you were one of them, and he swore. He cursed you terribly. He can't figure who or what you are. So I thought you might not be one of them, and would help me."

"This brother-in-law of yours," he said. "Is his name Chester Wilson?"

She stared at him. "How did you know that?"

"Is he?"

"Yes." Slowly, as if by no conscious effort on her part, her hands came up to her cheeks and pressed there, pressed until the fingers sank in. "You're one of them, too!" she said thickly.

"Sit still and shut up," he said. "And be ready to crawl under something that might be bulletproof."

A station wagon came chugging up the driveway to the side door of Stripe Lodge, a shiny varnished station wagon moving between walls of shoveled snow. It was a sleek genteel vehicle and it looked as innocent as an angel on Sunday.

On its top was a rack for skis, and on the rack two pairs of skis, short jumping skis with three grooves for steadiness. Two men were in the front seat, both wearing parkas with fur-fringed hoods that disguised their faces almost as well as masks.

Something in the back of the station wagon was covered with canvas.

The vehicle was slowing to a stop at the side door when Thaddeus Fay turned around in his chair—he was sitting now in a deep overstuffed chair upholstered with the skins of two species of bears—and rested his right fist on the back of the chair. The gun in his fist was very small, because its presence was hardly noticeable until fire and noise came out of Fay's fist.

Fay's bullet made a round hole in the door glass, and other round holes successively in the storm door, the window of the station wagon, almost the exact mathematical center of the forehead of one of the men in the front seat.

Fay turned his head.

"Joe Powell," he said. "What we want is under the canvas in the back of that station wagon."

Sheck, standing by the fireplace, now had opened his ski pack. He stepped to one side of the fireplace, and threw the pack very hard at the dancing flames, but holding on to the pack so that the pack's contents alone went into the fire.

The pack had held three half-gallon glass jugs and they broke when they hit. They were filled with gasoline. It must have been high-test aviation gas. Half the room seemed to fill with flame.

There was a rolling service cart, a portable bar of an affair, standing against the wall near the fireplace. Sheck went to that, picked bottles off it and threw them at the floor, the walls, the ceiling. These contained gasoline instead of liquor, and the contents caught fire.

Another spurt of fire and noise came out of Thaddeus Fay's fist. The second man in the station wagon rolled out on the far side.

"Let's go, Powell," Fay said. "Get up and turn over your chair and you'll find something you can use."

The chair, when turned over, proved to have an automatic pistol and four extra ammunition clips fastened underneath it with scotch tape. He tore the gun loose, and left all the clips but one. He jammed the gun in one coat pocket and the clip in another, then picked the heavy chair up and lunged with it against the large plate glass window which offered such a pleasant view of the skating rink. The window broke, almost all of the glass going out of the frame.

He seized the girl, picked her up bodily, and went out through the window with her, jumping far enough to cause him to fall and flounder.

There was an astonishing amount of flame inside the lodge lobby. The whole place seemed afire.

The business of the gasoline had seemed childish and overdone. But now, floundering out of the snow, he realized why it had been done. To go from one part of the lodge, or to leave any of the suites and go outside, it was necessary to pass through the lobby unless one used a window or a snow-blocked side door. With the lobby full of fire, the lodge was paralyzed.

The station wagon began moving, backing, skidding

down the driveway. He knew what had happened. The driver hadn't been hit by Fay's bullet, but instead had dived out on the opposite side of the station wagon, then reached back in and released the emergency brake and was steering the machine as it coasted back down the drive.

He hauled Edith Halcyon out of the snowbank. "Be still," he said. "Come on."

"You're hurting me," she said.

"The station wagon," he told her. "I'm going to get that if I can."

"But—"

"Chester Wilson is probably in it, under the canvas," he said. "Shut up."

He wanted Chester Wilson. Getting hold of Wilson—alive—was his job here, and the importance of doing so could hardly be underestimated. There had been no direct talk about his giving his life if necessary to get Wilson, but the fact had been implied.

He made for the station wagon. The girl did not hamper him, but she certainly did not help. When he drew near the station wagon, he dropped her in the snow.

He went on. He went behind the vehicle, which was not moving fast. As he had suspected, the driver was crouched on the runningboard looking back and steering with one up-reached hand.

The driver saw him, and made a snarling sound, but instead of trying to fight, pitched off the fender and shoved his arms above his head and began yelling, "Don't shoot me! Oh God, don't shoot me!"

He hit the driver on the lower right side of the jaw, as fast and hard as he could.

The man slid, as he went down unconscious, under the car, so that it was impossible to continue backing the car, or let it continue backing, without probably breaking the man's legs. He lost time hauling the senseless man out to the side.

Now Fay and Sheck had appeared. They came out of Stripe Lodge, chasing the station wagon.

He dived into the station wagon. What he wanted to do, what he intended to try, was to escape with the station wagon before Fay and Sheck could join him.

He didn't make it.

Fay and Sheck got there. And at about the same time, the girl got up out of the snow and reached the station wagon. She got in the back. Fay and Sheck climbed in the front.

"Get going!" Fay said. "For God's sake, get going!" And Sheck beat his fist against the dash and said about the same thing, but more profanely.

He was half tempted to try to club Fay and Sheck down and throw them out when the first of a number of bullets arrived. He changed his mind.

He got the station wagon going backward again. He tramped hard on the accelerator, manipulating the steering wheel. He could hear shooting, but the bullets were not reaching them because they were now down on the road, and the snow was stacked high.

"About a hundred yards down the road, they can see us for a minute," he warned. "Be careful."

They went through the dangerous spot, where the car could be seen from the lodge, in careening haste. They were evidently shot at several times, but only one bullet hit the car, cutting a rip in the hood.

Thaddeus Fay beat one fist against a palm in an ecstasy of glee.

"Joe Powell, you're great!" he yelled. "They would have gotten away with the station wagon if you hadn't gone through that window and headed them off!"

"Yeah, that was nice," Sheck said.

Fay was nearly gibbering with delight. He had lost control of himself. He said that Joe Powell had really done a job, as Fay had known he would, and a lot more in the same vein.

They traveled about a mile, Fay talking all the time, then the girl sobbed in the rear seat. She had climbed into the back, partly on the canvas, partly beside it. Fay's face suddenly got a pale sick look, and he turned around and demanded, "What's the matter?"

She threw the canvas back and said, "Look."

There was nothing under the canvas but some ski poles and more loose canvas which had been bundled up in what could have been the shape of a man. There was certainly no man there. No Chester Wilson.

VI

Thaddeus Fay was now stricken with a glaring silence that was as expressive as profanity. The wrinkles on his darkly tanned face appeared deeper and older, but his lithe crouching body seemed, strangely, more youthful.

"They sucked us in," Fay said. "Boy, did they let us jump out of a window! Right off the deep end, we walked."

Sheck complained, "What happened to us? I don't get it. They told us the station wagon was arriving with Chester Wilson."

Fay said, "Turn the next road north. Step on it. We're not sunk. We're in a little deep, but we're not sunk."

The next road to the right was ploughed, but narrow. It mounted steeply, winding, banked with snow, the evergreens snaking past in dark haste.

"Left the next house," Fay said.

It was an old house, an ugly frame thing, with a double garage adjacent.

"I've got two cars in the garage," Fay said. "But we won't use them yet. Come inside."

The house was cold, cheaply furnished. Fay, as they were waiting for him to unlock the door, explained that it was a summer place he had rented. He had taken it for two purposes, because he wanted a place to leave two cars they might need, and because it was high and looked down on Stripe Lodge.

Fay ran to a window. He had two pair of binoculars there, and he grabbed one hastily. Sheck took the other. They began watching the lodge.

Fay said, "Joe Powell, did they suspect you?"

"I don't know."

"I don't, either."

"Maybe the trap we fell into was set for me."

152

"No," Fay said. "No, it wasn't."

"How can you be so sure?"

"Did anybody besides me tell you that station wagon was going to be carrying Chester Wilson?"

"No."

"There you are. They told *me*. They told me and Sheck. That shows who they were aiming to suck in."

There was quite a fire down at Stripe Lodge. Actually the lodge was not more than a mile distant, airline, possibly less. They could see the fire, sheets of flame jumping out of the windows, and big black worms of smoke crawling up in the cold bright moonlit night.

Thaddeus Fay said, "I believe I know what happened. It's too bad I didn't think of it earlier. Sheck, watch that back road, the one to the left and up the hill. They'll leave that way, probably, if they haven't already left. But we'll be lucky if they haven't."

"I got my eye on it," Sheck said grimly.

"What happened to Chester Wilson?" Edith Halcyon asked. She sounded as if she was about to go over the edge.

He hoped Fay or Sheck would answer her, and along with it, say something that would tell him where the girl stood.

Fay talked without removing the binoculars from his eyes, watching Stripe Lodge and the road or path, whichever it was, back of the lodge.

Fay said, "They must have had Chester Wilson there at the lodge all the time. They told me that he was in a roadhouse over this side of Saranac Lake, but that was a lie to rope me in."

Fay removed the binoculars long enough to glance at the girl, then continued, "They got you up from New York, Miss Halcyon, and they let Chester Wilson look through a window at you. I bet they had him at the window when you and I were skating this afternoon. I can imagine that. Let Chester Wilson look through the window, then shove him down in a chair and tell him in detail how they were going to kill you if he didn't do business with them. And Chester Wilson must have done business with them, because the next thing they did was fool me into stubbing my toe and showing my true colors."

Fay glared and resumed looking at the lodge through the binoculars.

Edith Halcyon leaned back and looked bewildered. "I don't know what is going on," she said.

"You knew there was something, didn't you?"

"Yes," she said. "I knew that. I knew it because Chester Wilson called me and asked me where my sister—his wife—was to be found. I told her she was in Oklahoma visiting the folks, and he said not to tell anybody—tell no one, no matter who they said they were—where my sister could be found. I asked him why, and Chester said there was trouble, and that a threat against his family might be held as a club over his head."

Thaddeus Fay chuckled sourly. "Yes, that was the truth. And he had damned good reason to be scared, because we—any of us—would have killed his wife in a minute if it would have made him tell us what we wanted to know."

She put her hands to her checks. "That's unbelievable."

"Not a bit unbelievable," Fay assured her. "It's been done before. It's the regular thing in Europe, doing things to a man's family if he won't cooperate. Believe me, young lady, it's a very normal and effective way to get information out of a man."

She shuddered. "And then I got a summons to come up here to Stripe Lodge. The summons said to come quickly and act as if nothing was wrong, and not tell anyone who I was or why I was coming or where I was going."

"You thought Chester Wilson was asking you up here?"

"That's right."

"It wasn't," Thaddeus Fay said. "It was me."

"You!"

"That's right. But don't start getting a mad up at me because of that. I was merely ordered to get in touch with you to make you think Chester Wilson wanted you up at Stripe Lodge so he could talk to you."

"Why?"

"Why what?"

"Why was I wanted here?"

"You are stupid. You certainly don't think like you skate," Fay told her. "The plan was to use your safety as a club to make Chester Wilson talk. And that is what happened. Only they did it by just letting Wilson look through a window at you, which is something I hadn't figured on."

The girl stared at him.

"What does Chester Wilson know that you wanted to know?" she demanded.

"I don't think I'll tell you that," Fay said. "But it happens to be something important enough to—well, it's hard to describe." He frowned thoughtfully. "Very hard. It's a little like trying to put the Grand Canyon into words."

"But why all this confusion, this fight tonight?" she persisted.

"Well, I can answer that. You see, at first we were all one busy gang of rascals after what Chester Wilson knew, but some of us got greedy. I and Sheck got greedy. We thought how nice it would be to get Chester Wilson's information for ourselves. So we worked together. And then Joe Powell, as he calls himself, happened along, and we could see that he was branching out for himself, too. So we propositioned Joe, Sheck and I, and Joe helped us. And very good help he was, too, except that he was no more of a clairvoyant than Sheck or I, hence didn't know we were falling into a trap which had been set in order to see if we would betray ourselves."

Edith Halcyon turned and asked, "Joe?"

"Yes?"

"Is your name Joe Powell?"

"No."

"What is it?"

"Joe Powell for the time being," he said.

The girl was confused, and she was still frightened, and after she had clenched her fingers for a while, looking at them as she clenched them, she turned back to Thaddeus Fay, with the demand, "What will happen now?"

Thaddeus Fay had more of his normal manner and carriage than he'd had during and immediately after the fiasco at the lodge. He shrugged his shoulders slightly. But the answer he gave the girl was remarkably informing.

"Now they will take Chester Wilson and head for where he has told them to go," he said. "Of course they might leave Chester Wilson behind, dead, but I don't think so, because they will be afraid he hasn't told them the truth, in which case it would be too bad if they killed him. Mind you, I'm only guessing. But correctly, I hope."

"Where will they go?"

"I wish to God I knew!" Fay said fervently.

The girl, guessing, asked, "Is that—is that what—they wanted from Chester?"

"Where to go? That's right."

"Why don't you tell me everything?" she demanded.

"I don't see any sense in it," Fay said.

Sheck had taken no part in the conversation, had hardly removed his eyes from the binoculars through which he was watching the neighborhood of Stripe Lodge. But now he said, "Sister, you keep on asking questions, and it might be you would get to know so much somebody would have to cut your pretty throat."

The statement took more color out of the girl's face and shut her up.

They all watched the burning lodge. Various vehicles of the Lake Placid Fire Department were arriving, and at least two streams of water were being played on the blaze. The lodge probably would not burn down, but it certainly would be damaged.

Fay, sounding more and more like a man with confidence in himself, explained that this was why he had used the gasoline. So that the fire department would come out from town and firemen and policemen would swarm all over the place. Their presence would be a handicap to the other side, he had hoped.

However, he went on to explain, now that things had turned out as they had, the fire might not be such a good idea. It might mean the firemen or the policemen would rescue Chester Wilson, and that wouldn't be good.

After Fay fell silent, Edith Halcyon turned and said again, "Joe."

"What?"

"What is your name if it isn't Joe Powell?"

"Oh, be quiet," he told her.

"So you're just a gangster," she said.

This brought a loud but not especially gleeful laugh from Thaddeus Fay.

"Nobody in this thing could be called a gangster," Fay said. "So don't insult Joe, Edith. If you have to call him a crook, call him a very big one."

Sheck grunted, then pointed, "It looks like we fell in the mud and came out looking like a rose," he said. "Look."

After he had indicated carefully where to look, they could see with their unaided eyes the thing which had excited Sheck. There were several figures, single-file, working out of a thicket of evergreen trees. The short cavalcade climbed a hill—they were hidden from the lodge by another hill and quite a lot of trees—and worked to a road, then to a shed. They disappeared into the shed.

After they had been in the shed several times, and did not appear again, Fay said with conviction, "They will stick there a while. They won't dare go busting out on the highways with all that excitement at the lodge."

"It looks to me like they've got Chester Wilson with them," Sheck said.

"Yes, I'm pretty sure that was Wilson third from the front."

Edith Halcyon, suddenly intense, said, "You have a telephone here. I saw it. Call the police. Have them arrest those people and take Wilson away from them."

Fay, smiling again without humor, said, "Don't be quite so naïve. You know better."

"But you owe them something for trying to kill you—"

"Remember the goose that lays the golden eggs?" Fay said dryly.

"What about it?"

"You don't kill it. Wilson is that goose." Fay shrugged. "I'm being childish, am I not? The fact is, my graceful angel, we hope to get Chester Wilson away from them."

"You could take Wilson away from the police."

"The minute Wilson is found, he will be surrounded by the United States army, navy and marines, quite likely. And without doubt the first thing Wilson would tell the police is the very information we are all after—and which I'm afraid our friends down yonder already have forced out of him—and then it would be useless to us. Perhaps not useless, but we'd be in for a race against considerable opposition—and believe me, I speak conservatively, for the best efforts of every allied nation would be pitted against us—to reach our goal. No, I wouldn't care for the odds. Those fellows down there are much easier meat."

The girl said nothing more.

Turning slowly, Fay said, "Powell, we'll have a bit of a

wait. Sheck and I will go check the cars to be sure they run. You stay here and keep an eye on that shack."

"Righto."

He watched Fay and Sheck walk out of the room, then glanced at the girl, but she gave him a disgusted glare. She looked, he thought, quite frightened. She should be. She would be lucky if she came out of this with her life. There was no reason why Fay and Sheck should not kill her, none whatever, and every reason that they should. At the present, of course, they were keeping her alive so that they could use her to make Chester Wilson tell *them* what they wanted to know.

A grim impulse pulled him to the door. He followed Fay and Sheck. He followed them through two rooms, moving silently—and met them face to face unexpectedly.

"What're you following us for?" Sheck demanded harshly.

"The binoculars. You took them with you."

"I put them on the hall table," Sheck growled. "Here, I'll show you."

Sheck went back and showed where he had left the binoculars, and Fay followed him with an expressionless face. Then Fay and Sheck left again. They went outdoors, stepping out of a side door.

He watched Fay and Sheck stop on the porch. He could see their faces quite clearly, because the hall light in the room behind them was on, throwing illumination through the door glass.

He saw Fay and Sheck stop quite close together and stand staring at the distant shack to which the group from Stripe Lodge had fled.

He saw Sheck say, "He was following us just then!"

He saw Fay say, "Naturally."

That he saw them speaking was the literal truth, and he was damned glad, as he had been a few times before, that he'd had the days and days of patience that it had taken him to learn lip-reading, and to become skilled at it. He'd learned the trick quite a number of years ago, become fairly good at it, good enough to become smug about himself. Now, in the next minute or two, he wished fervently he'd kept practicing, kept his skill at more of a peak. Because he missed some of what they said.

He missed what Sheck said next. But it must have been a question.

Answering, Fay said, "Of course he would follow us. Don't you know who he is?"

"A guy who says his name is Joe Powell, an orchestra—-"

Fay interrupted, and what he said was also missed. The news, whatever it was, shocked Sheck. It took the insides out of Sheck for a moment.

Fay said, "Don't act so surprised, you fool!"

Sheck did the normal things a man does to get control of himself, staring fixedly at an unimportant object—in this case, the porch railing—and rubbing the palm of his right hand over the closed fist of his right.

"You are sure he is Doc Savage?" Sheck demanded.

Fay evidently said he was certain.

"Good God!" Sheck said.

"Don't let on!"

"Oh, murder!" Sheck said, and his lips were stiff enough to make reading them difficult.

"Take it easy. He has no idea I have guessed who he is."

"When did you?"

"The way he got around when the mess started at the Lodge. I guess it was in the back of my mind before that. I knew he was somebody important, and then it dawned on me who he was."

"But Savage doesn't look like this bird?"

"A good disguise job."

Sheck turned his back now, so the remainder of his part of the conversation was guesswork.

Sheck said something, evidently a query.

"Oh, the American government put him on the case, probably," Fay said. "He's the man they would naturally assign on such a big matter."

Sheck, another query.

"Yes. dammit, I'm mortally sure he is Savage."

Sheck, evidently with an idea.

Fay told him, "Listen, you take my orders, brother. And lay off Savage. Don't let on."

Sheck spoke.

Fay said, "Because of all the people in the world likely to get what they go after, Savage is the most apt. So he is helping us. So we get Chester Wilson, with Savage's help. So then Savage doesn't know we suspect him and we will—if I may use a tough phrase—knock him off."

Sheck, apparently an objection.

Fay: "By damn, you'll do it if I say so."

The two walked on toward the garage.

He stared after Fay and Sheck, and he was grimmer than he had been at any time so far. It always disgusted him when he took elaborate pains, and hatched a flop. Suddenly his faith in his disguise dropped like water going down a drain.

Sure, he was Doc Savage. There actually was a Joe Powell who had a barrelhouse orchestra, but he was now keeping out of sight and sound at the request of the State Department, by way of aiding the general plan.

So now they knew he was Doc Savage, not Joe Powell. At least Fay and Sheck knew it, and were keeping it to themselves hoping to make use of him. The deceivers were deceiving the deceived, and somebody was going to get, in the end, a sudden and quick death. If he weren't careful.

Doc turned back into the room.

Edith Halcyon was staring at him.

She examined him in a fixed, unwinking strange fashion for the space of three or four good long breaths, then she came to him, stepping with a quick, dramatic haste. She got close to him before she spoke, and then she kept her voice low.

"Aren't you Doc Savage?" she asked.

He said glumly, "Is there a sign on me?"

VII

He shouldn't have admitted it, he saw. Because she hadn't known who he was. She had been guessing.

She said, "Oh, you big juke box!" And she turned away and sat down.

He was puzzled as to how she had managed to tag him, and turning the matter over in his mind, finally decided she must have taken some kind of a random guess. But he didn't quite understand how he had guessed his name out of thin air.

Oh, well, he thought—she doesn't think I am Doc Savage, so no harm is done.

Unless—and he began to shudder at the possibility—she made some facetious remark to Fay and Sheck about thinking he was Savage. That wouldn't be good. Fay and Sheck wouldn't dare let a thing like that pass.

He said, "Miss Halcyon."

"Yes."

"Say nothing to Fay or Sheck about what you just said to me."

"You mean about your being Doc Savage?"

"Yes."

"Why not?"

"Just keep it to yourself," he said.

She stared at him. "Say, you're not really telling me you *are* Savage?"

He did not think there was much chance of her believing it, or he would have. There was no percentage in starting a long argument to convince her who he was. Particularly an argument with a woman.

"This is no time to sell you the idea," he said.

He used his normal speaking voice, which was deep and controlled—or should have been considering the amount of voice training he'd had. He had been, until now, speaking with a higher and slightly microphonish voice which was somewhat similar to the voice of the real Joe Powell. It was not a great change from normal, mostly a lifting of tone, and since excitement tends to make a man's voice get higher in pitch, he'd had no trouble with it. But now he spoke normally.

He saw the blankest of looks come over the girl's face.

He was puzzled at first. Then he realized that she was suddenly convinced that he was actually Doc Savage. He wondered what had decided her. His voice? How the devil would she know anything about his voice? He didn't give radio speeches, and kept pretty quiet in public.

She enlightened him. "You *are* Savage!" she said strangely. "I work in a doctor's office. He has a sound-picture of you making a delicate brain operation, and he has me run the picture before he makes an operation of that type. I've run it scores of times. Your voice—you are Doc Savage."

So that was how she knew.

"Keep it under your hat," he warned.

She nodded.

There was nothing to do but watch the shack where the people from Stripe Lodge had gone, and wait for developments. Doc Savage settled down to doing that, growing most uncomfortable because of the girl's attitude.

Discovering that he was Savage hadn't affected her as he had expected. He'd supposed she would accept it, show a little surprise, and continue her worry. She didn't.

Her attitude toward him changed. He could feel the difference. She tightened up visibly, and he got the impression she was stunned.

In the end, he was bothered. Why was she so affected? Because she was an enemy? That was disturbing.

He wished bitterly that women would stay out of the world's troubles, or at least that he could figure them out easier.

He got up suddenly and went to the garage. Fay and Sheck were there.

"Both cars are ready to go," Fay said. "There's nothing to do but wait for them to leave that shack, then follow them."

He frowned at Fay and Sheck and said, "Just how tough are you fellows going to be when I take the bit in my teeth?"

"Eh?" Fay frowned.

"I am going down to that shack."

"Why?"

"Because I suddenly can't wait around here any longer."

"Take it easy," Fay said. "I know where they will go after they leave the shack."

"How do you know you know? It's been demonstrated that they suspected you of being a black sheep. How do you know they didn't give you a lot of misinformation?"

"Well—"

"I'll tell you what I mean by the bit in my teeth," he said. "I'm going down to that shack. I'm going to see what I can see and hear."

"I don't think—"

"The point I'm trying to make is that it won't make any difference what you think. I'm going. I'm not in the mood to sit around here and hope another of your schemes will work."

Fay didn't like it, and his neck got a little red. But controlling himself, he said, "This is a poor time for a fight, so we won't say any more about it."

"Want to keep track of me with the binoculars?"

"Yes."

"I'll take a flashlight. Either of you read the Morse code?"

They didn't.

He said, "Three flashes for danger, three and one for danger but come, one and three for come in a hurry and it's safe." He went on giving them a simple signal code. He had them repeat it.

Edith Halcyon gave him a white-faced, horrified look when he informed her that he was going. Maybe she didn't want him to leave her here alone. Was that it? Or was she worried about the gang in the shack?

The shack was not exactly the rattletrap which it had appeared to be through the night distance. It was large, and he decided, on closer inspection, that it was really a plane hangar, large, comfortable and probably steam-heated, on the edge of a rather cramped flying field.

He was lying in the snow—he had brought a white sheet from the house, and with his white skiing parka, he was not having trouble concealing himself, when a plane went over.

It came from the west, from the direction of Saranac, and it was slowly losing altitude. After passing, quite low over the shack and the small airport, the plane did a gentle three hundred sixty degree turn over the burning Stripe Lodge.

The plane occupant or occupants were not interested in Stripe Lodge, but in the little field by the shack. He was sure of that, because the plane bracketed one side of the field carefully coming and bracketed the other leaving.

The plane droned overhead. It was a large, snaky looking job in bright orange, two radial motors, and a fat roomy cabin. It was on skis.

It left.

A man came out of the hangar-shack, carefully wrapped a long yard-wide white cloth about him—it looked like airplane fabric—and replaced another man who had been crouching, unnoticed, in a snowdrift near the door. Lookouts were being changed.

Doc Savage tore his sheet into strips, and bound the white cloth over the parts of his clothing which were not white, and over his face, except for the eyes.

He could, now that he knew where to look, see the lookout's breath steaming occasionally. Hoping to prevent being betrayed by the same thing himself, he made a pad over his mouth of loose cloth, so that his breath at least wouldn't rush out in puffs.

He decided to take the risk of presuming there was just the one lookout. He crawled ahead. There was a little wind, whipping loose snow-devils along the surface of the drifts. These helped hide him.

He had no idea of overhearing anything. That would be expecting too much. But he did hope to find out whether they had an automobile or automobiles in the building, or whether there were planes. The place was about big enough for two planes.

He got a break, though, when a man—the fat man who had sat in the lobby of Stripe Lodge with the hunting rifle on his lap before the blowup—opened the door.

"See anything?" he called.

"No," the lookout said. "Damn, it's cold out here."

"We'll relieve you in a while."

"Why didn't the plane land?"

"Afraid to. They saw the fire at the lodge, and got nervous."

"Probably a good thing."

"Probably."

"How'd you get in touch with them? Thought they didn't dare use their radio."

"They've landed on a lake. They got to a telephone and called me, a minute ago. They've hired a farmer to bring them over."

"You think it's safe for them to drive up here?"

"They won't. They'll park a mile down the road, and walk it. Or rather, ski it. They've got skis. There'll be two of them, a thin man and a heavy one, so if you see them coming, it's okay."

"Do you know them personally?"

"No. I've just got the description they gave over the telephone."

"How soon will they be here?"

"Oh, not for at least an hour."

"I'll keep an eye peeled."

"Yes, and don't forget about Fay, Sheck and that stranger who called himself Powell."

"You think they're around?"

"Somewhere. Sure."

"Suppose they should tip the police that we're here?"

"Fay won't. Fay will think we have Chester Wilson here, and will try to get Wilson himself. He won't know we've got Wilson salted away where he's safe."

"What'll we do when these two guys come?"

"If they're willing to buy at our price, we'll all load into the two planes in this hangar, pick up Wilson, and get the job done."

"That'll be a load off my mind."

"Let's hope it weights down our pockets with money," the fat man said. He went back into the hangar.

Doc Savage lay still for a while. He suddenly felt very cold, benumbed and uncomfortable. It was probably disappointment. The temperature didn't seem to be much lower than zero, which wasn't very frigid for Lake Placid at this time of the year.

He began backing away from the hangar, going carefully so that the lookout would not discover him.

He decided to go to the lodge, which was still smouldering and attracting a crowd. His two aides, Monk and Ham, might have arrived by now.

He went rapidly when he was in the cover of trees, haunting the shadows. Drawing near the lodge, he removed the torn sheets, which would look suspicious.

Despite all the commotion, smoke and flame, Stripe Lodge had not been greatly damaged. The east wing, which comprised the big lobby mostly, was a ruin on which a single hose still poured water. Soot and dirty water had made a mess of the skating rink.

Not sure just what ideas the public and the police had about the fire, Doc did not make himself too conspicuous. Then he heard a voice saying, "One of the guests was carrying a gasoline stove across the lobby. It exploded. Set the whole place afire."

"Hurt anyone?"

"No, they were lucky."

Savage moved on, thinking: So that's the way they explained away the excitement. He made a mental note to notify Army Intelligence and the F. B. I. so that they could begin picking up the staff of Stripe Lodge before they had a chance to disappear. He was tempted to tell the local police, then decided against it, because of the lengthy explanations involved. He began looking for a telephone.

Before he found the telephone, he discovered Monk and Ham. Or rather, they found him, because he hadn't immediately recognized them. They were disguised.

"We got here about fifteen minutes ago," Ham explained.

Doc Savage examined them, and decided he didn't like their disguises. What Monk and Ham had done—which might be the reason he was irritated—was get themselves worked over along the lines which Jonas House, the Hollywood wonderboy, had used on Doc. But Jonas House hadn't done this job. Doc grimaced.

"That's a great job of disguising yourselves," he said.

Monk Mayfair, missing the sarcasm, said, "I'll pass that along to Dot. She'll be very pleased to know you were impressed."

"Who is Dot?"

"She's featured in that show at the Gleever Theater. Quite a little actress, Dot is. Helped us with these disguises."

Ham Brooks said, "She's one of Monk's tramps, and she meant well."

Monk, startled and indignant, wheeled and demanded, "Say, cut out that tramp stuff—"

"I said she meant well, didn't I?" Ham turned to Doc Savage. "Doc, I can see you're not so hot about us looking this way, but I thought the girl did a fair job on us. No false wigs, greasepaint or shell-teeth. But I suppose it was a little too much like Sherlock Holmes' double-billed cap."

"Forget it," Doc said. "You fellows came by plane?"

"That's right."

"You didn't fly over here a few minutes ago?"

"No, we were just getting here when that one went over."

He started to tell them about the plane—and an idea hit him. He stared at them, weighing his idea against their altered appearance.

Monk Mayfair was a short wide long-armed man with a surprising collection of resemblances to pleasant-faced ape. He had very carefully shaved the bristling red hair off the backs of his hands, mowed and reshaped his bristling red eyebrows, dyed them and his hair. Also he wore, for quite a change, clothes that fit him. The alteration was considerable.

Ham Brooks, who was a slender dapper man, wide of shoulder and somewhat too thin about the middle, was more difficult to change. He had blonde hair now, not dark, and his suit was cheap and ill-fitting.

Monk had been scowling at Ham. Now he muttered, "The more I think about it, the less I like this tramp stuff you are always putting out about my lady friends. The next crack you make like that is going to get you turned into a humburger."

Doc Savage interrupted hastily. He recognized the signs of a quarrel that had probably been in progress during their whole trip up from New York.

"Maybe Dot had something after all," Doc said.

"Sure she has!" Monk said. "If this foul-mouthed shyster lawyer keeps on riding—"

"Postpone it!" Doc said.

His nerves were on edge, and irritation got into his voice. Monk and Ham looked at him, startled, then embarrassed.

Monk muttered, "Ham and I were just having a little—"

"You have them twenty-four hours a day, I sometimes think," Doc said sourly. "Let's postpone this one fuss."

"Sure," Monk said hastily.

"All right," Doc said. "Now, here is what I meant by saying Dot might have had something after all. You fellows don't look like your normal selves, and that may give us a chance to pull something—if you want to take the risk."

"Lead us to it," Monk said.

"Don't you want to know what you're getting into?" He frowned, and became more sober. "Both of you know the size of the matter involved, and you should weigh that against the value of your own neck before you jump at anything."

Ham Brooks said, "That quarrel a minute ago may have sounded as silly as a couple of ducks, but none the less we have a general idea of what we're up against. We'll go the whole way. Count on it."

Monk asked, "What have you got in mind, Doc?"

"There were two men in that plane which flew over a while ago, judging from what I heard," Doc explained. "Apparently they are on their way to see the men who seized Chester Wilson, to make a financial deal."

"The pair may be foreigners, then."

"Possibly. On that will depend what I had in mind."

"Which is?"

"Palm yourselves off as these two fellows and see if you can learn where Chester Wilson is being held—or better, get the information which Wilson has and everybody wants."

VIII

The two men were dressed for the part, that of two exuberant and connubial skiing roisterers on their way somewhere or other.

One of them was lean and the other was thick and wide. Both wore ski outfits, and carried ski poles and slalom skis with metal edgings. They came swinging up the side road, overdoing it a little, because they were linking arms and singing a ski song in maudlin fashion.

Doc Savage stepped out in front of them. The road here was a snow-ploughed groove between tall snow-banks.

"Hello, there," he said, walking toward them with his hand out.

The pair stopped, managing to look not too startled. But it was an effort for them.

"Hy'ah, pal," one of them said. The edge of foreign accent in his voice was barely noticeable.

Doc examined them, decided they must be the pair he wanted, and said, "I thought you'd remember my voice."

They stared at him. The wider one finally said, "Are you Burroughs? C. D. Burroughs?"

"I thought I would come down to meet you," Doc said.

"Oh." The man seemed dubious. "Is everything safe?"

"Quite safe so far. It put a little crimp in the situation when you did not land at the field, but that's not too bad."

"We dared not land. That place burning, the fire and excitement—we thought better."

"You were probably right."

The thinner man took over the conversation, going bluntly into the matter at hand. "You have Chester Wilson?" he demanded.

"He is safe."

"And you have the information, Mr. Burroughs?"

"That's settled."

"The exact figures, the latitude and longitude?"

"You have nothing to worry about."

"Good. We will proceed."

Doc said, "We can, after we settle one other point, which is the matter of payment."

The man had expected that. "I have an adequate down payment on my person. You have our assurances for the rest. And you needn't fear that the money I am carrying is captured American invasion currency, or counterfeit, because it isn't."

Doc Savage, fishing for information, said, "Just exactly how do you plan to proceed?"

"That is in your hands, of course," the other said immediately. "We expect you to take immediate steps to get to the spot designated by Chester Wilson, make the rescue, and then let us have the prisoner and one plane of large fuel capacity and good radio equipment. We will do the rest. In the other plane, you can return to the States, or wherever you wish."

"That is all?"

"All. Yes."

He struck one of the men. He was confident that he could drop him with an unexpected blow, and he did so without difficulty. The short square man had impressed him as being the more capable of the two, so Doc tackled him first. He put the man down, by swinging his right fist.

Then, for a moment, he was sure he'd made an error. The slender man whipped backward, flinging his skis and one ski pole at Doc's head, at the same time grasping the remaining ski pole as a spear. A ski pole, with its steel point, would make a dangerous weapon. The chances were that the man had a gun, so evidently he wanted to avoid the noise.

But Monk and Ham were coming out of the snow. They had been hiding, crouching in holes they had made in the snow beside the road.

Seeing them, the fellow suddenly decided to use his gun. He jerked his jacket open with one hand and drove the other hand under his clothing after the gun.

Doc Savage closed with him, seizing him, and they went to their knees in the snow. Doc had hold of both the man's arms at the wrists, and twisted upward and inward to immobilize them.

Monk came in and grabbed the man by the hair, pulled his head back and belted the exposed chin. The man sagged down. Monk was on him instantly, searching him.

"Don't tear his clothes," Doc warned. "You have to wear them."

Ham had dropped aside the other man for the sake of safety, but the fellow did not move.

"Let's see who they are," Doc said.

Without trouble, they found papers which identified the men as John Lewis and F. Fayell Grundy, Detroit, Michigan, different addresses. There was an Airman's Identification for each man, and a private pilot's license for each, both of which were probably faked.

"Lewis and Grundy," Ham said. "If their names are Lewis and Grundy, then Tojo and Adolf are named Smith and Jones."

"They're foreigners, all right," Monk agreed. "Say, I think they've got on bulletproof vests."

He investigated what he had thought was a bulletproof vest. "Holy goats!" he breathed.

"What's the matter?" Ham demanded.

"Take a look at this vest."

"Mine's got one on, too," Ham said.

"Well, take a look at yours, then."

Doc Savage had moved up to the edge of the road, to peer over the drift tops at the distant hangar shed and the still more distant hill house where Fay and Sheck and Edith Halcyon were, he hoped, still waiting. He turned his head at Ham's dumfounded whistle.

"Money!" Ham blurted. "My God, both of these fellows have their clothes lined with hundred-dollar bills."

Doc came down to look. It was as Ham had said, except that all of the bills weren't hundreds; some were twenties and fifties. He examined a few to learn whether they had the yellow seal of invasion currency. They seemed genuine.

Monk, digging through the bills with growing excitement, gasped, "There must be fifty thousand dollars here!"

Doc said, "Better change into the clothes these fellows are wearing."

"Who takes the money?" Ham asked.

"You do. It's a payment you are supposed to make, so it is important."

While they were stripping the two men of their clothing, Monk spoke, and uneasiness was in his voice for the first time. "They're liable to ask us some questions we don't know the answers to."

"They probably will."

"I may get confused."

Speaking from experience, Doc Savage thought, you probably will. I did. And it isn't a relaxing feeling.

"Good luck," he said when they were ready to go. "Try to leave a trail that I can follow."

Ham and Monk said they would do their best. They set off up the road.

Ham strode along jauntily. His clothing, purloined from the thinner of the two men they had waylaid, fitted him poorly, which he figured would help conceal his identity. Monk's suit, on the other hand, was tight and uncomfortable. But Ham reflected that as a whole Monk didn't look like Monk.

"How do you feel?" he asked.

"Like a walking mint," Monk muttered. "I hope Doc doesn't go off and let those two birds freeze to death, even if they've probably got it coming to them."

"He won't. He'll put them in our clothes and turn them over to the police or somebody."

Ham squinted ahead. "That's the place yonder, that big shed?"

"I guess so. Looks like a landing field beyond it."

The matter was settled when a rifle—apparently a disembodied rifle, because the man who held it was concealed in the snow and under white cloth—appeared and menaced them. "Take it easy," a voice advised. "What do you want?"

"We talked to a man on the telephone," Monk said.

"Yeah? What do you want with him?"

Monk had the impression his hair should be standing on end, but he felt Ham's probably was. Were they being asked for a password? If so, they were licked.

Monk, sounding much more airy than he felt, said, "We wanted to go skating with him. What do you think?"

The lookout grinned without too much enthusiasm, said, "We'll see if he will skate."

The man then took them to the hangar, and they met the fat man, whom they recognized from Doc's description.

The fat man said coldly, "Who are you gentlemen?"

"Lewis and Grundy," Ham said just as coldly. "What is this, a children's game?"

The fat man grinned. "I'm Burroughs," he said. "Come on in. You will identify yourselves farther, of course."

There were six other men in the hangar, some of whom Monk and Ham identified from Doc's description of different people who had been at Stripe Lodge before the blowup.

"Your identification," said the fat man, Burroughs.

Ham hoped he didn't look as pale and frightened as he felt. While he was wondering what on earth they would do about identifying themselves—when they had no ghost of an idea exactly who they were supposed to be—Monk came across with a performance which was inspired.

Monk tossed out the stuff, the private pilot's license and the Airman's Identification card, identifying him as F. Fayell Grundy, Detroit, Michigan.

Burroughs looked at these, said, "Phony. Phony as hair on a bird."

"If you think we carry any other identification, you're dancing under the wrong tree," Monk told him.

"We aren't satisfied," Burroughs said flatly.

Monk scowled at him. "Are you a direct man?"

"I like directness, yes."

"Then let's be direct," Monk said. "I think we have some identification that a direct man would like."

Monk began taking money out of his clothing. Ham got the idea, and did the same thing. Together, they shucked out money and piled it on a table which had been a hangar workbench.

Ham's mouth began to hang open. He took a revolver out of his clothing, one which had been on the owner of the suit when he was caught, and put it conspicuously beside the growing pile of currency.

There was an astounding amount of money.

Ham glanced about at the men in the hangar. They were pop-eyed and moistening their lips. He didn't blame them.

"Want to count it?" Monk demanded.

There was a rush for the bench.

Burroughs, suddenly sounding violent, said, "Keep away from that bench. I'll count it. Rice, you help me."

Rice was a lean man with thick dark hair over his ears, but a perfectly bald shiny pate, and thin competent lips. He was evidently second in charge. He looked capable.

They began counting. The totaling went on and on. Ham, listening to the figures, felt his mouth going dry. He glanced at Monk, and Monk rolled his eyes.

"One million, four hundred thousand," Burroughs said finally.

Monk was impressed. He was practically knocked speechless. Monk was a capable chemist, with a wide reputation. He drew large fees when he worked, but unfortunately he preferred to spend his time chasing excitement with Doc Savage, so he was continually broke. He was in the habit of thinking fifty dollars a comfortable sum.

Monk had an inspiration. He walked over and selected a few bills, which he pocketed.

"For my expenses," he said blandly. "I forgot to hold them out."

Ham looked as if he wished he'd thought of the same idea. He told Monk, "We'll need more than that for expenses."

Monk said, "That's right," and selected some more money.

Burroughs scowled at them. "What did you expect to do, dazzle us? During the arrangements, we were talking more money than this."

Monk shrugged. "That's our identification."

Burroughs snorted. "How do you figure that proves who you are?"

Monk glared at him, made his voice loud and disgusted, and said, "Who the hell else do you think would be walking in here and planking down over a million dollars in cash? My God, what kind of a dope are you!"

Monk overdid it, and sounded so much like an angry American that Ham, remembering they were probably supposed to be foreigners, was worried.

"Ich halte es für des beste, nicht zu gehen," Ham said violently.

Burroughs whirled. "What'd you say?"

Ham bowed coldly. "I said that I think it best not to go. Meaning not to go ahead with this. You are too difficult."

"Now, wait a minute," Burroughs said. "I just don't like to take chances, and I was making sure."

"You were making a fool of yourself," Ham told him haughtily. "That money is all the credential we need. If you are not satisfied, nothing will satisfy you."

Burroughs eyed him, said finally, "You're not much of a diplomat, are you."

"You said you were a direct man."

"I—"

"We want action," Ham said. "That money is a down payment. You get the rest later. Now, do we get action?"

Burroughs thought that over.

"You get action," he said. He turned to the other men. "Let's go, boys. Open the hangar doors, and start rolling out those planes."

The two planes in the hangar were large private ships, ski-equipped. The men began rolling them out, or rather skidding them outside, a not inconsiderable job since it had to be done by main strength and awkwardness.

Ham and Monk stood aloof from the labor, pretending the effort didn't fit their station, but actually to get a chance to confer.

"We've got to get a line on where we're going," Ham whispered.

"You mean so we can leave a trail for Doc to follow?"

"That's the idea."

"We better dig the information out of this Burroughs fellow."

They approached Burroughs, feeling far from certain about how they were going to get what they wanted. Monk indicated the two planes, asked, "By any chance, are you figuring on making the whole trip in those?"

Burroughs was surprised. "Naturally not. Your people are going to furnish us two large, fast planes, aren't they?"

"Eh?"

"Aren't they?" Burroughs looked alarmed.

"Naturally," Monk said airily.

Burroughs wiped his forehead. "For a minute, you had me worried. Your people will have the planes there, you're sure of that?"

"They had better be," Monk said. "Incidentally, do you know the place where you were to meet them?"

"I've got the location I was given."

"Repeat it, please. We wish to check on it."

Burroughs wasn't suspicious. He rattled off a location on an aeronautical chart in degrees of latitude and longitude.

"Good," Monk said.

When Monk and Ham had sauntered back to the rear of the hangar, Ham demanded, "You know where that is?"

"Sounded like up around Greenland somewhere, if I remember my geography."

"All right," Ham said. "I'm going to scuff a mark on the floor that Doc will see, and you think of some way of leaving him the figures."

Monk nodded. He went over and picked up his skiis. He examined them, as if he was checking them over, and while he was doing that, used his fingernail to scratch the latitude and longitude figures in the dark ski wax on the bottom of the ski.

Doc couldn't miss the writing on the ski bottom, Monk reflected. He put the skis back in a corner.

The men had the plane outside.

Monk whispered to Ham, "I put the dope on the bottom of one of the skis."

"Good enough," Ham agreed.

Burroughs came inside saying, "Get aboard the plane. We are all ready to go."

"What about Chester Wilson?" Ham demanded.

"We'll land and pick him up enroute. He is being held elsewhere."

"Far away?"

"Not very."

Monk and Ham went outside with Burroughs. They all climbed into the two planes, the motors of which were rumbling and spitting fire.

Suddenly a man came running and tossed a pair of skis into the plane with Monk and Ham.

"You'll need these," the man said. "Better take them along."

Monk stared sickly at the skis.

The planes began moving, gathered speed, rocked a little, finally lifted off the field and climbed sluggishly up into the cold night.

Monk picked up one of the skis, glanced at the bottom, then gave Ham an ill look. The ski was the one he'd intended to leave behind with a message for Doc Savage.

IX

The plane climbed and bored into the night northward and westward. The pilot, Monk reflected bitterly, was taking no chance of getting too close to the heavy red line on the air navigation charts marked "Boundary of Active Air Defense Zone." The line here approximately followed the New York-Vermont state borders. That was tough, Monk thought sourly, because the air defense agencies wouldn't be likely to keep track of them.

Doc Savage would have no idea where they had gone. Monk scowled sickly out of the window, reflecting on the injustice of the bad break. He made up his mind to personally kick the stuffing out of the helpful rascal who had picked up the skis and tossed them into the plane. But the resolution was not a remedy for the mishap.

It was a major tragedy, in reality. Everything, as Monk saw it, now depended on himself and Ham Brooks. Ordinarily he wouldn't have minded, and he knew Ham would not have. But the present matter was too drastic, too vital. In plain words, it was so big it scared him. He wished Doc Savage was on hand. Monk's state of mind was black.

Burroughs came back and plunked in a cabin seat where he could shout happily at them. Getting into the air had worked a change in him. All his fat round curves radiated delight.

He had a bag which he had made by tying four corners of a square of airplane fabric together, and in this he was carrying the money. He looked quite self-conscious about carrying around so much money. As, Monk Mayfair thought sourly, who wouldn't.

"We have had a series of bad breaks, but now I don't see how we can fail," Burroughs said, adding no cheer to Monk's state of mind.

"An American army plane may shoot us down," Monk said, almost hopefully.

"Not a chance. We have a radio, and we filed a flight plan the regular way. Civilian flying is permitted now, you know, and we have done nothing to arouse suspicion."

"Did you give your actual destination in the flight plan?"

Burroughs laughed. "Naturally not. But nobody will bother us until we get over waste country where there will be no one to bother us. Yes, indeed, the monkey wrenches are all out of the plan. Skies are blue. The goose hangs high." He smirked at Monk and explained, "All of those are American expressions meaning that our troubles are over."

The best American expression I can think for you is a good bust in the kisser, Monk thought gloomily.

Monk said, "You had troubles?" He hoped he would get some satisfaction out of hearing about the other's troubles.

Burroughs leaned back, hooked his fingers together over the fat cloth pouch containing the money, and said that he'd had plenty of trouble.

"I don't know what is coming over the world, the way it is getting so you can't trust your lifelong friends," Burroughs complained. "This fellow, Thaddeus Fay, has done work off and on for me for years. He was with me in Poland, when we performed certain services for your government in nineteen thirty-nine. And later he was in Italy with me, and France, and we have worked along together very well here in the United States since Pearl Harbor. You wouldn't think a fellow like that would doublecross you."

Ham said, "Ah, you have had disaffection among your associates?" He hoped he sounded like a supercilious foreigner.

Burroughs grimaced. "He did not fool me, though."

Monk and Ham found themselves listening to a long story concerning the cleverness of Mr. Burroughs, the undependability of mankind in general, and more of the cleverness of Mr. Burroughs. The man was a braggart, but a rather intelligent one, so that a fellow didn't immediately realize that almost everything he said was a buildup for Mr. Burroughs.

Burroughs, Monk and Ham gathered, followed a profession that could be best described as a free-lance internationalist in affairs of profit. That was the way he put it. A simpler way was to say that the man specialized in anything shady that would turn a large dollar.

Not that Burroughs was a direct crook, though. He did not knock people over the head and lift their billfolds. He was more refined, and anyway the average billfold wouldn't contain enough to interest him. Burroughs was mortally afraid of risks, and he had to be well paid for taking them.

The man was—and he probably wasn't bragging about this—a mastermind only. He laid the plans, arranged for others to do the actual doing and be where the bullets arrived, if any arrived.

Monk asked, "How did you happen to get your hands on this particular plum?"

Now it got interesting.

"I was under the tree with both hands ready," Burroughs said, "when the plum fell."

"Meaning?"

"That I had long foreseen certain possibilities connected with these international get-togethers such as the one concluded last week. So I have kept my eye on them, and made my contacts."

"Contacts?"

Burroughs smiled. "Take Chester Wilson, for example."

Monk got a sudden cold feeling of illness. Was Chester Wilson a crook? Had he sold out? No one believed such a thing was possible. The chance that it could be had been investigated, it was true. But Chester Wilson, U. S. Army Flier, had been cleared as of good character.

"If Chester Wilson was working for you," Monk said, "how come you had to kidnap him?"

"Oh, Wilson is lamentably honest," Burroughs said. "What happened was this: I had noticed that he was assigned to flight missions of this type whenever one occurred, and so I got in contact with him. I did so indirectly—that is, I put on sheep's clothing. I pretended to be a book publisher.

"I signed Wilson to do a book about his experiences, and paid him a substantial advance. We worked together rather closely, and it was impressed on Wilson's mind time and time again that if anything spectacular happened, he was to contact me immediately. In case it was a matter which censorship would not release, he was to contact me anyway, in order that I could be prepared with the publicity. In other words, so we could be set to take advantage of the situation."

Monk said, "Won't this book-publishing connection with Wilson draw the attention of the State Department and the F.B.I. to you?"

Burroughs laughed. "I don't mean I personally did it. It was through an agent. The agent is already in Argentina, where they'll have a hell of a time catching him."

"Oh."

"So you see," Burroughs finished, "when this wild thing broke, the first thing Chester Wilson did was contact me—or my agent. Wilson was excited. He was so excited that he was a fool. He called us before he gave his information to the State Department. So we lost no time in kidnapping him, and with luck, got him before he could reveal the vital location to the State Department."

Monk, with a bland approval he was far from feeling, said, "Very nice. Very profitable. When do we pick up Wilson?"

"Shortly."

Their plane settled down on a frozen lake to get Chester Wilson. The lake was a small one, and neither Monk nor Ham were sure of its exact location. Still in upstate New York, they believed. The pilot made a shoddy jackrabbit landing which stood Monk's hair on end.

A car came rolling out on the lake ice until Burroughs jumped out of the plane screaming for them to go back, did they want to break the ice and dump everybody in the lake? The car went back. Two men came from it, leading Chester Wilson.

Chester Wilson, it was plain, had been roughly handled. His nose was swollen, his eyes black, his fists skinned. He was tall and reddish, with the kind of a mobile face that registered all of his emotions, of which he was having plenty.

Wilson scowled at Monk and Ham.

"Is Edith Halcyon all right?" he demanded. "By God, I want to know about that!"

Monk and Ham, presuming they were to know nothing about Edith Halcyon, looked properly mystified, and turned to Burroughs.

"Oh, yes, Miss Halcyon," Burroughs said. "As a matter of fact, she is out of our hands. She escaped."

"When was that?"

"Shortly after you saw her through the window of Stripe Lodge, and so kindly decided to talk."

"There was nothing kind about it!" Wilson snapped.

"Well, it was wise, anyway."

Wilson glowered, and went into a dark discouraged silence. He did not speak again, not during the entire trip, nor did he as much as trouble to look out at the ground.

Burroughs told Monk and Ham, "The girl, Edith Halcyon, is his sister-in-law. We had to use a threat to her safety to get him to talk."

Monk, sympathizing with Wilson because of the load of anxiety and strain the pilot was carrying, made an effort to relieve Wilson's mind somewhat by asking, "The girl got away from you, eh?"

"Yes. When that crook, Thaddeus Fay, doublecrossed me."

"Then the girl is still alive?"

"I imagine so."

"That is no advantage to us," Monk said.

"No, it isn't."

Which, Monk reflected, means that they probably plan to kill Chester Wilson in the end, anyway. After Monk had watched Wilson for a while, he decided Wilson knew that.

The plane flew north, then east, then north, then west. Mostly, though, it went north and east.

The day came with a slate-colored reluctance, the sun dull behind a heavy convection fog. The fog dissipated slowly and they could see the snow-covered country below.

Chester Wilson continued to stare fixedly at the plane floor between his feet. Once he lifted his head, and Monk got set to join in, thinking he was about to start a fight, but nothing happened. Wilson's head dropped again.

Later their pilot began to worry. He did some wing-wagging at the other ship, which was flying alongside them. Monk watched him making gestures—motions of peering downward, scratching his head, holding both palms up—and decided the fellow couldn't find what he was hunting for.

The pilot beckoned Burroughs, and they conferred.

Monk leaned over and whispered to Ham, "They can't find the other planes, the big ones, they were to meet."

Ham nodded. "I hope to God they don't ask us where they are."

A moment later, Burroughs came back to them, and asked, "What were those rendezvous figures again." He was looking at Ham.

Ham stared at him stupidly. To save his life—which was possibly what it amounted to—he couldn't remember the figures.

Monk stepped into the void blandly. He gave the figures which he had scratched in the wax on the ski back at Lake Placid.

Burroughs said, "Damn!" explosively. He ran forward to the pilot, jabbed his finger at the chart they were using, and said something violent that Monk and Ham couldn't catch.

Monk whispered, "What was the matter with you when he asked you the figures?"

Ham shivered. "My brain cut out on me. I couldn't think of them."

Monk grimaced. "Brother, I'll never forget those figures."

Burroughs rejoined them, and he was grinning. "You know what? The silly pilot wrote down a five where it should have been a three, or his three looked like a five."

"Oh, then we're still all right?"

"We're not lost yet, anyway."

Burroughs began whistling cheerfully, and Monk was tempted to take a swing at the man for his good spirits. Monk leaned over, and being careful that no one could overhear or see his lips, whispered, "What's gonna happen to us when we get to this rendezvous?"

"Why bring that up?" Ham asked uneasily.

They were flying north. The day was gray. The cabin heater wasn't doing much good, so it must be very cold outside. Ham, looking out of the cabin window, could see rime ice on the leading edge of the wing, and he worried about that on top of everything else. The plane didn't have de-icing equipment.

It was an anti-climax when the pilot turned and gave them all the circled thumb-and-forefinger signal that everything was fine.

"There they are," Burroughs said.

If Monk and Ham had not already been impressed with the magnitude of the thing in which they were involved, the size of the two planes would have given them a by-golly-I-didn't-know-the-ocean-was-that-big feeling.

The planes were Heinkel HE 177s, four-engine ships with sharp taper, wings well back from the nose, and an exceptionally thick wing. Both big ships were on skis, and the skis seemed about the size of canoes.

The craft were well hidden, the upper wing surfaces being painted white, and in addition each ship was draped over with a white netting.

Monk and Ham, having heard that two planes would be there, did not expect any others. It was a shock when Burroughs said, "That wasn't a bad idea either," and pointed.

Ham jumped violently when he stared under the netting and discovered another ship, this one also a Heinkel, but a HE 113, with a fifteen-hundred horsepower Daimler Benz DB 603 motor.

"How the devil did they get that pursuit job over here?" Ham asked Monk in a low voice. "Maximum range of those things is supposed to be around six hundred fifty miles."

"Auxiliary fuel tanks maybe."

"They couldn't load enough fuel on it to get it this far."

"That's among our lesser worries," Monk said. "Here comes the head guy of the outfit with these big planes."

"I hope he don't know us."

"If he does!" Monk made a gesture which he could make well and expressively, the gesture of drawing a finger across his throat. "Geek!" he said.

The pantomime was effective enough to cause Ham to look a little ill.

They watched Burroughs meet a man who looked as if he was mostly jaw and mean eyes. The two talked for a while, in English, then Burroughs brought the jaw and the eyes over to Monk and Ham.

"This is Blohm," Burroughs said.

"So you are Lewis and Grundy," Blohm said, and his voice was quite pleasant, although his looks weren't.

"I'm Lewis," Monk explained. "This is Grundy." Then he wondered why Burroughs was staring at him with such a strange expression.

"You are Grundy," Burroughs reminded Monk. "And the slender man is Lewis."

Monk's neck crawled. My God, he thought! What a time to make a dumb mistake!

But Blohm was smiling and shaking hands with them, and saying, "I'm very glad to meet you two. You have done some very fine work."

"How soon will we proceed?" Monk asked.

"The supercharger on the pursuit ship went bad, and there is about half an hour of work on it," Blohm said. "Then we can get going."

Monk had an inspiration, and said, "All right. In the meantime, we'll keep an eye on Chester Wilson."

As they were walking back to the smaller plane, Ham told Monk, "That was nice going, you forgetting who you are?"

Monk said a bitter nothing.

They got a break. They found Chester Wilson guarded by only one man in the plane, and the guard said, "You fellows want to watch him while I go over and take a look at those Heinie planes. I never saw one before."

"Sure, go ahead," Monk said.

The guard scrambled out of the ship.

Monk lunged to Chester Wilson's side. He said rapidly, "Don't ask a lot of questions, Wilson. We're Doc Savage's assistants, Monk Mayfair and Ham Brooks. We trapped Lewis and Grundy and took their places. We planned to leave a trail so Doc Savage would be able to follow us, but we flopped, or I did. Now, answer me this: Do you believe us?"

Chester Wilson frowned at them. "I don't know. I'll act as if I do, because I don't see where that would hurt anything."

"Good," Monk said. "First, did you give them the straight dope on where the plane went down?"

"Yes."

"That's a hell of a note," Monk said bitterly. "You should have lied to them."

"They were going to kill Edith Halcyon."

"They would probably have murdered her anyway."

Wilson nodded, but he lost color. "Is she safe now?"

"She's with Doc Savage. I don't know how safe she is. Doc is with the two guys who tried to steal you, Thaddeus Fay and Sheck, and they think he's one of them."

"She's safe with Savage, probably," Wilson muttered.

Ham stood up. "We've got to leave some kind of a message here for Doc."

"What good'll that do?" Monk growled. "Doc won't find this place."

"Of course he will."

"Huh? How?"

Ham grinned at Monk and said, "Well, while you were wasting your time leaving the hieroglyphics you call handwriting on the skiis, I left a nice little note on the sidewall of an old airplane tire that was lying around. And I marked it so Doc will be sure to find it."

"You left a note," Monk said. "You left a note. You left a—" He shut his eyes tightly.

Monk stood there, pinching his eyes together tightly, thinking of the actual physical sickness, to say nothing of the mental fungoes, which he had undergone in the past few hours thinking they hadn't left a trail for Doc Savage to follow. All of which could have been avoided by a few words from Ham.

This, of course, was one of Ham's little jokes. Ham was full of them. Monk was full of them, too, but not as much as Ham, he frequently thought. He wished violently that Ham would confine his practical jokes—if one could call one like this practical—to times when they didn't have anything else on their minds. Monk did not follow this policy, but he wished Ham would.

He turned all this over in his mind, hid his relief carefully, and told Ham, "If you were not supposed to be my brother conspiritor, I would plant my foot on your behind, take hold of your ears, and turn you inside out. Later, as a matter of fact, I am going to do exactly that."

Chester Wilson, excitement rushing through his voice, said, "If you think Savage will get here, for God's sake leave him the location of the spot where the plane went down!"

"Where was it?" Ham demanded.

"Close to latitude sixty-five north and longitude fifty-seven west," Wilson said. He gave them the exact minutes and seconds.

Ham glanced at Monk. "You want to leave a message this time, too?"

"It's not funny, you shyster," Monk muttered.

They left the information for Doc Savage without trouble. Monk kept his eye on Ham, and saw that Ham wrote his on the wrapper of a candy bar, which he carelessly tossed aside.

Monk considered his own method more subtle. He used paper and pencil to write the note, then rolled it into one of four snowballs which he made. Then, when they were out of the plane, he slammed Ham on the back of the head with one snowball, and popped him between the eyes with the other when he turned around.

Ham indignantly scooped up snow and returned the fire. Monk laughed and ran—going off and leaving the snowball containing the note lying in a conspicuous spot.

He ran, as it happened, toward Burroughs and Blohm. He joined them, dodging and laughing.

"You are in good spirits," Burroughs said.

"Why shouldn't we be?" Monk asked him amiably. "We are just about at the end of the trail, aren't we?"

Burroughs looked queerly at Blohm. "Are they? What would you say, Blohm?"

"I think so," Blohm said queerly.

Monk lost his gleeful expression. "Something wrong?"

Ham came up and asked, "What's going on?"

"*Achtung!*" Blohm shouted suddenly. "*Nehmen sie sich in acht!*"

He was speaking to his men, the crew of the two big planes. Most of these, Monk and Ham realized suddenly, were much too close at hand. Furthermore, all of them suddenly produced guns.

Blohm turned back to Monk and Ham. "It is immaterial whether we shoot you now or later," he said.

Monk stared at him. "What the hell!"

Blohm showed the tips of his teeth in an expression that wasn't at all a smile. "You two men are Lewis and Grundy, agents of my government?"

"That's right," Ham snapped. "Who else do you—"

"Oh, no."

"Eh?"

"Oh, no," Blohm said. "You see, I know Lewis and Grundy personally. They happen to be friends of mine."

Monk, speaking against the terror that came toward him like a black wall, said, "Listen, brother, if we are friends of yours—"

"Then you're not Lewis and Grundy," Blohm said. "Which you aren't. Don't you think you'd better put up your hands?"

X

Thaddeus Fay, Doc Savage, Sheck and Edith Halcyon were flying northward in a plane which Fay had produced with the confident air of a magician saying, "Well, you see I had a rabbit in the hat after all."

The plane, a big single-motored private ship of the type used by millionaires back in the days when there were millionaires, was about five years old, but still airworthy and capable of a hundred and sixty cruising. Fay had had it in a hangar near Saranac Lake. Planted there, Fay had explained, for such an occasion.

Doc Savage had visited the hangar at Lake Placid after the men they were following had fled in the two planes. Doc's purpose, of course, was to see whether Monk and Ham had managed to leave a message, but he couldn't tell Fay that was his object. Fay had not favored wasting time on the hangar, but Doc had insisted, and Fay was still puzzled about that.

Doc had found Ham's notation, latitude and longitude figures, on the old airplane casing. Ham had scratched the figures there with his fingernail and initialed them, and they were quite legible. Doc had committed them to memory.

He had done one other thing immediately: He had contacted Wister of the State Department by telephone, and explained the situation, giving Wister the figures. "Give us five or six hours, then get up there with every man you can scrape up, would be my advice," Doc told him.

"Do you suppose those figures are the spot where the plane went down?" Wister demanded anxiously.

"No. Apparently they are a rendezvous location, a spot where larger planes, probably long-distance craft from Europe, are waiting."

189

Wister said that he would take steps. He added that he would try to do so more sensibly than he had previously. But he sounded every bit as nervous and frightened as he had at any time.

Doc Savage, to keep his identity as Joe Powell intact with Fay and Sheck, informed them bluntly that he was calling his two pals from New York, telling them to stay around Lake Placid if they couldn't find him.

Then they had gotten Fay's ship.

They had been flying about five hours. In the wrong direction. They were going north. The correct course was north and east.

Fay's ideas of the rendezvous figures didn't agree with the ones Ham had left. Doc had no way of knowing which was correct. There was plenty of gasoline in the fuel tanks, so he concluded to let Fay try his spot. If it proved a blank, then Ham's figures would be right.

Doc spent most of the five hours in the air wishing he hadn't allowed them to bring Edith Halcyon along. He might have prevented that. He didn't know.

His reason for allowing the girl to come, now that he thought it over, didn't seem too good. He hadn't been entirely convinced that she was what she said she was. He suspected her.

His reasons for suspecting her now seemed inadequate, his allowing her to be brought along struck him as reprehensible.

Still, her attitude *was* strange. She seemed to be afraid of him. Why should she be afraid?

After they had flown about six hours and spent another half hour circling, he knew that Fay had been handed a wild goose to chase.

He gave Fay the correct destination, and it caused the uproar which he had known it would. Fay looked at him with bleat intentness. "That is the destination?"

"Yes."

"How do you know that?"

Doc asked, "What did you think I did before I connected up with you, stumble around with plugs in my ears?"

Thaddeus Fay was a very quick man, because now he made a gesture with the same smoothness that went into his skating figures, producing a gun. The weapon, a pistol of the sort that would be carried by a man who was a marksman and who loved fine guns, was in an unhandy place, a sheath inside his parka. But he got it smoothly and expertly. He stood there holding the weapon, not quite pointing it at Doc.

"What else do you know?"

Doc told him, "That they were to meet two enemy agents who would make a payment for the information, after which they would pick up Chester Wilson and fly to this spot I've just located for you, where larger planes with proper equipment for reaching the spot where the crash occurred, would be waiting."

Fay said, "That's long-winded, but it's the facts." He was a little hoarse because of tension.

Doc said nothing. He watched Fay. Fay was flying, or rather letting the ship fly itself at the moment, and concentrating on holding his gun and frowning at Doc Savage.

"Where'd you get this dope?" Fay demanded.

"By keeping my eyes open."

"Let's not be facetious," Fay said.

Doc shrugged.

Fay was very still for a while, except that he was trying out different kinds of frowns on his face. Finally he demanded, "The girl tip you?"

"Don't be ridiculous."

"It does seem ridiculous," Fay agreed. "She didn't know about this arrangement to get larger, long-distance planes from Europe. Or she wasn't supposed to know."

"Why are the larger planes necessary?"

"There are no civilian planes around loose these days that could make such a flight. Anyway, those guys on the other side were plenty willing to furnish the planes."

"They would have furnished you sixteen battleships, if it would do any good," Doc said.

"That's right, if they had sixteen battleships left, which I doubt."

Doc said, "The information is straight. The rendezvous location, I mean."

"You reckon they could have tricked you, too?"

"Maybe. We can see."

Fay continued scowling. Finally he decided, "The girl told you." He whirled on Edith Halcyon. "My dear, you've been holding out on me. I really don't like that."

"Don't bother her," Doc said.

"She's with you, eh?"

"Leave her alone," Doc said.

Fay put his gun away.

"What's the new course?" he asked.

They found the spot, but there was nothing there but tracks of plane ski runners in the snow, and a large white camouflage net which had been used to cover the planes. Doc Savage, Sheck and Fay walked around looking at the snow marks.

"Two Heinkel 177s, and a Heinkel 113," Fay said.

This information astonished Doc Savage, although he had reached the same conclusion himself. He hadn't supposed that Fay knew so much about planes, and he had been quite proud of himself for being able to identify them from the tracks of the skis. The incident spilled some of his confidence.

"How do you know?" Doc asked.

"I was in Norway when they were using them to go after convoys headed for Murmansk," Fay explained.

"Oh, you've been a German agent, then?"

"Not at that time," Fay said, and chuckled. "As a matter of fact, I was doing a little high-class skullduggery for Uncle Joe at the time."

"Russia?"

"That's right."

"You get around."

Fay was either pleased, or his nervousness was making him talkative. He said, "I've been at this sort of thing a long time. About twenty years in fact."

"You're old in the game, then."

"Older than they usually get," Fay agreed. "I quit it for a few years, but those stinking Nazis stole so much of my property in Europe that I had to go at it again." He sighed bitterly. "I had a resort in the Tyrol, the most beautiful place you ever saw. A fat louse of a fellow from Dresden has it now."

"But you're doing business with them now."

"You're damned right, or I will if I come out on top of this. And maybe you don't think they'll pay through the nose!"

Sheck was impatient. "What do we do now? We've found where the planes were. But what do we do?"

"Let's ask the mystery man if he has any ideas," Fay said. He eyed Doc. "Have you?"

"We'll look around," Doc said.

He found both notes which Monk and Ham had left, the one on the candy bar wrapper and the one in the snowball. It took him half an hour of hunting, but he located both.

He showed Fay the notes, but did not let him see the figures. Very quickly, he destroyed both by popping them into his mouth and chewing them until they were unrecognizable. He kept a gun in his hand while he was doing it.

"Life insurance," he told Fay.

"Really, I'm not bloodthirsty enough to dispose of you if you had given me the figures," Fay told him.

"No?"

"Anyway, I need your help. I'm beginning to think you are fairly capable."

"Thanks."

"Who left those notes for you?"

"A friend."

"Obviously," Fay said. He did not try further to find out who had left the information on the candy wrapper and in the snowball. But his facial expression indicated the puzzle was far from being out of his mind.

They took off and flew north. Doc occupied the co-pilot's seat, and worked for a while with an aeronautical planning chart which he found in the map case. The scale of the chart, five million to one, or about eighty miles to the inch, was too general for much accuracy. But it didn't matter. Landmarks in that section were not charted with sufficient accuracy to be of much value.

He fussed with the drift sight and worked out windage and set up his triangle of velocities on a computer. Then he took over the controls.

Fay, astonished, said, "You can fly, too?"

"A little."

"I noticed how little. You handled that computer like a stenographer uses her typewriter. You've had plenty of experience."

Instead of answering, Doc suddenly put the plane into a spiral. He pointed downward. "Two planes down there," he said.

Fay said he'd be damned, and stared with anything but ease of mind while Doc circled the spot. The planes were private ships with United States NC numbers. Fay identified them as the two planes which had been in the hangar at Lake Placid.

"It may be a trap," Fay warned, when he saw Doc intended landing.

"The probabilities are that it isn't," Doc said. "That other field back yonder, where they met the big planes, is close to a patrol route which a Canadian Mounted Police plane makes twice a week. They wanted to leave their planes to be picked up for the trip back, but didn't dare leave them at the other field. So they brought them this far. That would be my guess."

But Fay was gray-faced with nervous uneasiness until they had landed and made sure it was not anything specially arranged for them.

Doc examined the plane fuel tanks. "Another reason for the planes being left here," he said. "This was as far as they could go and still have enough fuel left to get back to something resembling civilization." He started digging around in the ships. "Look for something to shift the fuel from these planes to our own," he said.

There were no buckets or cans, so finally they cut a slab of fabric off the belly of one of the ships and made a cup affair which they used. They had trouble, because the wind was coldly violent, but finally the fuel was transferred.

Fay raged with impatience. "We'll be so far behind that we won't be able to do any good."

"Maybe not," Doc said.

"Meaning that your friends with Burroughs will take care of things for you?" Fay demanded.

Doc wondered just who Burroughs was.

They climbed back into their plane and then two of them had to climb out again, and struggle with their weight against the tail in order to keep the craft from wind-vaning while they taxied downwind. The girl and Sheck did the pushing, and when Edith Halcyon climbed back into the plane, she hurried and slipped into the pilot's seat beside Doc Savage.

"I'm scared!" she whispered. She sounded very frightened. "I'm afraid they will kill me any minute. There is no reason why they shouldn't, is there?"

"Get hold of your nerve," Doc told her.

Her fingers were biting into his arm and her lips were thin and tight over her teeth. He had the sudden frightened conviction that she was about to scream and go into hysterics. He put his face close to hers and said violently, "Stop it! You're acting a fool! You'll give us away!"

The words produced no effect on her at once, but then they soaked in, and she withdrew.

Thaddeus Fay had seen the exchange. He came forward, told the girl, "You ride back in the cabin."

She didn't look as if she was going to obey, but she did, and Fay took her seat. He told Doc angrily, "No more talking behind my back!"

Doc ignored him.

"Is she working with you?" Fay demanded.

Doc took the plane off without answering. They were loggy getting into the air, because of their heavy load of fuel. Fay sat there with perspiration visible on his forehead until they were in the air, letting Doc fly the ship.

Then Fay demanded, "Who left those notes you found? I want to know!"

Wondering how to shut the man up, how to avoid a quarrel, Doc began to have a loose, wild feeling that he was going to lose control of himself, that the door was going to fly open and the wildness rush out. He was awfully tempted. He wanted to strike Fay, to smash him with every bit of violence, and Sheck as well; he wished to shake the girl, or at least do something to show her that women had no place in such violence and tension as this. Still, she wasn't at fault, he supposed. Not if she was what she said she was, innocent Edith Halcyon who had tried to help her brother-in-law and been used as a pry to get information from the man instead.

All the wildness climbed up inside him. Not much was really happening, which made it worse. So much was at stake, and he seemed to be getting hold of nothing really decisive. Just enough to lead him on headlong with the hair-raising tension increasing and the uncertainty growing.

His doubt and suspense was worse now, for good reason. He had intended to summon help as soon as he got the location of the plane, the location which Chester Wilson had known. Now he had it. Now was when he had been going to summon help. But he had a sick feeling that no aid could reach the lost plane in time to be of any use. He might reach the plane himself. There was a chance. But help couldn't.

Altogether he was in no mood for an argument with Fay.

"Sit down and shut up!" he told Fay.

Fay almost didn't hold himself in. His face looked bleak and almost fleshless as he sat there.

The fellow isn't exactly in an enviable position himself, Doc reflected. He knows who I am. He knows he has to dispose of me violently. But first he has to use me, because he needs my help.

Doc tinkered impatiently with the controls, the throttle, the carburetor heat, watching the tachometer and airspeed indicator. He wished they had another hundred miles an hour speed. He was afraid, mortally afraid, that they weren't going to be in time.

He debated whether to get rid of Fay and Sheck now. Probably he could do it, although they would be half expecting trouble. In the end he decided against it, for he needed their assistance. They were capable.

He asked Fay, "Have you a plan?"

"Have you?" Fay countered.

He said, "I am only getting a third. For that, am I supposed to give the orders?"

Fay closed his eyes for a while. "There is no landing place where the plane was forced down. There is none for miles. If there was, Chester Wilson would have landed. That means they will have to land somewhere else, and make the trip afoot. That gives us time."

Fay opened his eyes and said, "If we can catch them afoot, going across the ice or across whatever they have to cross, we may be able to shoot them down."

"With what for guns?"

Fay went back into the cabin. There was a case lashed in the baggage compartment, and from this he took a small machine gun and two carbine rifles. He had three boxes of cartridges for the rifles and about twenty boxes of .45-caliber for the little machine gun.

"This will have to do it," Fay said. He stood one of the

rifles in the control cockpit, gave Sheck the other rifle and kept the machine gun for himself.

Doc said, "You are overlooking one thing."

"Eh?"

"Chester Wilson was flying a seaplane. Maybe the other plane came down in a spot where ski-equipped planes can land. Maybe Wilson didn't dare set down because he had a seaplane."

Fay moistened his lips uneasily. "Maybe you're wrong. You better hope you are."

Doc Savage loaded the carbine rifle which Fay had stood in the cockpit. It was a 30-30, lever-action, short-barreled and not much of a fighting weapon in these bloodthirsty days when a 30-06 calibre machine gun was generally referred to as a peashooter. But it was better than no gun.

He put the rifle aside as soon as he had it loaded, for handling it was giving him a coldly depressed feeling. He didn't like firearms, and almost never carried any kind of a gun. He had often imagined that, subconsciously, he must be afraid of guns. But the logical explanation he gave himself was that a man with a gun in his pocket got too much in the habit of depending on the gun to solve everything. A gun wouldn't do that.

It was cold. The cabin heating wasn't adequate. The external thermometer indicated it was about thirty below zero outside. Checking frequently with the drift sight, he could tell that the wind here was about forty miles an hour, and that worried him, so he dropped down to get the surface wind. It wasn't as bad, quite. About thirty miles. That wouldn't be so tough, unless they got a bad crosswind landing.

Altogether, the wind and cold wasn't as bad as could be expected for the Arctic winter. In fact, it was a rather calm day.

He checked the course, running the groundspeed and elapsed time problem on the computer.

"Fay," he said.

"Yes?"

"It isn't much farther."

Fay looked at him uneasily. "What are you going to try to do first?"

"Knock the bombers out—and the fighter plane—if we can find them."

"That fighter!" Fay said hoarsely. "We haven't got a chance against it!"

Doc Savage went back to watching the Arctic waste below, and it was not more than five minutes before he saw the two bombers.

XI

They were over land, rolling snow-covered coastal country. Far to the north and east would be the Greenland mainland, and north was Jones Sound, then Ellsmere Land. So this must be Devon Island in midwinter.

He searched the terrain intently. And suddenly, as if a curtain had gone up in a theater, the whole situation was in front of him.

The big U. S. Army transport was piled up in the snow. It had lost its undercarriage and part of a wing, but the fuselage was intact. The pilot had done well with what he had to work with. There simply hadn't been enough runway when the ship iced up and he had to come down, but he had made a safe landing.

The big plane wasn't very impressive, lying there crippled in the snow. It certainly wasn't a sight that lived up to the uproar its loss had caused in Allied circles. It didn't look like something around which the future of nations quite probably hinged. It was just a big Army transport which had gotten lost in the Arctic, iced up and made a forced landing in which it had suffered some damage.

The two Heinkels, the big ones, were down about two miles to the east. They were down in a good spot, a long level stretch which was ample for their landing and take-off needs.

About half way between the wrecked American Army plane and the two Heinkels, a group of men were making their way on skis. There was a ridge of hills, and they were having slow going.

Fay, after staring through the binoculars, pointed at the skiing group and yelled, "That's Burroughs! They haven't gotten to the downed plane yet. We've got a chance."

Doc took the binoculars out of his hands. He tried to conceal his own anxiety. He was concerned about Monk and Ham, wondering where they were. If they were with

199

the bombers, in the ships, that meant he didn't dare dive and fire on the Heinkels at random.

He couldn't spot Monk and Ham.

He saw Burroughs and his men stop and stare at the plane.

He knew the pursuit ship must be above somewhere, since it wasn't on the ground.

There was no time to kill. He dropped a wing and peeled off in as much of a dive as the civilian plane would take.

"Give me that machine gun!" he shouted at Fay. "We will try to knock out the motors on the bombers."

Fay astonished him by handing over the light machine gun without an argument. He took it, jammed it down beside him, and gave his attention to getting the plane down, killing its speed with a slip, and floating in on the two bombers.

The Heinkels got larger, the way things on the ground seem to do when you come down on them from the air. He watched the plastic gun turret windows, alert lest they should man some of the turret guns.

He told Fay, "Take the controls. Bank around them as close as you can."

Then he saw a man jump out of each bomber. The men ran madly, getting away from the ships, and flattened out in the snow and began raking snow over them with their hands.

"Glory be!" Fay said gleefully. "They've been trained to get the hell out of grounded planes when there's an air attack. They think we've got bombs."

Doc aimed carefully with the little machine gun, and gave one of the Heinkel engines a burst.

Then he saw Monk and Ham. They had rolled out of one of the Heinkels. They were tied hand and foot.

Doc put the gun aside instantly. He could see that Monk and Ham were tied with rope, so he dug a pocket knife out of his clothing. He hauled out the chart case, dumped the charts, and put the knife in the case, which he zipped shut.

"I'll take the controls," he told Fay.

He banked the ship sharply again, estimated wind direction, got the cockpit window open, and let fly the map case. He watched it. The case landed close to Monk and

Ham, and both of them made for it, flopping with their bound hands and feet, ludicrously like fish out of water.

One of the men who had fled from the Heinkels now got up out of the snow with a gun. Fay began shooting at him deliberately. Back in the cabin, Sheck's rifle also whacked methodically.

The man in the snow suddenly got down on his hands and knees, then spread out loosely, face down, and did not move again.

Monk had reached the map case. He had trouble with the zipper. Evidently his hands were numb with cold. Ham helped him. They got the case open, and used the knife on their ropes.

They got up, both of them, and Monk ran for one Heinkel, Ham for the other.

Shortly they appeared in the top turrets, swinging the pairs of Rheinmetal-Borsig machine guns.

"Do they know how to use those guns?" Fay demanded.

"They should."

Edith Halcyon shrieked now. She was pointing upward, gesturing.

Doc, knowing what had horrified her, condemned himself for a fool, and put the old plane in a hard, tight bank to change its course quickly. Below him, even as he turned, he saw the hot sparks and wisps of tracer bullets, and the little racing storms which the slugs tore up in the snow below.

The Heinkel one-thirteen was coming down the sky like a black widow spider on a string, the gun ports filling with flame for the brief intervals that ten and twenty shot bursts took.

Doc watched the ship. When it corrected, he put the wheel hard over and slipped earthward. He got the wing down until the plane was almost falling free. He kept the nose high, so airspeed would be at a minimum.

It was a well-known trick he was trying, a maneuver used by army grasshopper planes to thwart enemy fighters. This was no grasshopper in maneuverability, but it would function fairly well. The idea was to do a terrific slip nearly to the ground, flatten out about ten feet off the earth, and hope the enemy fighter couldn't pull out of his dive—he had to dive, because he could only aim his guns by pointing his plane at the target—in time to prevent a crash.

It was a maneuver that looked and sounded goofy, but it would make a fool out of a fighter plane.

But the Heinkel fighter pilot wasn't sucked in. He had his flaps cracked, and he hauled back in ample time. He got out of the dive.

Doc Savage climbed his heavily laden plane slowly, banking, turning away from the two Heinkel bombers. The fighter plane arched upward, got some altitude, and came around to attack from the rear, the most desirable place for a target run.

As Doc had figured, the run carried the fighter over the two bombers. The pilot evidently didn't know that he no longer had friends in the two ships, because he came in low and fast and almost directly over the bombers.

Fay, watching, said, "A sitting duck!"

Monk and Ham started firing almost together. They knew something about aerial gunnery, at least how much to lead the target.

Nothing outwardly visible happened to the Heinkel fighter when they got it. The Heinkel kept boring ahead, in a slanting dive, not swerving right or left or up or down. It was doing perhaps three hundred miles an hour when it hit, and made the sudden giant splash of flame that is always such a shocking sight when a plane is shot down and crashes.

Sheck came forward suddenly. He was excited, and yelling, "The guys on the ground have about reached the wrecked plane!"

Doc Savage nodded. He had been aware of that, but the fighter had been so much more important that he had hardly given the matter thought. Now he brought the ship around, and sent it toward the crashed army transport.

Edith Halcyon came lurching along the cabin. She said, "There is something coming out of our wings. It looks like gasoline."

Doc turned and looked. She was right. It was gasoline, and it was coming out through six or eight holes where bullets had gone through the wing. There was a stitching of bullet holes along the rest of the wing.

Scowling, Doc thought: I must be really scared, not to hear or feel that burst when it hit us.

Fay demanded, "Where did those holes come from? The fighter plane didn't hit us, did it?"

"It must have," Doc said.

He was switching to the other fuel tank when the motor stopped.

It didn't seem very tragic at first, the motor stopping. They had a starter, and there was a nearly full tank of fuel in the other wing. He took a gliding angle, and got the other tank on, and got the starter going.

The engine wouldn't start. It wouldn't fire a single time. It had cooled off too quickly, or something. It wouldn't start. They were up for a forced landing.

Doc did some guessing about the angle of glide. He had never flown this type of ship, and he wasn't too sure about the gliding angle.

He decided to take a chance on making the level stretch where the American transport was wrecked. He set the glide for that spot.

He thought, feeling as tight as if a gun was aimed at him, of several little things. Things like the habit a man acquires from doing something one way for a long time. In this landing, for example, he would have no time for a standard one-hundred-eighty degree pattern approach. He would have to come straight in and set down, and it was tricky. It wouldn't have been tricky if he hadn't been making the other kind of approaches exclusively. Or was he just scared?

It was very still in the plane with the motor dead. And the cold came in with biting force. He closed the open cockpit window, not wanting the icy blast to water his eyes too much.

"Get in the seats and fasten your safety belts," he warned. "Even if we make it, it's going to be a rough one."

Thaddeus Fay went back in the cabin with Edith Halcyon and Sheck, and it struck Doc Savage that this was a strange thing for Fay to do. So he watched Fay. He saw Fay test the girl's safety belt after she fastened it. That was all right. A man would do such a thing, probably.

But Fay tested Sheck's belt after Sheck fastened it— then hit Sheck a terrific blow on the jaw with his fist. Sheck sagged back, dazed.

Fay beat Sheck's jaw and temples with his fists until there was no chance that Sheck was still conscious. Then Fay came back to the co-pilot's seat.

Fay sank into the seat and fastened his safety belt. He sat staring at the approaching snow-covered earth, his face bleak and frightened.

"I guess that was the wrong thing to do," he said.

"Why did you do it?" Doc asked.

"Lay Sheck out?" Fay said. "It seemed like the time to do it. Maybe it wasn't. But I think it was."

"Why?"

"I have been afraid he was going to shoot you in the back," Fay said. "I've been afraid of it a dozen times. I've watched him. That's what he planned to do, and I was afraid he would do it before I could stop him."

Doc watched the airspeed—and Fay. He thought they might make it. That is, they might make a landing near where the transport lay, but it wouldn't be a good spot for a landing.

"Why should Sheck want to shoot me?" Doc asked.

"He knew you were Doc Savage," Fay said.

Doc didn't get it. He didn't get it at all. He had known that Thaddeus Fay knew he was Doc Savage, and Sheck had known it. But now was a queer time for Fay to admit it.

He thought they had about twenty seconds more for talk.

"What gave Sheck that idea?" he asked.

"Back at Lake Placid, when we were in the house on the hill, watching the airplane hangar, Sheck decided that was who you were," Fay said. "He told me. Sheck wasn't dumb. He said he was going to shoot you. So, to cover you up, I pretended to be a mastermind who was using you to help us get Chester Wilson and do the rest of the job. I told Sheck we must use you for that, because of your ability, then knock you off."

It sounded all right. It sounded like what Fay and Sheck had said when Doc got their conference with his lip-reading at the Lake Placid place.

But it didn't make sense that Fay should admit it now.

Doc hit Fay suddenly with his right fist, on the jaw. The blow made a loud sound, and Fay slept with his mouth open and his eyes rolled up.

The plane came in, wobbling, straining to finish out its glide. Doc scowled at the spot where they were going to have to land. It wasn't good. They would probably wrap up in a ball when they landed.

A few bullets began hitting the plane. These came, he was sure, from Burroughs and his men.

He turned his head and said, "There may be a fire when we hit. You can never tell about those things. Get out of the plane as soon as you can."

His voice was very loud, because he had been in the habit of shouting over the plane noise. He must have shouted the same way during his talk with Fay, and not noticed it. He felt silly.

Edith Halcyon looked at him fixedly. She did not nod or anything.

XII

The landing was fifteen seconds that stood his hair on end. They took snow and ice off a ridge with a grinding metallic crash, bounced to another ridge, hit with a sickening shock, sailed off nearly out of control. In the middle of it he thought: The pilot of that transport should get a Congressional Medal of Honor for the landing he must have made with that iced-up ship.

They hit the ground again, and stayed down, metal grinding and fabric ripping in a blinding cloud of snow. He knew one wing had gone, felt the ship ground-loop. He did what he could so fast that he was not sure what he did.

Then they were still. He was hanging upside down from the safety belt, and he broke his fingernails on the belt release. He got loose. He crawled back on the roof of the plane cabin which was now the floor.

"Are you all right?" Edith Halcyon asked.

"Yes," he said. "Pile out into the snow. But don't stand up and run. Get down. Burrow into the snow until we find out the situation."

She dropped out into the snow.

He unfastened Fay and Sheck from their belts, and tossed them out, then followed himself.

They were not more than seventy yards from the wrecked transport. He stared at the big ship. He had not, he realized, seen any sign of life around it, or in the plane itself.

As he waited, the cold stillness affected him like a sickness. Everything, all this trouble and strain, was based on the idea that the transport had gotten down with the occupants alive. Now he was afraid that it hadn't.

He lifted his voice.

"Ahoy the transport!" he called. "Doc Savage, of New

206

York, assigned by the State Department to finding you fellows. What do you say?"

There was more stillness. He could hear the small brittle crackling sounds that bitter cold makes.

Then he got an answer.

"You better identify yourself a little more," a voice said.

For a while he was speechless with relief. He didn't know where the voice had come from. A little to the left of the mangled transport, he thought. He wasn't sure.

"Where are you?" he asked.

"Crawl toward the transport," the voice said. "But keep down. Some guys are lying out there in the snow with rifles, and they're pretty good shots."

He searched intently, trying to locate the speaker.

He said, "You had better do some identifying yourself. Who are you?"

"Gaines," the man said. "Lieutenant General Gaines."

That was all right. Gaines was one of the men who had been on the transport.

He told the girl, "Stay here until I make sure of this."

The occupants of the wrecked transport had gone native and built themselves an igloo of packed snow blocks and stone. Snow had drifted over the structure, hiding it almost completely. That was the explanation for their being invisible.

Gaines' voice said, "Turn left. Crawl in that hole you'll find."

He saw Gaines then, or saw a rifle barrel which he presumed Gaines was holding. He crawled until he found the hole.

Out on the ice, Burroughs' men must have discovered him, because there was a brief storm of lead, some of it quite close. From near at hand, from the igloo, rifles whacked angrily in reply.

He dived into the hole, and a man met him instantly with a gun muzzle. The man scowled at him. "You don't look like Doc Savage."

"I changed my looks a little when this began," he explained.

The man was undecided.

Doc said, "There's a light machine gun in the plane, if you fellows are short of ammunition."

Back in the igloo, someone said, "My God! Go get that gun!"

Instantly men were crawling past him, out into the biting cold.

He called, "There is a girl out there." He lifted his voice, shouting, "Miss Halcyon! They are coming after you and the guns. Help them, but be careful!"

The man who had met him said loudly, "This doesn't look like Doc Savage."

Gaines' voice said, "Bring him in here."

The igloo was not large, but it was warm. They had rigged an ingenious burner for the plane fuel, and torn the seats out of the plane and made fairly comfortable furniture in the igloo.

There was a ledge around the wall of the igloo, and men were crouching on this. They had poked portholes through the snow at various points, and were watching for Burroughs' men.

"Hello, Gaines," Doc said to Gaines. "I don't know how to straighten up this matter of identification. I haven't any credentials on me, naturally."

Gaines eyed him thoughtfully. "Where did you last meet me?"

"Cairo, about six months ago. You were with a very striking blonde Englishwoman named Celia."

Gaines laughed. "I guess that identifies you."

Gaines then went to a porthole to watch the men who were crawling to the plane to get the machine gun. His intense interest in the operation indicated that there was very little in the way of arms and ammunition on hand.

Gaines, still watching, moved his head a little as if surprised. He whistled softly. "Speaking of tall blondes, you haven't done badly yourself," he said. Then he asked, "Who is she?"

Doc Savage didn't answer, because he was looking at the man who had been standing watching through a porthole on the other side of the igloo. The man had turned. He had a rifle.

Using the deep, amiable voice which millions had heard over their radios, the voice which could ring with confidence or rasp with the determination of a bulldog when necessary, the man said, "I have one of them spotted. I am not a very good shot with a rifle. Would someone care to do the honors?"

Doc Savage had wondered, initially in New York when Wister of the State Department had first tossed into his lap the frightening job of finding this man, what his feelings would be when, and if, he did find him. He'd had the same thought often as matters developed, turning his possible reactions over in his mind, because it was an interesting mental item to chew upon.

Mostly his reaction had been that this man had better have stayed home, safely guarded by the millions of soldiers he commanded, and the ingenious young men who made up his personal bodyguard. A man with so much responsibility had no business gallivanting around the world and getting himself lost in the Arctic wastes.

Doc had met the man before, twice. The other meetings had been in the man's executive offices, in surroundings of efficiency and executive activity. Doc had received the same impression that everyone did, that the man was really fitted for the job he was doing, which was guiding one of the four Allied nations through the most complex, scientific and bloodletting war so far in history. It was hard, meeting the man in his office, to visualize him in a setting of primitive danger. One just didn't think of him as being in a battlefield foxhole, or in an igloo in the Arctic with a rifle in his hands, quietly asking someone else if they'd shoot a man whom he didn't think he could hit.

But the man sounded and looked as if he belonged here. His manner—and his manner was a composite of what was in the man, his courage, his training, his ability, his allotment of the stuff called guts—was impressive.

He *is* a great man, Doc thought.

Which was an unnecessary reflection. The man had to be great, to guide his country through what it had undergone, to stand at the head of his nation, a tower of courage that had become a symbol of the dogged persistence of his people.

The man got down off the ledge.

Another man took his place with the rifle, aimed carefully, fired, then got a blankly sheepish look which indicated he had missed.

"I missed him, dammit, Sir," said the man who had fired.

"Don't worry about it."

"Thank you."

The man came to Doc Savage. He put out his hand, saying, "How are you, Savage?" And he followed that with a direct question, "What is going on, anyway?"

"The wrong people found out about your being lost up here."

The man nodded. "That's quite likely. The enemy planes ran into my escort by accident, I think, but they evidently had information which led them to realize what they had stumbled on to. They threw everything they had into trying to shoot us down. We had to run for it, and for safety, headed into a cold front which offered the only thing in the way of a refuge."

He grimaced. "You know what a cold front is? I didn't. I assure you it's nothing for an airplane to get mixed up with. This one scattered us like chaff. When we came out of it, the Jerries weren't around, but neither were any of my escort. Except one. An American army plane. Then we iced up, and had to make a crash landing here. The American plane flew around. It was a seaplane and couldn't land, but we signalled we were safe, and the pilot signalled that he would fly out and get help. He didn't dare use his radio, because the Jerry planes might be in the vicinity, or might pick up the radio signal."

Doc said, "Here is the rest of it. The American pilot got back to the States safely, but the Nazis had evidently tipped off their American agents. The agents were waiting, and they had a beautiful piece of luck, managing to kidnap the pilot. Finally they forced him to reveal the location of the crash. Then there was a race up here to get you. The race, as you can see outside, came much too close to being a tie."

"They're infernally anxious to get me, aren't they?"

"Naturally."

The man shrugged. "I'm not my nation. Not by a long shot. If I was a prisoner in Berlin, it wouldn't make one whit of difference in the progress of the war."

"There is another way of looking at that."

"Eh?"

"Yes. You happen to know all the Allied military plans."

"Do you think I'd tell a word of them?" the other asked sharply. "They're all in my head. I destroyed every document as soon as we crashed."

"Plans can be gotten out of a man's head with a little work," Doc said.

The other considered the point for a while. "You're correct enough," he said finally. "No man likes to think he could be made to tell such things. But I suppose it could be done scientifically, and he couldn't help himself."

There was shooting outside, a rattling flurry of it. Then Edith Halcyon came inside. She was followed by the men who had gone after the machine gun. They had the gun, and two of them were dragging Fay and Sheck.

Fay was conscious. He told Doc Savage, "You should have let me finish."

"Finish what?"

"Explaining that I—" He stopped, because a man at one of the portholes was yelling.

"Smoke!" the man shouted. "There's a lot of smoke coming up from the east!"

Monk and Ham had set fire to one of the Heinkels, Doc knew after he had watched the rising smoke for a moment. Or he hoped that was what it was. He waited, listening for the motors of the other plane to start, growing tight with anxiety.

Finally the first Heinkel motor started, then the others. Their thunder came faintly across the two miles of Arctic waste, the sound almost dying out at times as it was buffeted by the wind. It seemed that the motors warmed for an hour, and it was impossible to tell when the plane actually took off.

The Heinkel appeared above the snow-covered ridges.

"Who is in it?" Gaines asked.

"My two associates, Monk Mayfair and Ham Brooks—I hope," Doc said.

"I hope so, too," Gaines said. "You know, as a last resort, the Jerries would gladly drop a bomb on us."

Doc watched the Heinkel climb, circle, get altitude, then listened to it thunder overhead. When nothing happened, a coldness crawled all through him. If it wasn't Monk and Ham, they were indeed in bad shape.

Doc said, "We had better get out of here. Scatter and

charge the enemy. If the plane is with us, we can smoke the enemy out where they can gun them. If it isn't with us, at least we'll be scattered."

They held a conference about that. Then they began crawling out of the igloo. And the shooting started, a scattered shot here and there at first.

The Heinkel came thundering back. It went over, and the bomb bay doors were open. A stick of bombs came out. They seemed directly overhead, but that was only an illusion, because they hit two hundred yards beyond, driving up a procession of geysers of earth, stone, snow.

"It seems to be with us," Gaines said.

The rest of it seemed to take three or four minutes to finish. Actually the elapsed time was more than an hour, during which the big plane made nearly thirty runs either bombing or machine-gunning.

But in the end, there was no more shooting, and three men, all of them from Stripe Lodge, crawled out of the snow where they had been hiding, holding their arms in the air.

The captives were taken into the igloo and searched.

Thaddeus Fay pointed at one of them, the fattest of the three. "Burroughs," he said.

"Who is Burroughs?" Doc asked.

"Their bull," Fay said cheerfully. "The head one. The man with the ideas."

Burroughs looked at Fay and cursed him with a low furious intensity, cursing him in German, Czech, English and French. Then Burroughs put his face in his hands.

Doc asked, "What about McGillicuddy? There was talk about a McGillicuddy earlier in this thing."

Fay indicated Burroughs. "Him. That's one of his names, and he never liked it much, so pretty nearly everybody called him McGillicuddy behind his back."

"You've known him some time?"

"A long time," Fay admitted.

Doc scowled at Fay. "And just who does that make you?"

Fay grinned. "We'd better wait until Wister gets here. You might not take my word."

Wister of the State Department arrived with the first swarm of American army and navy planes. The ships began getting in about six o'clock in the evening of the following day.

Monk and Ham had flown out in the Heinkel, going alone because there was an unhealthy possibility that some American pilot might sight the Heinkel coming in over the Canadian or Maine coast and shoot it out of the sky without benefit of ceremony.

Wister was full of apology. He introduced Fay.

"This is Thaddeus Fay," Wister said. "He is an operative for the State Department, and has been working with Burroughs for about three years. Burroughs trusted him and Fay had access to the information which enemy agents were getting, which was a handy thing for us to know. So handy that we let Burroughs keep operating, and fed him now and then a piece of information which was poison for — his employers."

Doc told Wister bitterly, "You might have told me you already had a man planted with the gang who had kidnapped Wilson."

"We didn't want to give Fay away. And Fay figured you could accomplish more by yourself."

Fay said, "As it turned out, we should have told you."

Doc Savage wheeled suddenly and went outside and stood watching the planes landing and taking off and circling. The place looked, he reflected, as busy as an English bomber field on an afternoon when visibility was good over the Continent.

He was irritated, but he supposed he shouldn't be. Everything had come out all right. Probably the secrecy, the withholding of information from him, had been a prudent precaution on Wister's part. There was so much at stake. Wister couldn't take chances. Wister was a good man. He had been excited this time, but he was still a good man.

He watched a group of men nearby. The man who had been the cause of all the trouble, the man who was the head of an Allied nation, was the center of the group. No one else in the cluster seemed to be less than a Lieutenant General. They were getting ready to leave on one of the planes.

The man who was the head of a nation saw Doc Savage. He waved, and smiled. He didn't say anything about gratitude, but his smile and gesture were a great deal more expressive. They said enough.

Doc watched him leave. It was worth it, Doc reflected. Very much worth all the tension and worry and frightening effort, to preserve a man who was so important to humanity.

Monk and Ham and Edith Halcyon and Chester Wilson were waiting beside one of the planes. They were going back together, all of them. They were waiting on Doc.

Doc went back to Wister.

"No hard feelings," he told Wister.

"I'm certainly glad," Wister said. "Next time we work together, I hope I keep my head a little better."

"Next time!" Doc said. "God forbid."

He went to join Monk, Ham, Wilson and Edith Halcyon. Edith Halcyon was smiling, and suddenly he felt fine. He felt very good indeed.

RELAX!

SIT DOWN

and Catch Up On Your Reading!

☐	13098	**THE MATARESE CIRCLE** by Robert Ludlum	$3.50
☐	14491	**THE HOLCROFT COVENANT** by Robert Ludlum	$2.95
☐	13688	**TRINITY** by Leon Uris	$3.50
☐	13899	**THE MEDITERRANEAN CAPER** by Clive Cussler	$2.75
☐	13396	**THE ISLAND** by Peter Benchley	$2.75
☐	12152	**DAYS OF WINTER** by Cynthia Freeman	$2.50
☐	13201	**PROTEUS** by Morris West	$2.75
☐	13028	**OVERLOAD** by Arthur Hailey	$2.95
☐	13220	**A MURDER OF QUALITY** by John Le Carre	$2.25
☐	13471	**THE ROSARY MURDERS** by William Kienzle	$2.50
☐	13848	**THE EAGLE HAS LANDED** Jack Higgins	$2.75
☐	13880	**RAISE THE TITANIC!** by Clive Cussler	$2.75
☐	13186	**THE LOVE MACHINE** by Jacqueline Susann	$2.50
☐	14463	**ICEBERG** by Clive Cussler	$2.75
☐	12810	**VIXEN 03** by Clive Cussler	$2.75
☐	14033	**ICE!** by Arnold Federbush	$2.50
☐	11820	**FIREFOX** by Craig Thomas	$2.50
☐	12691	**WOLFSBANE** by Craig Thomas	$2.50
☐	13896	**THE ODESSA FILE** by Frederick Forsyth	$2.75

Buy them at your local bookstore or use this handy coupon for ordering:

Bantam Books, Inc., Dept. FBB, 414 East Golf Road, Des Plaines, Ill. 60016

Please send me the books I have checked above. I am enclosing $_____
(please add $1.00 to cover postage and handling). Send check or money order
—no cash or C.O.D.'s please.

Mr/Mrs/Miss_____

Address_____

City_____ State/Zip_____

FBB—9/80

Please allow four to six weeks for delivery. This offer expires 3/81.

OUT OF THIS WORLD!

That's the only way to describe Bantam's great series of science fiction classics. These space-age thrillers are filled with terror, fancy and adventure and written by America's most renowned writers of science fiction. Welcome to outer space and have a good trip!

☐	13179	**THE MARTIAN CHRONICLES** by Ray Bradbury	$2.25
☐	13695	**SOMETHING WICKED THIS WAY COMES** by Ray Bradbury	$2.25
☐	14323	**STAR TREK: THE NEW VOYAGES** by Culbreath & Marshak	$2.25
☐	13260	**ALAS BABYLON** by Pat Frank	$2.25
☐	14124	**A CANTICLE FOR LEIBOWITZ** by Walter Miller, Jr.	$2.50
☐	11175	**THE FEMALE MAN** by Joanna Russ	$1.75
☐	13312	**SUNDIVER** by David Brin	$1.95
☐	12957	**CITY WARS** by Dennis Palumbo	$1.95
☐	11662	**SONG OF THE PEARL** by Ruth Nichols	$1.75
☐	13766	**THE FARTHEST SHORE** by Ursula LeGuin	$2.25
☐	13594	**THE TOMBS OF ATUAN** by Ursula LeGuin	$2.25
☐	13767	**A WIZARD OF EARTHSEA** by Ursula LeGuin	$2.25
☐	13563	**20,000 LEAGUES UNDER THE SEA** by Jules Verne	$1.75
☐	12655	**FANTASTIC VOYAGE** by Isaac Asimov	$1.95

Buy them at your local bookstore or use this handy coupon for ordering:

Bantam Books, Inc., Dept. SF, 414 East Golf Road, Des Plaines, Ill. 60016

Please send me the books I have checked above. I am enclosing $_____ (please add $1.00 to cover postage and handling). Send check or money order —no cash or C.O.D.'s please.

Mr/Mrs/Miss _____

Address _____

City _____ State/Zip _____

SF—9/80

Please allow four to six weeks for delivery. This offer expires 3/81.

FANTASY AND SCIENCE FICTION FAVORITES

Bantam brings you the recognized classics as well as the current favorites in fantasy and science fiction. Here you will find the beloved Conan books along with recent titles by the most respected authors in the genre.

☐	01166	URSHURAK	
		Bros. Hildebrandt & Nichols	$8.95
☐	13610	NOVA Samuel R. Delany	$2.25
☐	13534	TRITON Samuel R. Delany	$2.50
☐	13612	DHALGREN Samuel R. Delany	$2.95
☐	12018	CONAN THE SWORDSMAN #1	
		DeCamp & Carter	$1.95
☐	12706	CONAN THE LIBERATOR #2	
		DeCamp & Carter	$1.95
☐	12970	THE SWORD OF SKELOS #3	
		Andrew Offutt	$1.95
☐	14321	THE ROAD OF KINGS #4	$2.25
		Karl E. Wagner	
☐	14127	DRAGONSINGER Anne McCaffrey	$2.50
☐	14204	DRAGONSONG Anne McCaffrey	$2.50
☐	12019	KULL Robert E. Howard	$1.95
☐	10779	MAN PLUS Frederik Pohl	$1.95
☐	11736	FATA MORGANA William Kotzwinkle	$2.95
☐	11042	BEFORE THE UNIVERSE	$1.95
		Pohl & Kornbluth	
☐	13680	TIME STORM Gordon R. Dickson	$2.50
☐	13400	SPACE ON MY HANDS Frederic Brown	$1.95

Buy them at your local bookstore or use this handy coupon for ordering:

Bantam Book Catalog

Here's your up-to-the-minute listing of over 1,400 titles by your favorite authors.

This illustrated, large format catalog gives a description of each title. For your convenience, it is divided into categories in fiction and non-fiction—gothics, science fiction, westerns, mysteries, cookbooks, mysticism and occult, biographies, history, family living, health, psychology, art.

So don't delay—take advantage of this special opportunity to increase your reading pleasure.

Just send us your name and address and 50¢ (to help defray postage and handling costs).